I0641212

THAT REILLY BOY

NEW YORK TIMES BESTSELLING AUTHOR

shannon stacey

For Her Royal Hiney, the Pretty Pretty Princess Minibella Louise Stacey. I miss your sassy, furry little face every hour of every day.

Chapter One

CARA

"What are we going to do about that Reilly boy?"

It isn't the first time that question's been asked in this town, by any means, and I know it won't be the last. But it's the first time I've heard that question come out of my mother's mouth because the Gambles and the Reillys haven't really spoken to each other since...well, however long four generations is. Ignoring each other in a town the size of Sumac Falls, New Hampshire isn't easy, but somehow our families have managed it.

Until now, apparently.

I ignore the familiar pang in my chest whenever I hear the Reilly name. She has to be talking about Aaron—the Reilly boy who did *not* leave town like his ass was on fire the day after graduation—but I don't know why Mom would be talking about him.

"What about him?" I ask, my curiosity piqued. I've never been told how the low-key feud started, which was awkward considering I went to school with the two Reilly boys.

"One of them wants to buy the house," my mom replies, and judging by the way she's scrubbing the counter with a wet rag, she

1

isn't thrilled by the offer. Gin Gamble can scour the finish right off a hardwood floor when she's in a mood.

My first grooming appointment of the day is in twenty minutes, so I *had* been making my way toward the door, but the bait of a potential buyer for this house hooks me.

It's the first offer we've had on the house since my dad's heart gave out on him five years ago, which makes sense because it's not on the market. It would be, if only I could convince my mom we *really* need to sell it. But apparently, on his deathbed my father made my mother promise she'd keep the house in the Gamble family. Unfortunately, a trust fund to *maintain* the house hadn't been part of the inheritance and I should be logging things in the checkbook register with red ink to indicate the danger level.

Whether she wants to admit it or not—and she definitely doesn't—we're in trouble.

"Can you imagine?" my mother continues, either not noticing or not caring that I didn't respond. "A Reilly living in the Gamble house?"

"To be fair, once the sale is final, it would be the Reilly house." Feud or no feud, our lives would be easier if the house sold, so I care a lot less about whose name is on the mailbox than she does. But Aaron and his wife already have a really nice house, so I'm confused. "Which one wants to buy it?"

"The older one."

Hayden. That pesky pang in my chest hits a little harder this time, and I'm even *more* confused. Why would he want to buy our house?

"I forget which one that is, besides one of those Reillys," Gin continues, "but he's back in town and told his real estate agent or lawyer or whatever he is to contact me."

Oh, I know who Hayden is.

I spent every study hall block of my freshman year staring at his gorgeously brooding profile from two desks over and one desk back. He'd been a sophomore at the time, and that study hall had been my favorite forty-six minutes of every school day.

2

And then came the glorious moment Hayden had bumped into me on our way out of class. The way he'd put his hand on the small of my back had made my skin feel hot and prickly all over—a sensation I'd never felt before. His blue eyes were even prettier up close, and a shock of dark hair had fallen over his forehead. I left fingernail marks in my textbook from the effort to keep from smoothing it back.

"Sorry, Cara."

I'd forgotten how to breathe because Hayden Reilly knew my name.

Of course he did because, again, small town with a small school, but logic had been no match for my raging teenage hormones.

We had two classes together my sophomore year, and Hayden talked to me whenever he had the chance. I can still picture him leaning against my locker, smiling at me in a way that made my common sense go right out the window.

When the school year ended, we found a secret spot in the woods. Whenever we could sneak away, we'd sit on a boulder by the river, eating ice cream and talking about anything and everything. Eventually we did less talking and more making out. That summer, Hayden became my entire world.

When school started again—my junior year and his senior—secrecy and stolen kisses weren't enough anymore, and he asked me to be his very public date to the fall homecoming dance.

My parents didn't know I was even seeing a Reilly and I knew they'd be angry, but I didn't care. I was going to homecoming with Hayden.

And then...well, I don't like to think about how the story of our star-crossed romance came to an end. It wasn't tragic on a Romeo and Juliet level, by any means—nobody died or anything—but seventeen years later, my heart's still a little broken. It's not as if I'm still madly in love with him after almost two decades, but the old wound still hurts if I poke at it.

Hearing his name is a pretty hard poke.

SHANNON STACEY

"Your father would roll over in his grave if I sold the house to a Reilly," my mom says.

Is there a good reason my dad doesn't find me lying awake, wondering if this is the month I'll have to choose between fuel for my car or fuel for the furnace, to be more roll-worthy than doing business with the Reilly family? "I don't get it. Why does our family hate the Reillys so much?"

She sniffs. "We don't like to talk about it."

There has to be more to it than which grandmother brought better homemade pickles to be judged at the fair. I'm on the verge of asking my mom if she even *knows* the story, but my phone rings. It's Brenda Eccleston, whose Irish setter is supposed to walk through the door of my shop in about eighteen minutes.

"Cara, we're running a few minutes late. Peaches is in a mood and she buried her collar in the new garden. And yes, I know June is late to be putting in a garden, but I just got the urge. Anyway, as soon as David finds it, we'll be on our way. The entire patch was just turned over, though, so it might take him a few minutes to find the freshly dug spot."

"I'll be there whenever you get there, Mrs. Eccleston. Thanks for letting me know."

As I slide my phone back into my pocket, my mom wrinkles her nose. "I'll never understand why you insist on grooming animals instead of cutting hair for the ladies in town, who certainly smell better."

"Because those *ladies* never stop talking, and I like animals more than I like people." Also, people smelling better isn't neces-sarily a given, but I keep that thought to myself.

I also don't point out that Sumac Falls didn't have a groomer before I opened Pampered Pets Grooming, but if you add up the barber shops, salons and the stylists who work out of their homes, I think there's a chair for every roughly two and a half residents in this town. I don't know how they all stay in business, but I knew I couldn't afford to scrounge for customers in an oversaturated market.

4

Mostly I'm in it for the dogs, though. With the exception of Mrs. Brophy's Chihuahua, they never judge me.

"We need to consider his offer," I tell my mother, bringing the subject back to Hayden.

"No." She scrubs harder, and I feel bad for the speckled countertop that needed to be updated before I was born. "This house has been in the Gamble family since the day it was built. I made a promise to your father, and I'm not going to be the one who loses it."

No, that's going to be me. My sister, Georgia, is two years older than me, and she managed to get away before I was old enough to beat her to it. And as much as Mom likes to go on about the Gamble *family*, it's down to just us. My mother, Georgia and me.

Oh, and my Aunt Tess. She's my paternal great-aunt, and she's never been okay with the house passing from her father to her older brother to *my* father while her inheritance consisted of an ugly broach and a fancy dinner setting for twelve. She won't contribute to the upkeep of the house—not that I blame her since it's not hers—but she never misses an opportunity to remind me of my *legacy*.

That's a weighty word for a money pit of a house. And honestly, there's more value in the ten dollar bill she still sends me in a birthday card every year than in "the Gamble legacy."

The bottom line is that if I leave, my mother will be alone. And despite what Georgia says, I don't think me walking away would give Gin the kick in the pants she needs to move on from this house. I think she'd stay, and then she and the house would deteriorate together. And no matter how many Instagram posts I see urging me to set boundaries and live my life, I can't do it.

She's my mother. I've already lost my father, so she's the only parent I've got.

But I can tell by the set of her mouth and the way she's intensely focused on an imaginary stain on the counter that the conversation is over.

For now.

I'll give her some time to stew about it, but we're going to talk about that offer again. And again and again, until I get her to at least consider hearing him out.

We scrape by okay—most months—but selling the house sure would relieve some of the pressure.

Even if we sell it to Hayden Reilly.

Chapter Two

HAYDEN

"There's no way Gin Gamble is going to sell you that house."

My younger brother isn't usually a pessimist. "Have you seen that house, Aaron? If she doesn't sell it, it's going to fall down around her."

"I'm not saying she won't sell. But she sure as shit ain't going to sell it to *you*."

"Bet me."

The familiar challenge from our childhood makes him smile. "Too easy. There's no chance."

He's wrong. Gin *will* sell it to me because buying that house is the only reason I'm back in Sumac Falls, and I don't fail. If her baseless hatred for my family is stronger than her need for the money I'm prepared to offer her, I'll find another way to get it.

Sure, I could have paid somebody to conduct this business for me, but that wouldn't have been nearly as satisfying. This is personal and I'm ready to get my hands dirty because I made a promise to myself when I was eighteen, and it's time to keep it.

One way or another, the Gamble house is going to become the Reilly house.

7

"I know you're a smart guy," Aaron says. "If you weren't, a bunch of very rich people wouldn't trust you with their money, so I'm pretty sure you could have figured out how to hide your name and make an anonymous offer."

He's not wrong, but I never considered hiding behind a trust or a shell corporation's name. I *want* her to know it's me. I want her to have to surrender to the inevitability of a Reilly owning her house.

I'm saved from having to cough up some kind of plausible explanation by our mother entering the room. She'd popped home during her lunch break to see me, and I'd let her know about the offer. After a lot of yelling, she'd called my brother to come give his two cents, assuming he'd also be outraged.

Her cheeks are still flushed with annoyance at me. "I'm going back to work. Aaron, talk some sense into your brother."

She's gone before either of us can respond, the front door slamming like an angry exclamation point at the end of her words. We wait in silence for about twenty seconds and the door opens again.

She grabs her keys off the stand where she'd tossed them and then points at me. "I don't want to hear any more about this nonsense."

The door slams again and Aaron gives a low whistle. "This is going to be a fun visit. How long are you staying?"

"Until I close on that house."

"I hope you brought everything you own because it's not going to happen. And I'm glad we're two streets over. As long as we keep the windows closed, we might not be able to hear the yelling." He snorts. "I'm sure Hope's going to get an earful at work.

Hope's my sister-in-law, and one of the most popular orthodontists in the region. Our mother has been the office manager there for years, which was how Aaron and Hope met. Mom doesn't have to work anymore—I've told her that repeatedly—but she refuses to let me pay her way. Plus, she says Hope needs her and since she hates gardening, she'd have nothing to do all day.

She also refused to let me buy her a new house. While it isn't big or fancy, this is the home she made with her husband and where she raised her sons. She was staying and none of the photos of lovely homes for sale I emailed would budge her. I was able to talk her into letting me pack up all of her belongings, though, so she and her best friend could go on a long cruise while professionals totally renovated the house—inside and out.

Key to the renovation was an addition to the house that put a primary suite, complete with a killer bathroom, and the laundry room on the ground floor so my mom only has to use stairs if she wants to. Another piece of the renovation was selfish on my part, making a guest suite with a bedroom, sitting area and bathroom upstairs. I rarely come back to Sumac Falls—preferring my family visits me in Boston—but when I do, I want to be comfortable.

"Mom's coming over for dinner tomorrow," Aaron says. "Every Wednesday, actually, because there's some show she and Hope watch together. Even though Mom will be in a mood, you should come. I know Hope and the kids would love to see you."

Aaron's six-year-old daughter, Daisy, and four-year-old Aaron Junior—who's only ever been called AJ—are the greatest kids in the world, hands down. I'm biased, of course, but they're definitely the best Reillys yet. If only I could talk their parents into moving anywhere but here, but Aaron wants to stay close to Mom, and she loves Sumac Falls. I don't get it, but she's definitely the parent I get my stubbornness from.

"You can bring the dog," Aaron adds. "And speaking of the dog, why is she just sitting there like that?"

I turn to see Penelope Louise sitting a few feet away, her body turned away from me and her back rigid. "She's punishing me for bringing her here."

"She's a dog."

"She's a Shih Tzu." I don't bother trying to get her attention. She'll give me the cold shoulder until her desire for something she wants grows stronger than her desire to stay mad at me. "She doesn't like changes in her routine."

"I tried to pet her because she's seen me enough times to know who I am, but I changed my mind. She has pretty fierce facial expressions for a dog."

I laugh at Aaron's understatement. "Penny hates everybody. Except me."

She hears her name and twitches, almost turning before she remembers she's mad at me. I usually have her favorite dog sitter —or the one she dislikes the least, anyway—stay with her in my Boston apartment when I have to travel. I'm not sure how long I'll be in Sumac Falls, though, and—while it's hard to judge by her current attitude—she doesn't like being away from me.

The feeling is mutual.

"Well, your dog might like you, but when it comes to the Gambles, they hate *all* of us. Even you," Aaron says. "Or maybe *especially* you, for some reason. There's no way Gin even takes your call, never mind considers your offer."

"Gin isn't the only Gamble who lives there, though," I point out, even though I've been away for seventeen years and Aaron never left Sumac Falls. It's information he already has, but Aaron is focused on the woman who actually owns the house.

He's forgetting Gin's daughter.

I, on the other hand, have never forgotten Cara. When we were teenagers, she was so pretty, I could have happily stared at her for hours. I didn't talk to her, of course. She was a Gamble and Gambles didn't lower themselves to speak to Reillys. And Reillys liked it that way.

Most of us, anyway.

Then, one day coming out of study hall, I'd bumped into her. I'd spent so much time imagining her in my arms, my hand went straight to the small of her back before I realized what I was doing. She'd looked into my eyes and, in the space of a heartbeat, every-thing changed.

I lift my hand to my chest, my fingertips running over the

tattoo hidden under my shirt. We only had one magical summer and a bit of autumn together before her father destroyed all of the hopes and dreams I'd had.

"Cara?" Aaron snorts. "She's been stuck in that house with nobody but Gin since Marcus Gamble passed away like, what... five years ago? What makes you think she'll break from the family pack?"

I give my brother a smile that's usually reserved for board-room victories. "She'll break precisely *because* she's been alone in that house with nobody but Gin."

Aaron sits back in his chair, shaking his head. "Diabolical."

I am at times, which is how I've amassed a fortune—by Sumac Falls standards anyway. I don't have enough to make the potential Netflix documentary roster, but I can be fairly brutal when it comes to business. Buying the Gamble house isn't business, technically, but it's a goal I set for myself a very long time ago.

And, again, I don't fail.

"How are you going to get around Gin to get to Cara, though? She doesn't like you any more than her mother does."

Maybe not, but she used to. I turn to look at Penny, who's still giving me her back. "I have a plan."

Chapter Three

CARA

Hayden Reilly is back in town and I know I shouldn't care, but I kind of do. A lot.

It takes me five minutes to drive from our house to my tiny little storefront shop on the main street of Sumac Falls. Usually I walk because walking is free, but I'm already running behind due to the conversational bomb Gin dropped on me. And it's supposed to rain later in the afternoon.

Five minutes is a long time to focus on *not* thinking about Hayden Reilly, and I fail miserably. I know he's been home before. I haven't seen him, of course, but people are always talking in this town and sometimes they're talking about Hayden being home to see his mother and brother.

Because my best friend, Mel, made me pinky swear many years ago I'd never look him up on the internet, I don't know how much he's changed over the years. I always thought he was the hottest boy ever born in this town, and I know I wasn't alone in thinking that. But it's been seventeen years since I've seen him and I can't help but hope the years have taken a toll on his looks. I try to be a kind person, but when it comes to the boy who stood me up on homecoming night and broke my heart, I can be petty.

He'll probably leave town before I see him, anyway. He's good at that.

I try to put him out of my mind as I roll past Pampered Pets. Ironically, it's the second business from the end of the long, red brick multi-unit building called the Gamble Block. I don't get a family discount on the rent, though, because my grandfather sold it to somebody else before I was born. There are four blocks on my side of the street and five on the other. Some are red brick and some are gray. There used to be five on each side, but the Reilly Block—built during the family's flush years, and the only one not constructed from brick—had been on the far end. It burned in the winter of 1946.

Over the years, some vocal members of the Reilly family have claimed a Gamble must have lit the match, of course, but the fire department said the upstairs tenant was trying to keep warm with an open fire in a cast iron pot and overdid the flame. They'd demolished what was left of the building and eventually the town took the property for unpaid taxes. Then they planted grass on the lot, plunked down a couple of wooden benches, and called it a park.

I find a parking spot behind the row of businesses, in a lot designated for people who work on the main street. Thanks to an SUV the width of a tank on one side and a car who thinks the parking lines are more like suggestions on the other, I have to hold onto my door to keep it from banging the SUV while I suck in a breath and squeeze through the opening. Sumac Falls wanted to keep the main street parking for visitors and customers, which is great, but they underestimated how much space the business owners and employees would need—and how big vehicles have gotten over the years. It's another reason I try to walk whenever possible.

I pause, as always, in front of Pampered Pets Grooming to savor the little jolt of pride and happiness I still feel every time I see it. I bartered three grooming sessions with a Dachshund-owning artist who painted a variety of cartoon dogs and cats on my front window, happily galivanting around the name of my business. She even painted little paw prints on the glass door, and I'm smiling as I unlock it and pull it open.

This is my happy place. It's all mine, for better or worse. There's no drama, other than trimming the nails of a dog who thinks it's being murdered. And thanks to alleged pet dander allergies, Gin never comes here. Other than pick-ups and drop-offs, it's just me and the town's furry friends.

If I lived in an apartment or even a tiny starter house, the business would probably make me a comfortable living. But I don't. I live in a giant money pit with a mother who thinks working part-time for her friend the florist means she's doing her part to keep our house standing.

My phone chimes with a message from my client.

BRENDA ECCLESTON

Found the collar. Leaving now.

CARA

I'm here. See you soon.

With at least ten minutes to kill—maybe more if they weren't actually in the car, but still chasing Peaches around with the recovered collar—I send a message to my sister.

CARA

Did Mom tell you Hayden Reilly is back in town and also wants to buy the house?

I set the phone on the counter because Georgia's a nurse in a very busy emergency department in Portland, Maine. Sometimes she responds right away, but more often than not an hour or more will pass between each message in our conversations.

Not only does she respond right away, but she calls. That's rare. "Hey, Georgia."

14

"He's back? Have you seen him? Why does he want to buy that shitty old house? Is he going to burn it down? Did you see the offer? Did Mom's head explode?"

I laugh at the barrage of questions. "Take a breath. I haven't seen him and I didn't see the offer, but Mom isn't going to sell it to *anybody*, never mind a Reilly. And I doubt he'd come back and buy our house just to burn it down."

A familiar growl of frustration vibrates through the phone. Georgia doesn't have a lot of patience when it comes to our mother. "I'm tempted to burn the place down myself."

"If you do, we're coming to live with you and Tony. Both of us." Her husband is a graphic designer with flexible office and work-from-home hours. And they have a studio apartment. It's a good threat.

"Why don't you just leave?"

I've lost count of how many times she's asked me that. The first time was the day after I graduated from high school, and I think we've had maybe three conversations over the years since then that haven't included my least favorite topic.

"I can't," I say for the umpteenth time. Because she left first and now I'm stuck here.

"Yes, you can. Just throw some stuff in your car and start driving."

I laugh, even though that's basically the dream. "Have you seen the price of gas? I'd be lucky to make it to the state line."

"I won't give you a dime for that damn house, but I'll send you a bus ticket to get here. Or gas money, if your car's in any better shape than the house."

"Barely," I confess. It probably isn't going to pass inspection in September, even with Mel's husband—the town's mechanic— giving me a wife's-BFF discount.

I won't start losing sleep over that until mid-August or so, though. The things that keep me up at night make for a long list, so worries have to wait their turn.

"I know it's hard to leave," Georgia says, her voice softening. "But it's worth it."

I want to. But I don't feel like I can, and we both know I won't. "If I go, she'll be alone in that house and it'll crumble around her."

"Or maybe she'll be forced to do something about it." Georgia's voice goes hard again. "And her life choices are on her, not you."

"She's our mother."

"Which means she should have cared more about us than about that town and a bunch of gossipy shit and a promise she made to Dad when he was barely conscious. She doesn't deserve you, Cara."

She's not wrong, but I can't bring myself to acknowledge that truth out loud. Luckily, I see the Ecclestons' SUV doing a slow drive past the window, looking for a parking space.

"My client's parking now, so I have to run."

"Do whatever you have to do to get her to accept Reilly's offer," Georgia said in her stern big-sister voice.

"Sure, because I've had so much luck influencing her in the past."

"Cara, I'm serious. I know our family and the Reillys don't get along because there's nothing better to do in a small town but nurse grudges you can't even remember the origin of. And I know Hayden Reilly is an asshole. But you might never get an opportunity like this again—an offer on a house with a value that's dropping faster than a smartphone depreciates at this point. This is your chance, so do *whatever* it takes."

My client is about to walk through the door, so I promise her I will and get off the call, even though I have no idea how to *keep* that promise.

She's not wrong, though. I have to do whatever it takes or all of my tomorrows will look just like my yesterday. And yesterday sucked.

Chapter Four

HAYDEN

I'm not a patient man where business is concerned, so I'm frustrated by twenty-four hours—give or take—passing with no news from Matt Woodrow, the real estate lawyer I hired to deal with Gin Gamble. Though it's tempting to nudge him before leaving for dinner at my brother's house, I resist the urge.

There's a very slim possibility her straits are dire enough she'll consider selling—even to me—and the best thing I can do is let her come to that conclusion on her own.

I'm almost to the front porch of Aaron and Hope's brick Colonial when my phone rings and my smartwatch flashes Matt's name. "Mom, I need to take this. Go ahead without me and I'll be there in a few minutes."

She sighs and waves her hand. My workaholic ways are usually at the top of her maternal complaint list, but everything got bumped down a notch when I mentioned Gin Gamble's name yesterday. "Five minutes, and then we're sending the kids out here after you."

I nod and slide the bar to answer the call before it can go to voicemail. Penny sighs dramatically and plops down with her face on my shoe. "Talk to me."

"That woman does *not* like you."

"That was never in doubt." I watch my mom walk through the front door and close it behind her. "The question is, does she need money more than she hates me?"

"No, actually." He pauses to let the curses that come out of my mouth run their course. "I've been in this business a long time and I'm confident this is the first time I've ever told the owner of a rundown house in a small town that a client is offering them *significantly* more than the property's worth, and been told my client can shove his filthy money up his ass."

The word *filthy* crawls under my skin, triggering an old, deep-seated rage. "That sounds like Gin."

"That was one of the kinder things she said, actually. I know you wanted this house for whatever reason, but I can have an agent scout some comp properties for you."

"No." I don't want similar houses. I want *that* one. "Keep the file on top of the stack and I'll be in touch when she's a little more open to what you have to say."

"I don't see that happening." There's a pause and then an awkward chuckle. "No duct tape, zip ties or baseball bats, Hayden."

"Not my style. Talk soon," I say, and then I hang up.

It's time for Plan B.

I glance at my watch and judge I have another minute or two before my mother sends the kids out after me. It's not usually a threat she follows through on because she knows work is important to me, but Colleen's in a mood. Plus, I haven't seen my niece and nephew since Christmas, other than video calls, so they'll be eager to see me.

I pull up the contact info for Cara's grooming business, which I saved in my phone before leaving Boston. Rather than taking a second to think about what I'm about to do—giving any uncharacteristic second guessing of myself a chance to creep in—I hit the button to make the call.

She answers on the third ring. "Pampered Paws Grooming, Cara speaking. How can I help you?"

I thought I was ready to hear Cara's voice again after all this time, but I wasn't prepared for how the years have aged it like fine wine. Her voice is deeper now—and slightly husky—and my body tightens in response.

Once upon a time, I was head over heels for Cara. But that was a long time ago, and now she's a means to an end. I need to remember that.

"Good afternoon," I say, as casually as I can manage. "Do you have availability for a canine nail trim? I'm not sure how, but my dog has a ragged edge on one nail and I don't want her chewing at it or catching it in her hair."

"Of course. I can squeeze her in tomorrow at ten. Have you been here before?"

"No. I'm in town for a short time, visiting family."

There's a long pause and just when I think she's placed my voice, she clears her throat. "Okay, let me just take down some information, then. Your dog's name?"

"Penelope Louise." The dog looks up at me, her head cocked as if trying to figure out why I'm talking about her.

"That's a big name."

"She has a big personality."

"On a scale of one to five, how well is she trained?"

"It's hard to say. You don't really train a Shih Tzu. They either like you enough to want to make you happy—if they're in the mood, of course—or they don't."

Her laugh is soft, and I close my eyes for a second to savor it. "So a one, then. But I can't wait to meet her. And your name?"

It's the moment of truth. "Hayden Reilly."

Nothing but silence. I'd think she hung up on me, but I can hear her breathing. Based on the slight force behind each exhale, I assume she's trying to control her temper. The odds are against me—there's a good chance she's going to refuse to let me through her shop door—but I'm banking on a pet groomer in a town this small being very reluctant to turn away business.

"I have you down for tomorrow morning at ten o'clock," she says. There's definitely no warmth in her voice now. "Are you actually going to show up?"

Ouch. I probably deserve that. "I'll be there."

"I'm charging you double," she says curtly.

"That's reasonable for a short notice appointment, I guess."

"Actually it's because I don't like you."

I know I shouldn't, but I can't help myself. "You used to."

"Tomorrow, ten o'clock," she says, and then the line goes dead.

I smile as I slide the phone into my pocket, which signals Penny it's time to move. My smile fades, though, when I turn and see my mother standing on Aaron's porch with her arms crossed and the door open behind her. "What was that about?"

"Penny has a ragged nail I need to get trimmed," I say, thankful my dog isn't exactly welcoming when it comes to anybody but me touching her feet. My mom's not going to be able to confirm or deny my claim.

"Where are you taking her?"

"Pampered Paws Grooming, which is the only groomer in town. And you know that."

As I expect, her jaw clenches and she presses her lips together before shaking her head. "Trying to buy that house is bad enough, but now this? There's no reason to be giving a Gamble *any* of your money."

"You wouldn't say that if you'd ever tried to trim Penny's nails."

Her eyes narrow. "I might believe Princess Penelope over there needs her nails done if she didn't have a standing appointment with her own team of groomers who visit her at home."

"That's a little dramatic, Mom. The *team* is the two sisters of my IT manager—one of whom is a teacher and the other a stay-at-home mom—who are trying to get a home dog grooming business off the ground around school hours. They get to use me as a reference in my neighborhood and I don't have to rearrange my schedule for grooming appointments."

"Are you denying she's spoiled?"

I laugh. "Oh, she's absolutely spoiled, as she should be. But not as ridiculously as you make it sound."

And she's worth it. Penny keeps me from disappearing into my work entirely. She came into my life at a time when I was at risk of becoming all focus and hard edges, and loving her softens those edges. Penny gives me a reason to close my laptop, walk in the park, and relax on the couch. She loves me with her whole heart and there's nothing I wouldn't do for her.

"Why do you have to stir up trouble?" Colleen asks in a low voice when I reach the porch. "You barely come home over the years and now you're here *indefinitely*—and don't get me wrong, I love having you home—but you're poking at the Gamble hive with a sharp stick and I can't figure out why."

"I haven't even sharpened the stick yet." Temper flares in her eyes and her hands go to her hips, making me regret the careless words. "Mom, I'll explain it all to you someday soon, but for now trust that I have my reasons and I'm not going to stir up trouble."

There's almost no chance she believes me, but as she's opening her mouth to give me a piece of her mind, Daisy and AJ explode through the open door.

"Uncle Hayden," they yell in unison as Penny skirts them and rushes inside to find her favorite spot behind Hope's knitting basket. She's only been here twice, but she figured out on her first visit she's almost invisible there.

The kids hit me with enough force so I have to shift my foot to brace myself and keep us all from tumbling down the three porch steps. Then I laugh and crouch so they can give me proper hugs. With the opportunity for a maternal lecture lost, my mom goes back inside.

Grabbing a kid under each arm and making monster noises to make them giggle, I straighten and follow her inside.

Chapter Five

CARA

How did I not recognize Hayden Reilly's voice?

I was obsessed with him in high school. We even dated...kind of. To me, dating means driving to the movie theater in the city or two straws in one frappe at the diner. But two small-town teens whose families despised each other couldn't do any of that.

Instead, we spent one glorious summer hiding in our favorite spot—sitting on a big, flat boulder on the riverbank. It felt so much more intimate than dating.

I also thought about him constantly after he broke my heart, of course, remembering things he'd said to me over and over in my mind. His voice was a record I played on repeat.

I still think about him when I see Aaron or Colleen from a distance. Or when a song from our high school days comes on the radio. He's certainly been on my mind since Gin told me he's in town and looking to buy our house.

So ten minutes ago, I would have sworn I'd recognize Hayden's voice instantly.

I didn't. The deep voice threaded with confidence and a hint of authority caught my attention on a purely chemical level, of course. It's the kind of voice that would top a list of things I find attractive in a man, along with sexy forearms, a solid sense of humor, and letting me have the last cookie. But it wasn't until he said his name that I realized it was Hayden.

I thought about hanging up on him. I'd even pulled the phone away from my face and hovered my thumb over the red X.

Then I heard my sister's voice in my head. *Do whatever it takes.*

Maybe if I spend time with him alone, in my shop, I can get more information about the offer he made. Why he made it, for one thing. Why would a man who's gone off and made a fancy life for himself in Boston—again, people talk—want to buy a house that's walking that real estate listing line between a handyman's special needing some TLC and a complete tear-down like a tightrope? And in a town he doesn't spend a lot of time in. If there's anything compelling I can use to convince Gin this is an offer she can't pass up, I need to find it.

Even if that means being alone with Hayden Reilly.

Since I don't have any more clients scheduled to come in, I start closing up. When Mr. Jensen is scheduled to bring in Aries, the family's husky, he's one of the few clients who has to stay through the session. And I always make sure they're the last appointment of the day. Aries is very strong, highly melodramatic, and has the vocal range of an opera star. It takes both of us to get him fully groomed and by the time they leave, I'm exhausted. There's also enough husky hair in my shop so I could spin it into yarn and knit an entire second dog.

Unfortunately, cleaning is a good way to burn off nerves, but it's not a great mental distraction. My hands are busy, but my mind is free to think about the fact I'm going to see Hayden tomorrow.

Here. In my shop.

My junior year felt endless after that disastrous homecoming dance that wasn't in October. I did everything I could to spend my days looking anywhere but at him. He seemed as devoted as I was to avoiding each other, so we rarely crossed paths. While I spent an overwhelming amount of time thinking about him, I rarely saw him and *never* spoke to him.

Then, about a week after the seniors graduated, I overheard two women standing in line at the market talking about the fact Colleen Reilly's older son had left town. Even though I was angry and hadn't spoken to him for months, I was heartbroken all over again.

Once I've locked up, I hurry directly to my car. I drove again because the weather forecast called for more rain, but they'd been wrong. The skies are blue, but I barely notice.

Even on the days I drive, I usually take a walk around the town square after work when the weather's nice, but today is different. Today, Hayden is somewhere in Sumac Falls and I absolutely don't want to risk running into him—especially after my wrestling match with Aries.

Even though I wouldn't give him a glass of water if he was on fire, a woman wants to look her best when she runs into an ex. And maybe my best isn't great, but I'm pretty sure my hair's rocking ragged husky fur extensions right now.

When I pull into the driveway, my mother's car isn't in its usual spot in front of the lefthand garage door. We haven't been able to park in the two-car garage since before my father died because it's so full of junk. And not useful junk, but stuff my parents collected over the decades thanks to a mutual love of yard sales. Everything in there needs just a little fix, a new cord, or a coat of paint.

Or a bonfire, I think. The property as a whole would make a great training exercise for our volunteer fire department. Except for the part where Gin and I would be left with nothing, of course.

But if I can talk my mother into considering Hayden's offer, we could start over. My mom could buy a cute little house and I could...do something. I don't know what, but I'd be free to figure it out.

I look at the enormous Victorian home that generations of Gambles have been born and raised in. My great-great-grandfather built it, showing off what mill money could buy when you were the owner.

It's three stories, with ornate trim and a deep porch. We don't use the third floor anymore, having sealed it off so we don't have to heat it. I go up there periodically to clean because the last thing we need is rodents or raccoons taking up permanent residency in our house, but we live our lives in the small, oddly-shaped rooms on the first and second floors. There was no such thing as open concept back in the day, I guess, but at least there are plenty of walls to decorate with Gamble family photos and yard sale paintings.

The outside was originally a deep yellow, with white trim and shutters. It's a faded cream color now, peeling and chipping because that much paint is expensive and a painting crew would cost even more. I manage to keep the porch and front door in decent condition, but that's about it.

Like a lot of New England mill towns that saw their mills close down, Sumac Falls was hit hard economically. But the Gamble family had already been living beyond their means and by the time my parents got the house, the money was gone. The house was the only thing left.

I talked to the bank once about taking out a personal loan. Gin refused to mortgage the property because that was a point of pride for her—she owns the house outright. But we needed money to update the electrical system.

Unfortunately, because of our income, we could only take a loan against the house, but they wanted the electrical system updated and the whole house painted first. We couldn't even afford to get a loan. And it's in worse condition now.

There's no sensible reason for Hayden Reilly to buy this house.

We absolutely *have* to sell it to him.

A chiming sound interrupts my thoughts and I groan when I

realize it didn't come from my phone. It's the light on my car's dashboard, letting me know it's going to run out of gas soon. Awesome.

I turn off the ignition, wanting to save every precious, over-priced drop of fuel I can, and then I lower my forehead to the steering wheel and try not to cry.

Chapter Six

HAYDEN

Dinner is a total waste of an excellent beef stroganoff. The vibe is so tense, the adults around the table are just shoveling the food in our mouths as an excuse not to talk. And the kids, who would rather have chicken nuggets, are mostly pushing it around on their plates.

My mother's silent, but visibly angry. Aaron and Hope can probably guess I'm the one responsible for her mood, and that it has to do with the Gamble family. But they won't ask about it and risk setting Colleen off with Daisy and AJ at the table.

Awkward silence only broken by the kids works for me because I don't want to have any deep conversations about the Gamble house with my family. There's only so much I can explain without sharing things I'd rather keep to myself—stuff I've never told them and hopefully never will.

My cover story about wanting to restore the old home to its former glory is thin, and it won't stand up to too many hard questions. Nobody in this room has ever heard me express an interest in the restoration of old homes. And even if I want to flip a house or keep it as an investment, the fact I picked the one belonging to a woman I hate in a town I rarely visit is pretty sketchy.

So the more the kids can distract them, the better.

"Can we get a dog?" AJ asks, as he does every time he's around Penny.

I'm not sure why my dog triggers the desire for one of his own, since Penny wants absolutely nothing to do with small children and will stay in her hiding spot until I tell her it's time to go. To be fair, she doesn't want anything to do with older children, teenagers or most adults, either. I'm Penny's person and she only seems to need one.

"We're not really a dog-friendly family," Hope says. "We're busy all the time, and it wouldn't be fair to a dog."

None of the adults at the table point out that Aaron works from home, doing freelance bookkeeping and tax prep for businesses around the state, and the kids don't seem to have made that connection yet. It won't be long before they do, and then Hope will have to come up with another excuse. She told me once that she'd love to get a dog for the kids, but all the breeds that would run and play as hard as her kids do are the overly shedding kind and she has a thing about dog hair.

"At least there's a groomer in Sumac Falls if you do get one someday," my mother says in a deceptively sweet voice, and Aaron and I both pause with forks midair.

Here it comes.

"Did you know Cara Gamble owns Pampered Pets Grooming?" she asked Hope, even though everybody in this town knows that. "Hayden made an appointment to take Penny in tomorrow."

There's a long moment of silence before Aaron clears his throat. "There's only one in town, so it makes sense he'd go to her."

"We haven't used her, obviously," Hope says, "but everybody in Sumac Falls seems to have well-groomed pets, so she's probably very good."

Aaron's gaze flicks to me, but I ignore the look. We both know the only reason I'm taking Penelope to Pampered Pets tomorrow is to get a chance to talk to Cara, but he keeps his mouth shut.

Before Colleen can say anything else, Hope gives her son a bright smile. "AJ, did you tell Grammy about your swimming lessons?"

I smile my thanks at my sister-in-law as the excited child launches into a minute-by-minute recitation of his swim class, including in-depth descriptions of his classmates and the instructor. When he's this wound up about a subject, he can talk for at least ten minutes without pause, so I turn my attention back to eating my dinner in peace.

Not that I *feel* peaceful at the moment. Even though I turned down the coffee Hope offered me earlier, the tension that's taken up residence in my body is going to keep me from sleeping tonight.

In a little more than twelve hours, I'm going to see Cara Gamble again for the first time since the end of finals in my senior year. I was in the office, signing myself out early because I'd completed my academic obligations, and she walked in.

My heart had stopped during the moment our gazes locked. Her eyes widened and her lips parted. I saw the hitch in her chest as her breath caught. The flash of hurt across her face. We hadn't spoken for months—not a word since we walked out of school and I told her I'd pick her up for the homecoming dance later. And then didn't.

Then Cara blinked and kept walking, straight into the principal's office with a stack of papers. She hadn't looked back and, after signing my name on the senior dismissal sheet, neither had I. Cara wasn't at graduation the following weekend—Georgia had already graduated and her close friends were in her own class, so she had no reason to attend—and I left Sumac Falls the following day. I couch-surfed in Boston all summer, working as many hours as I could every week until it was time to move into my dorm.

I channeled my pain and anger into being successful—taking the right classes and excelling at them and, more importantly, making the right connections. Jumping a few rungs on the collegiate ladder for my master's degree and making even better connections. Grueling internships. Then the job with the best investment company in Boston. A brutal schedule and ruthless moves until only a few very wealthy men who preferred country clubs to being in their offices remained above me on the staff directory. All the while, investing just the right side of recklessly until I had enough money to *almost* sleep well at night.

When I got tired of funding other men's golf memberships and summer homes, I started my own firm. I worked even longer hours, and once I'd achieved stability, I started a side portfolio earmarked for the one thing I hadn't yet checked off my list.

When I've taken the Gamble house away from the Gamble family and everybody in Sumac Falls knows I did it? *Then* I'll finally get a good night's sleep.

Tomorrow can't come soon enough.

Chapter Seven

CARA

When I woke up this morning, after a long night of tossing and turning, I thought I'd mentally prepared myself for seeing Hayden Reilly walk through my door.

I was so wrong.

The closer the time gets to ten o'clock, the less I'm able to concentrate on anything but seeing him again. I finally give up on making a list of supplies to reorder and just polish the stainless steel tub that doesn't need polishing.

Maybe he won't show up.

It certainly wouldn't be the first time. A guy who would stand a girl up on what was meant to be one of the best nights of her teenage life probably wouldn't hesitate to blow off a nail appointment for his dog.

But I think he *is* going to show up because I don't believe for a second Penelope Louise needs her nails done. He wants to feel out whether I'm as hostile to the idea of his offer on the house as my mother is and, if not, how he can use me to influence her.

As the time nears, I resist the urge to step into my shop's tiny bathroom to check my hair or look for residual cleaner or wet spots from the scrubbing I'd done. I don't want to give him the satisfaction of thinking I care.

At exactly ten o'clock, the door opens and my heart skips a beat.

He's a stranger, of course. It's been seventeen years, and I don't really recognize the man who steps into the shop. I'd know him if I passed him on the street, of course. He hasn't changed *that* much, but this Hayden Reilly isn't the Hayden I'd loved as a teenager.

Always one of the taller boys in his class, he's broader now. His shoulders fill out the casual light blue button-down shirt that highlights the icy blue of his eyes. The sleeves are rolled back, showing off the tan forearms cradling a white and tan Shih Tzu, and even though his jeans are well-worn and his shoes casual, I recognize them as expensive. His dark hair is neatly trimmed, as are the closely-cropped beard and mustache, which are new.

"Hi, Cara," he says in a much lower, huskier voice than he'd used on the phone yesterday.

Then he smiles, and there he is—*my* Hayden. The crinkling in his eyes and the way he grins while barely showing his teeth because he has a slightly crooked eye tooth he hates are so familiar to me, I almost move toward him.

Just in time, reality sets in and I fix my eyes firmly on the dog in his arms. "Hello. This must be Penelope Louise."

"Yes, though she'll also answer to Penny, of course. And Penny Lou and...well, I'll spare you the entire list of nicknames."

I gesture to where I've put a fluffy pillow on top of the stainless steel grooming table. "You can set her on the cushion, but clip the overhead lead to her harness before you take her leash off."

Usually I'd replace the harness with a slip leash, but Penny's only getting her nails done. And I prefer to do it myself, as a rule, but I don't want any chance of physical contact between Hayden and me. It's hard enough hearing his voice and seeing glimpses of his younger self. There's so much nervous energy coursing through me right now, our hands brushing might feel like a lightning strike.

Hayden does as he's told, and then backs up. He doesn't back away very far, though, so he can easily reach the dog if she decides to move. His brow is furrowed in an adorably concerned way, and he doesn't take his eyes off of her.

I'm usually a sucker for a man who loves dogs, but I am absolutely *not* going to soften toward this particular man.

I move closer so Penny can smell me and rest my hand on the cushion near her head. It's obvious she's professionally groomed regularly, but my shop and I are new to her, and I know Shih Tzus don't like changes in their routines.

Once it's clear she'll at least tolerate me, I give her a little scratch under her chin while stroking my other hand over her back. "Hey, sweetie. You're a pretty girl, aren't you?"

She gives me a happy expression and leans sideways just a little so I can stroke her belly.

"Huh." Hayden's body language relaxes when he realizes Penny isn't going to dive off the table to get away from me. "She's usually really unhappy if somebody besides me tries to talk to her or pet her."

"We're going to be friends, aren't we?" I ask the dog in that slightly higher than usual voice we use with pets, ignoring her owner.

"She's got a little rough spot on one of her nails and if she scratches her ears, it catches on her hair and annoys her."

I skim a fingertip over the edges of her practically perfect nails. "I don't feel anything."

"Maybe walking on the pavement smoothed it out, but if you give her a touch-up, I won't have to worry about it."

I roll my eyes at Penny, as if she and I are in on thinking he's ridiculous together, but I'll buff her nails. I wasn't kidding about charging him double.

"How old is she? I meant to ask yesterday." I don't admit I

also forgot to ask about her vaccinations because hearing his name knocked me off my game.

"She recently turned two."

I pull the rolling stool over, since it doesn't look as if this is going to end in a wrestling match. Between Penny and I, of course. I can't promise I won't be tempted to throw a punch Hayden's way before the appointment is over.

"How did you and Penelope Louise come to be together?" I ask to distract myself as I pick up her front paw. She sighs, but accepts it. "Did you get her as a puppy?"

"She was a baby when we met. One of my employees bought her for his mom so he wouldn't have to feel guilty about never visiting her. He neglected to ask her if she was allowed to have dogs in her building, which was a no, or if she even *wanted* a dog, which she did not. He brought her to work because he had a meeting and didn't know what else to do with her."

"He really didn't think any of that through."

"No, he didn't. Anyway, Penny got out of his office and found her way to mine."

"So it was fate?"

"It was more likely the roast beef sandwich on my desk. But when Kirk realized she'd wandered into the boss's office, he was embarrassed and mad, which made him a little mean. I didn't like the way he spoke to her or picked her up, so I took her away from him."

"And you kept her? Just like that?"

"More or less just like that. He didn't really put up a fight. Also, I did reimburse him for what she'd cost him, and then I fired him a week later."

"Because of how he treated Penelope?"

He chuckles and the sound makes my toes curl. "No, but the way Kirk had treated Penny may have been the reason I didn't give him the benefit of the doubt in the situation I *did* fire him for."

I stifle my amusement. I do *not* want to like this man, and I *definitely* don't want him to think I do.

I don't like you.

You used to.

Yes, I used to like him very much, and that didn't get me anywhere but crying into my pillow every night.

Now I don't like him at all, but I need to be civil until he's paid me, at least. And I still need to figure out how to bring the conversation around to the fact he made an offer on our house.

"So," I start, hoping I'll sound casual without being *suspiciously* casual. "What brings you back to Sumac Falls?"

Chapter Eight

HAYDEN

My guilt over making Cara go through the motions of small talk when she'd probably rather plunge the nail file into my heart is significant, and the way my pulse is still racing from the two of us being in the same room doesn't help.

As soon as I walked through the door, I realized that no amount of anticipating this moment could have prepared me for seeing Cara Gamble again.

The lush brown hair—a few shades lighter than her chocolate eyes—that I'd loved to run my fingers through is pulled up in a ponytail. She's curvier now, and my hands twitch with a need to skim over her hips. She's aged, of course—we both have—but she's still one of the most beautiful women I've ever seen.

And I'm pretty sure if I was on fire, she would pour a glass of water and then slowly drink it right in front of me.

But neither making Cara like me nor Penny's unnecessary canine pedicure are the reason I'm here. It's time to focus on my end goal.

"I come back now and then to see my mom. And Aaron, Hope and the kids," I say. And as awkward as it's going to be, I know this is my opening. "Every time I drive by your house, it breaks my heart a little."

She stills for a few seconds and then resumes filing. "My mother told me you want to buy the house."

"I do."

"Why?"

Considering the offer I made was for more than the property's worth and doesn't require inspections it would undoubtedly fail, I'm not sure it matters. "I have a soft spot for those big, old New England houses—especially the ones that haven't been converted into apartments—and seeing the most beautiful house in Sumac Falls fall into disrepair is sad."

Her cheeks flush, but there's really no way to dance around the subject. And it's not her fault her ancestors just assumed future generations would have enough money to maintain the property. She finishes with Penny's paw and I have to move as she slides the stool to the dog's other side.

"I'd love to restore it," I tell her. "But our families haven't exactly been friends over the years, so I'm anticipating some resistance from Gin."

She snorts. "So much understatement in one sentence."

Aaron was right, then. Gin might sell, but she sure as shit ain't going to sell it to *me*. "Since you live there, too, I thought maybe you would be...an ally, I guess."

"And you thought inventing a reason to come into my place of business so you can bring it up while I'm working would help your case?"

"You're filing my dog's nails."

She pauses and without letting go of Penny's paw, gives me a look that drops my core temp five degrees. "Insulting my profession is an interesting way to go here."

"I apologize. What I was trying to convey was my certainty that you can file and talk at the same time, and also I didn't really an invent a reason since you're actually doing it."

She turns her attention back to Penny's nails, and I resist the urge to fill the silence that stretches on.

"There has to be more to it than wanting to restore an old house," she finally says. "You know the history between our families, and even if I could finally convince my mom to sell it, there's almost no chance it would be to a Reilly."

There's a lot to unpack there. There *is* more to it than wanting to restore an old house, but I have no intention of sharing that motivation with Cara. And *almost* no chance isn't the same as no chance at all.

But most importantly, there are those two very telling words —*finally convince*—that snag my attention. Cara actively *wants* Gin to sell the house, and she has to know mine will be the best offer they can get.

"Did Gin give you the specifics of my offer?"

"Nope. She probably didn't think the details mattered since she's never going to consider it."

"Never?"

"Even if you weren't a Reilly, she won't let it go to anybody outside of the family."

Right. Because it's *the Gamble house*. It's quickly becoming the Gamble *ruins*, but apparently that doesn't matter to Gin. "Let me take you to dinner."

The file stops, but Cara doesn't look up. "Absolutely not. No."

It's hard to work with a hard, unequivocal *no*. There's not a lot of wiggle room there. That doesn't mean I'm not going to try. I've been told I can be very persuasive when I want something.

"We can go separately and meet in the city. Your choice of restaurant, and it'll be my treat for taking the time to hear me out."

"Still no." She stands and gives Penny a good fingertip rub, all the way down her back. "I think we're done here since her nails were immaculate when you came in."

She unhooks Penny from the overhead lead and clips her leash back to the harness. I expect my dog to turn her head in my direction, but instead she licks the back of Cara's hand. When Cara leans down and plants a kiss on top of Penny's head, I have to look away.

Once she's set Penny on the floor, she gives me the total and then runs my card. Even though she did charge me double, I add a generous tip. I'm always thankful when Penelope has a good experience with a service provider.

"Please think about dinner," I say, knowing I won't get a yes right now, but maybe I can plant the seeds. "We can get out of this town and talk about how my offer is not only in the best interest of the house, but maybe you and your mom, too."

"I use my cell for the shop, so I have your number in my phone. If I change my mind, I'll let you know, but I wouldn't hold my breath." Then, after making a kissing sound at Penny and giving her a final scratch under the chin, Cara gives me the fakest smile I've ever seen. "Have a nice day."

Chapter Nine

CARA

I'm still stewing over the nerve of that man to ask me out for dinner when I pull into the driveway after a long day. Besides my regular appointments, I also had the pleasure of trying to de-stink a something-doodle that had rolled in an unknown but persistently unpleasant substance.

How charming does Hayden think he is that he can just walk into my shop after seventeen years and expect me to share a meal with him? Obviously he's successful at whatever financial investment-type thing he does, but money and the promise of a fancy dinner can't buy my forgiveness.

His money could end my misery, though, I think as I enter the side door of the garage. It's stuffed with a ton of junk, but there's a laundry basket in one corner, with a shelf of clothes next to it. I strip down to my underwear and drop my clothes in the hamper, and then I pull on a clean T-shirt and shorts. It's a pain in the ass, but it's what I have to do to accommodate Gin's alleged pet allergy.

As soon as I walk through the back door into the kitchen, I can tell Gin's in a mood. She's tense and usually she hums or sings quietly while she cooks dinner. Today's she silent, and she's chopping a carrot with so much vigor, she's going to lose a finger if she misses.

That's fine with me—her attitude, not my mom losing a finger—because my mood isn't great, either. We can just stay out of each other's way and keep conversation to a minimum.

I take a quick shower and then set the table while my mother finishes up the sauteed chicken breasts to go with the salad. We still haven't spoken and I'm not sure why. She's not usually shy about voicing annoyances. The tension's getting awkward, but I don't have the energy to break the conversational ice.

I take my first bite of chicken, and of course she chooses that moment to cave. "Why was that Reilly boy in your shop today?"

And mystery solved. "His dog had a nail that needed to be taken care of, but it wasn't bad enough for him to go all the way back to Boston to see her regular groomer."

"How hard can trimming a dog's nails be?"

Says the woman who's never tried it. "I'm not really in a position to turn away business, no matter who it is. And I charged him double, if that makes you feel any better about it."

Gin makes a sound implying it actually does make her feel slightly better. For some reason that annoys me even more than her anger. I work my butt off, never saying no to a pet in need, even if it's after hours or a weekend. The night Hudson—a mischievous Westie—got chewing gum ground down to his undercoat, I'd already taken my bra off. But I put it back on and missed my favorite show at airtime, risking spoilers, because pet owners show their appreciation for me with their wallets.

Also, I love animals and I wasn't going to let Hudson gnaw at his sticky coat all night.

My mother doesn't get to interfere with that just because her name is on the deed to this house. Pampered Pets Grooming is mine alone, though it's the primary source of support for both of us, and I'll make my own decisions and they'll be in the best interest of my business.

Maybe it's petty, but her aggravation with the situation makes me want to push her buttons a little bit. "He invited me to go out to dinner with him."

Her eyes narrow. "He did *what*? Why would he do that?"

I'm about to tell her he wants to get me on his side, hoping I'll convince her to sell the house to him, but I change my mind. If Gin thinks he's using her daughter to manipulate her, she'll dig her heels in even harder. And, yes, that's what he's doing, but I don't need to say it out loud and confirm her suspicions.

"To catch up," I guess. "We were friends in high school, right up until he stood me up for homecoming."

Her mouth pinches, reminding me of all the tears and yelling and slamming doors that lasted for days after I finally worked up the courage to tell them I was going to the homecoming dance with a Reilly boy.

"Well, you're not going," she says flatly.

Did she seriously just say that to me with a straight face?

I'll admit I tend to go along with Gin in order to keep the peace a lot more often than I should, but I'm a thirty-five year old woman and I'll have dinner with anybody I damn well want to.

"Actually, I think I *am* going to go," I say and for a few seconds, it feels like some kind of vacuum has sucked all the sound out of the room. Even the refrigerator's fan motor seems to have quieted down.

Then there's a familiar rumbling sound.

"Did you hear that?" Gin holds up her hands as the house trembles just enough to make the nested mixing bowls on top of the fridge rattle together. "That's the sound of generations of Gambles rolling over in their graves."

"Funny how they timed their rolling with the fuel oil truck going by."

My mother doesn't think I'm funny. Actually, she throws her fork down and walks out of the room without another word. A few seconds later, I hear her bedroom door slam.

At this point, I'm ready to have dinner with Hayden out of pure spite.

I have to do a search of restaurants in Concord on my phone. We rarely eat out these days, but even when we did—maybe once a month before my dad died—it was at the corner cafe or the diner here in Sumac Falls.

After almost ten minutes of looking at menus online, I find an entree I want at a place I definitely can't afford. If nothing else, I'm going to get a heap of chicken parm out of this. It would be way too messy to order if it was a first date, but that's definitely *not* what my dinner with Hayden will be.

Before I can lose my nerve or talk myself out of it, I text him a link to the restaurant with a note that I'm available any night after six. That gives me time to shower and change. I might even rummage through the drawer in the bathroom and see if I have any unexpired makeup.

It's not even a full minute before I get a response.

HAYDEN

I'll make a reservation for Saturday at seven.
I'm looking forward to it.

I toss my phone on the table and bury my face in my hands. I probably should have run this idea by Mel first, but she's on a camping trip. This is the worst possible time for my best friend to have no cell signal.

Thanks to house-induced financial desperation and Gin-induced spite, I'm actually going out to dinner with Hayden Reilly.

Chapter Ten

HAYDEN

I'm pouring myself a second glass of water from the glass pitcher, annoyed they don't use an insulated carafe so the condensation doesn't drip on the tablecloth, and wondering if Cara is going to stand me up.

Just like she thinks I did to her all those years ago.

She's been standing outside the restaurant for at least three minutes, her arms folded as she paces a tight circle, clearly torn about having dinner with me. I'm sure she doesn't realize I can see her from our semi-private table in the back of the place, and with the lighting so dim, I doubt she could see me even if she looked this direction.

I'd like to send her a text asking her to come inside. Actually, I'd like to go out there and take her by the hand, leading her back to the table. But I'm fairly confident she only accepted my invitation to spite Gin. I'm not one of Cara's favorite people, by any means, and there's a good chance if I get pushy, she'll leave and not look back.

When she finally yanks open the door and steps inside, I

45

breathe a sigh of relief. Then I turn my attention back to the menu, even though I've already decided what I'm having. Me watching her walk the length of the restaurant might make her feel self-conscious, but the image of her stays in my head, torturing me.

Her dark hair is loose in a shiny cloud, and she's wearing a sundress that hugs her curves. I wish she wasn't wearing a cardigan over it so I could see her shoulders—I used to kiss the freckles there and I want to know if they've faded over time—but the restaurant's gone a little overboard on the air conditioning. I want her to be comfortable more than I want to see her shoulders because the fewer excuses she has to get up and walk out on me, the better.

Once I can see her in my peripheral vision, I look up at her and smile before getting to my feet. "Hi, Cara. Thank you for coming."

She gives me a tight smile and takes her seat before I have a chance to walk around the table and pull her chair out for her. After she's settled, I sit and then I have to swallow a growl of frustration when the server immediately appears.

I do *not* want this evening to be rushed.

Cara orders a glass of white wine, and I nod at the carafe to let him know I'll stick with the water for now. After our server leaves the menus and walks away, she finally turns her attention to me. "We should set some ground rules for this dinner."

I don't point out the time for her to negotiate ground rules was before she joined me at the table and ordered a glass of wine. I don't think she'd appreciate it. "Okay, you go first."

"Fine." She pauses, taking a deep breath. "This is not a date. I'm here to talk about the house. We're not going to take any strolls down Memory Lane, stepping in the garbage and potholes along the way."

I drop my gaze back to the menu again, trying to hide my wince at the unexpected gut punch her words deliver. Garbage and potholes? I know I deserve her anger, but that's harsh.

"And no flirting," she says emphatically. My eyebrow quirks because I didn't see that stipulation coming. "I'm just saying, you're not going to be able to charm me into making my mother accept your offer."

"Ah. Understood." Not necessarily agreed to, but understood.

When the server brings her wine, we order the chicken parm for her and a NY strip steak for me, and I refill my water glass again. My mouth feels inexplicably dry because no matter how firmly she denied it, this feels like I'm finally on a real date with Cara freakin' Gamble after all these years.

"Tell me about the offer," she says.

"Did Gin share any details with you?"

"She didn't bother, since she has no intention of accepting it."

Because I'm hoping Cara will become my unofficial partner in this transaction, I lay it all out. The offer for more than it's worth. No contingencies. No inspections. I'll pay all costs incurred. It's recklessly generous on my part and as uncomplicated as possible for her mother.

"Essentially, I've made her an offer she can't refuse," I say in summary.

Cara snorts. "And she's refusing it."

"I know our families haven't always gotten along, but it's a good offer."

Rubbing her thumb up and down the stem of her wine glass in a way I find incredibly distracting, Cara thinks about it for a moment and then looks me in the eye. "That's the part I don't get, and why I'm not sure I want to push my mother to reconsider her position."

"I don't know what you mean by that."

"The offer is *too* good. I don't believe for a second that you're willing to make a bad business deal to restore the one house in the thousands of old New England houses needing restoration that happens to belong to the family *your* family hates."

I'd hoped Gin would see the number and jump at it, not looking too closely at my motivation. But now Cara's involved

47

and she's going to kick over every rock to see what she can find out.

The one thing she *won't* find is the honest reason I'll do whatever it takes to own the Gamble house. Only two people know. One is me and the other died five years ago.

"Does it really matter?" I ask, careful to keep my tone light despite the rage that sparks any time I think about Marcus Gamble.

"I think it does." She takes a sip of her wine, watching me over the rim of the glass.

"It's not necessarily a bad business deal. The increase in value if the house was totally restored and modernized would be significant." I shrug. "And it's the one house in the thousands of old New England houses needing restoration that's in my hometown."

"Right. How could I forget your close bond with Sumac Falls?"

Sarcasm is practically dripping from her voice, making me smile. "I'm busy and don't get home often, but it's still my hometown."

Her eyes narrow, but before she can challenge how I feel about the town, the server steps up to our table with our meals. It takes a few minutes to get everything settled, and Cara declines another glass of wine. I pour her a glass of water from the carafe while she snaps her napkin open and lays it across her lap. Then we take the first few bites of our food while my mind works, trying to determine the next step in my plan. But I'm having trouble focusing on the house at the moment.

Now that Cara has a rather impressive plateful of chicken parm in front of her, I think she's probably less likely to storm out if I ask her the question I've been struggling not to ask since she walked through the door. Actually, since my visit to Pampered Pets, if I'm being honest.

"How come you never got married? I thought Jacob Brophy would have been down on one knee the day after graduation."

"Jacob told me his parents convinced him making commitments before going off to college is a bad idea. He started his freshman year in Maine and brought a fiancée home for Thanksgiving. Then he brought a different fiancée home for spring break in his sophomore year. Neither of those women was the fiancée he married two summers later."

"Aaron was invited to his third wedding."

She smiles. "I heard his mother bought a sheet cake for the reception."

"Pretty strong statement from a woman who owns a bakery."

"Listen, that woman can be petty. Even though her son dumped *me* years ago, basically at her suggestion, I think Mrs. Brophy has deliberately trained her Chihuahua to hate me." She sets down her fork and glares at me. "Wait. I started dating Jacob Brophy during my senior year. You were already gone, so how do you know about me and Jacob dating? And don't tell me gossip from your mom because there's no chance she was sending you cheery little updates about the Gamble family goings-on."

I don't like to expose my weaknesses, as a rule, but I'm not going to get anywhere with Cara if I don't. "Sometimes, if I had too much to drink, I'd sneak out of a party and text Aaron to ask about you."

Her expression changes, and I have a hard time reading it. There's annoyance, of course, because I lost my right to know anything about her life on homecoming night. But there's something softer, too—almost sad—and I can't help but wonder what might have been if I'd reached out to her instead of to my brother.

Then she shrugs it off. "Believe it or not, in this town it's not easy to find a man you've haven't been annoyed by since preschool. Or a man who wants a wife who comes with the baggage of a falling down house and Gin Gamble for a mother-in-law."

"You wouldn't move out if you got married?"

"And leave her alone to try to take care of that house by

herself?" Her pretty eyes lose their sparkle. "I can't bring myself to do that."

This is the moment—the opportunity to bring Cara around to my side of the negotiating table. "This is our shot, then. Help me make this deal happen and I'll save that house and you'll be free to live the life you want."

Chapter Eleven

CARA

You'll be free to live the life you want.

Hayden's words echo around in my head while I savor the truly delicious chicken parm. Living the life I want sounds like a wonderful thing, even if I can't really picture what that would look like.

My father managed a lumber yard two towns away, and I grew up knowing my family lived paycheck to paycheck. But since losing my dad, Gin and I are basically living day to day—from grooming appointment to grooming appointment. Every day I wake up hoping nothing goes wrong and then I go to bed at night, only to lie awake shifting income projections and expenses around in my head. That doesn't exactly leave any space for daydreaming about what I'd rather be doing.

"Do you have any kind of insider information about this town?" I ask abruptly, not willing to let him believe he has the upper hand so easily.

"What do you mean?"

"Is there something that's going to happen, like a business

moving in or something else being developed, that's going to make our property worth a ton of money in the future?"

His smile makes my skin hot, and I take a long sip of my water. "That's a good question, and no, I don't have any information along those lines. There are no external factors at play here—just me wanting to restore what used to be the most beautiful building in town."

I lean toward believing him, mostly because if there was so much as a whisper about something big coming to Sumac Falls, it would be the worst kept secret ever. I probably would have heard about it at the market already. "Okay."

"Realistically, how much longer do you think you can live there if nothing changes?" he asks.

I want to bristle at the question, but it's one I ask myself practically every day. "We do what we can, but it's a lot for two women alone. Just heating the place eats up more money than you can imagine, so there's not a lot left for painting and repairs. If something goes wrong structurally...not long."

It hurts to admit that out loud, but it's not as though it's a secret. Anybody even randomly driving by can see Gin and I aren't able to keep up the property the way it deserves.

"Every day, the condition and value of your property drops, and it's already unlikely a buyer could get a mortgage approved for it at any price. Not without a ton of work being done to get it past the necessary inspections, anyway." He's speaking matter-of-factly, with no judgement that I can hear. "She's never going to get another offer like mine. Not today and definitely not weeks or months or years from now."

"I know, and that's the only reason I'm here." Did he flinch slightly at those words? Maybe. Or maybe it's just my imagination acting up because I'd like to think he regrets blowing his chance with me.

Seventeen years ago, I remind myself. The time we spent together was such a small blip in time, he probably barely remembers we were even a thing.

I don't like you.

You used to.

"Maybe I don't even care what your motivation is," I say quickly, not wanting to get too bogged down in those mental weeds. "What do I care what you spend your money on if it means Gin and I get out from under that house?"

"Then let's do it," he says, his lips curving into a smile. There's a little triumph in his eyes, but not enough to cross over into being smug.

I laugh. I can't help it. "I think you missed the part where the actual owner of the house would rather sit on a pile of its ashes than sell it to you."

"If there's anybody at all who can sway her towards selling, it's you."

"This may come as a shock, but I've tried—more than once over the years, actually. I think the first time I suggested the house was too much for us, I was talking to my dad." The familiar pang of missing him squeezes my heart for a moment and I take a long drink of water. "Needless to say, I've been fighting a losing battle."

"Maybe you just needed the right ally to come along."

Oh, he's *good*. My heart remembers well the potent combination of Hayden's low voice, warm eyes, and disarming smile. My head, though? That's a different story. I need for my brain to stay tuned into the fact he's only here—and looking at me like this—because he wants something from me.

To be fair, he wanted something from me then, too, but I wanted those kisses by the river and his hand sliding under my shirt as badly as he did. Colluding with him against my mother is something else entirely.

His smile slowly fades, probably because I haven't said anything, and his eyes grow serious. "Look, I screwed up in high school. I was young and stupid, and I'm sorry I treated you that way."

I'm surprised by the apology—and I didn't realize until he said it how badly I wanted to hear the words—but I don't want to dig into those emotions right now. "I told you I don't want to talk about that."

Hayden's jaw tightens, and then he nods once. "Okay. Is there anything you think I can do to make my offer more palatable to Gin?"

Unfortunately, he can't go back in time and make the offer under another name, hiding his identity. That's what he should have done in the first place. Honestly, I'm surprised a man who's supposedly so good at business he can afford to throw money at an old house he doesn't intend to live in didn't think of that.

And, even more importantly, I can't go back in time and stop Gin from making that promise to my dad as he was dying—a promise that had ensnared me, too, because I don't have Georgia's ability to walk away and establish rock solid boundaries.

Sometimes I wonder if our birth orders were switched, with me graduating first and going off to college without looking back, would Georgia still have left? Maybe she truly was wired for *every adult for themselves*. And perhaps I would have returned to Sumac Falls, degree in hand, because I'm just not wired to leave our mother to fend for herself. It's a moot point, of course, but something I think about from time to time—usually after I've talked to Georgia.

"Cara?"

Hayden's voice drags me back into the *actual* reality I'm stuck in, and it takes me a second to remember the question. What can he do to make Gin accept his offer?

"Keep a low profile," I tell him. "Don't do things like being seen in my shop or taking me out for dinner. Wait, no—you didn't take me out. We met for a discussion at a restaurant. Anyway, don't antagonize her and I'll do what I can to make her see she can't pass up this opportunity."

"I'm pretty sure I antagonize her by existing, being a Reilly and all."

I laugh, surprised by how easily the amusement bubbles up inside of me, and he laughs with me. It was like this before—so easy between us when we were alone. It was as if the rest of Sumac Falls, especially our families, faded away and we were free to be ourselves.

I've missed that. I've missed *him*, even though I've been mad at him for a lot of years. Sure, it had all mostly faded away to that nostalgic remembrance of a broken heart, but I'd also shared a lot of my hopes and dreams with Hayden over those months together.

And now, if I want a chance to hope and dream again, I have to let him back into my life.

Chapter Twelve

HAYDEN

I don't want the evening to end.

Laughing with Cara unlocked something inside of me, allowing the good memories of my time spent with her back in the day to push back the more painful memories of how it all came to an end. I don't even take a second to savor my triumph in gaining her as an ally because, right now, I don't want to focus on my objective. I just want to spend more time with Cara.

"I checked out the dessert menu on their website earlier," I tell her. "There are photos, and the cheesecake looks amazing."

When Cara groans, waving her hand over her chicken parm, I'm afraid she's going to say no. She ate less than half of her meal, but it was served on an oversized plate and it wouldn't surprise me if she's full.

Then her lips curve into a mischievous smile. "Good cheesecake is hard to pass up."

In a stroke of fortunate timing, our server appears at the perfect moment and I'm able to order cheesecake and decaf for each of us before Cara can talk herself out of it. What I'd really like to do is order one slice of cheesecake and share it with her, but one dessert with two spoons might be pushing my luck.

As we dig into the dessert, I'm reluctant to bring up the house again because we ended that conversation on the right note. And I'm definitely not bringing up *our* past again. But maybe the past in a general sense is safe ground.

"Did you know my great-great-grandfather and your great-great-grandmother were in love?" I ask after we've both savored a few bites of the rich, creamy cheesecake.

"What? You're kidding. My family refuses to talk about all that, which makes no sense to me."

I shake my head. "Not kidding. Isaiah Reilly and Jonas Gamble worked at the mill together, but Isaiah was also doing every odd job he could scrape up, trying to earn enough to buy Esther Fitzwilliam a ring. He probably took longer than he should have, but her family had a lot of money so he felt some pressure to buy her something prettier than he could afford. And while he was shoveling manure for a few extra coins after a full shift at work, Jonas Gamble figured out if Isaiah—his *best* friend—married Esther Fitzwilliam, he'd be the mill owner's son-in-law. Eventually, since there were no Fitzwilliam sons, the mill owner himself."

"Our great-great-grandfathers were best friends? Really?"

"They were, until the night Jonas got Esther to drink a little too much and managed to get her into an indelicate situation in a place they were sure to be caught. There was a shotgun wedding, and Jonas Gamble inherited the mill and built that big house on the hill, and Isaiah Reilly tried to drown his broken heart with bootleg liquor—it being Prohibition and all. Then he started *running* that liquor and probably made more money than Fitzwilliam himself had. But eventually Isaiah got caught and sent to prison, and so the reputation of Reilly boys was set."

"That had to be almost a hundred years ago." She doesn't actually roll her eyes, but I can hear the reaction in her tone. "And that's the *Reilly* version of the story."

"The fact I actually know the story and your family refuses to talk about it speaks for itself."

She laughs, and points at me. "Good point. So you want to... what? Buy the house and burn it to the ground to avenge your great-great-grandfather's broken heart?"

"It would be a crime to burn that house. And I don't mean legally—although it would definitely be illegal—but because it's beautiful and I want to restore it."

It's not exactly a lie. I do want to restore it to its former glory. But I don't tell her the part where I want to restore it so a Reilly saved something the Gambles let go to shit.

After savoring another bite of cheesecake, she points her spoon at me. "I can understand a generation or two holding a grudge, but *still?*"

"I think as long as the mill was in operation, my family having to work for your family kept it fresh. And it seems to have taken on a life of its own with each generation—like your grandmother tampering with my grandmother's pickles to steal the blue ribbon at the fair."

She gasps and then laughs, clearly shocked by the accusation. "That blue ribbon has hung in a glass shadowbox frame on our kitchen wall since before I was born."

"It would be hanging on *our* kitchen wall if not for the sabotage."

Her eyes narrow, but a smile is tugging at her lips. "And did your grandmother have any proof that my grandmother tampered with her pickles?"

"I don't know."

"Maybe your grandmother's pickles just sucked."

"Gram's pickles did *not* suck."

She grins, sending a sizzle of heat through my veins. "You can say that because you never had *my* gram's pickles."

We laughed about the pickles for a while—which is ironic because neither of us really care for them—but the inevitable moment when the server brings me the check and Cara her boxed leftover chicken parm arrives. I'm thankful she doesn't leave right away, but waits for me to settle the bill so we can walk out together.

"I'll walk you to your car," I say once we're outside. Anything I can do to prolong this time with Cara.

She points to an older vehicle sitting only four spots down the sidewalk. "I think I'll make it there safely."

Of course she wins the parking spot lottery tonight, of all nights. "So what's next?"

"As I said before, keep a low profile. Give me some time—a few days, at least—to work on her without it feeling like pressure. It won't be easy to convince her to look past your last name, assuming I can even make her let go of the promise she made my dad not to sell. I'm not hopeful, but I have to try."

The weary resignation in her voice tugs at my soul, strengthening my conviction to win this real estate battle. Not only will I own the house I wasn't good enough to step foot in, but maybe freeing Cara from Gin's grasp can be my way of trying to make up for what I did to her in the past.

"Let's have dinner again next week to touch base and assess how it's going," I say, already desperate to spend time with her again.

I watch feelings filter through her eyes—she wants to, but she's talking herself out of it—and then disappointment makes me sigh when she shakes her head. "I'll text you. Thank you for dinner. And the dessert. It was delicious."

"It was my pleasure." That's an understatement. She's starting to turn away from me, but there's nothing left to say and no reason to keep her here on the sidewalk with me. "Goodnight, Cara."

"Goodnight, Hayden."

I wait until she's in her car and it's running before I head for my own car. It means turning my back, but I hear her car back out onto the street and then drive away. Staring after her would have been weird, but I can't help turning back once, just in time to see her taillights as she turns onto the main street.

I *have* to get this deal done. For me. And now also for Cara.

Chapter Thirteen

CARA

I asked Hayden for a few days to work on Gin, but we're on day three now and she's still barely speaking to me. Her silence and pinched expression every time she sees me makes it hard to have any conversation at all, never mind a productive one.

Usually her displeasure with me burns itself out in forty-eight hours or less, but when I got home from work today, she was clearly still in a mood. Now I'm clearing the table after another uncomfortable supper, not sure how to break the ice.

She didn't even share the leftover chicken parm with me Sunday night, because she knew Hayden paid for it.

That's next-level petty, even for her, and it's triggering something more like actual anger than the usual annoyance in me. I don't care how many generations of Gambles and Reillys haven't gotten along—there's no reason for her to hate Hayden so much. She hasn't had a conversation with him as a grown man and never —as far as I know—had a conversation with him when we were growing up.

My phone—sitting faceup on the counter—chimes and the

text message is so short, the entire thing shows in the preview when I pick it up.

MEL

WTF?

I realize, in all the turmoil, I lost track of when Mel was due back from camping. I should have sent a message, letting it hang there so she'd get it the second she had cell signal again.

It's unthinkable I forgot to update the one person I've been telling every single thing in my life since third grade. Melinda Pearson and I ran with a tight group of four girls right up through graduation. Two went off to college and never came back. Mel went off to college, but she *did* come back. She married a mechanic and they're the only reason my car passes inspection every year. He gives a really good *wife's-best-friend* discount.

Truthfully, I didn't *entirely* forget. The fact I need to update Mel on the unexpected developments in my life has crossed my mind several times, but I didn't tell her I was having dinner with Hayden, whether she could read it right away or not. I'm not sure what my best friend's reaction is going to be when I tell her I'm basically touching a hot stove that's burned me before.

Another text message comes through while I'm trying to pull up the app to respond to the first one.

MEL

My mom went into Sherry's to buy Harry 7.0 and overheard your mom telling Sherry that you went on a date with HAYDEN FREAKIN' REILLY.

I smile as I type.

CARA

Harry 6.0 didn't make it very long.

Harry was the name given to the cactus Mel's dad gifted her mom for their anniversary three years ago. When he teased her about hoping something that didn't require much care might survive her, Mel's mom swore Harry the Cactus would outlive *him*. Unfortunately, making the vow didn't come with a miraculously green thumb, so she kept having to replace Harry with a fresh *alive* version, hoping her husband wouldn't notice.

Emily and Bob Pearson have always been like bonus parents for me, which might be another reason I haven't updated Mel. They've been dropping a lot of hints lately about how I should find somebody other than my mother to share my life with, and I don't want them getting their hopes up.

Mel responds to my text with a flurry of emojis that translates roughly to yelling about how she's so annoyed with me right now, she'd probably throw her phone at me if we were together. Since she's the type to actually get in her car and drive to wherever I am to do just that, I cave.

CARA

It wasn't a date. It was more like a business meeting.

MEL

I'm too busy to call or to text all the thoughts in my head right now. Basically, LIAR. Spill.

I definitely don't want her to call, since Gin—who's washing the dishes I cleared—would be able to hear my side of the conversation. I type out an overview of everything that's happened so far, ending with a plea not to call because my mom's nearby and not happy about it.

After a few seconds, her response comes through.

MEL

Is he still hot?

CARA

Yes. And he has an adorable dog.

63

MEL

NO. That's very bad. Do you remember when you cried so hard you blew a blood vessel in your eye and looked like something out of a horror movie? You're not doing that again.

CARA

I just want him to buy the house, Mel.

MEL

Gin will never.

She's not wrong, but I'm not ready to give up hope yet.

CARA

Maybe not, but I got free Chicken Parmesan out of it. And cheesecake.

MEL

If anything else happens, you better tell me IMMEDIATELY.

CARA

I will. Gotta go.

"Who was that?" Gin demands when I slide the phone into my pocket so I can wipe down the stove.

"Mel," I say, even though I'm not a teenager and it's none of her business who I'm talking to. But I'd like to put an end to her sulking, not make it worse.

She makes a sound that implies she doesn't believe me. "I don't like you running around with that Reilly boy."

I laugh, even though I know it's the wrong thing to do. "First of all, he's not a boy. And secondly, I'm not going to refuse to talk to a man I like because my great-great-grandfather stole his great-great-grandfather's girlfriend. It's ridiculous."

"There's more to it than that."

"Then explain to me why you won't sell a house we can't afford to keep up anymore to Hayden Reilly even though his offer is more than generous. There has to be a reason beyond a very old family grudge and a promise you made to Dad even *he* knew you wouldn't be able to keep."

"Cara, why can't you leave this alone?"

"Because we sell the house or we *lose* the house, Mom." I'm done dancing around the subject. "We can barely pay our bills now, even though we keep the heat so low in the winter, we have to wear heavy cardigans and wool socks. And it's decaying. The house is falling apart and someday it'll reach a point where we can't live in it anymore, but it'll be too decrepit to sell. Assuming we haven't lost it for back taxes by then."

Gin looks startled by my tone—or maybe by the hard facts— and I have to fight back guilt. There's no reason for me to feel guilty. It would be worse to let my mother keep pretending everything is okay until the moment we actually lose everything. Making her understand our circumstances are dire is the right thing to do.

"What's your plan, Mom?" I ask, wanting to dump some of the emotional and mental responsibility back on her shoulders. "Are you hoping we'll win the lottery? That'll be tough since we can't spare the cost of the tickets and you have to play to win. How do you see this playing out?"

Gin lifts her chin. "In a perfect world, you'll marry some guy from Sumac Falls. You'll live here and fix it up and fill it with children, and I'll have a little mother-in-law's space until I die. Then it'll be yours."

I don't even know how to respond to that. We can't even use the third floor because we can't afford to heat it, and we have a window we can't open because we're afraid too much pressure will make it fall out of the wall. But she thinks somebody's going to want to marry me enough to put all of his money into updating this house? To say nothing of renovating some part of it into a little apartment for his mother-in-law?

I know most of the men in Sumac Falls and I'm more likely to win the lottery. And since I wasn't kidding about not spending my money on buying tickets, that says a lot.

"That's not going to happen," I say firmly. "I've lived here my entire life and I've yet to meet a man I want to marry. I don't have the time or energy to date. And even if I *do* somehow meet a guy I'm interested in, do you really think he's going to want to sink his money into this house and supporting you?

"It could happen."

There's a tightness in her face and body that actually scares me. The conviction in her eyes makes me aware of just how many years have slipped by while I've told myself she'd come around. At first, I believed my parents would see their friends downsizing and embrace letting go of the generational debris. That didn't happen. After my dad passed, I thought in time the grief would fade and take the weight of her promise with it. That also didn't happen.

At some point, it just became the way it was—Gin in denial and me so busy trying to get through each day, I don't even think about the future anymore. And now I know she's never going to change. If I don't do something, this is going to be how I spend the rest of my life.

"Mom, can you—"

"*Enough*, Carolina." She dries her hands and then tosses the towel on the counter instead of pulling it back through the metal loop screwed into the cabinet door. "I'm going for a walk, and when I get back, I don't want to hear another word about this. I'm not selling this house. Period. Ever."

Chapter Fourteen

HAYDEN

I'm on the highway, heading north out of Boston, when my phone rings. Cara's name appears on the hands-free screen and even being cut off by a jacked-up truck in a hurry can't wipe the smile off my face as I hit the button to accept the call.

"Hi, Cara. How's it going?"

"Gin Gamble is the most stubborn woman I've ever met," she says, clearly frustrated. That's not a good sign.

Penny lifts her head when she hears Cara's voice. The dog is clipped into a very comfortable carseat, but she looks around as if Cara magically appeared in the car. Considering how often Penny ignores the business calls I make and accept almost constantly while I'm driving, her reaction is interesting.

"We knew it wouldn't be easy," I remind Cara.

"We had it out a bit last night and she's not going to budge, Hayden. She'll let it fall down around us rather than sell."

Her voice is heavy with resignation, but I don't surrender that easily. "I'm on my way back to New Hampshire as we speak. Let's get together and regroup."

"I didn't know you left."

"I set up a few meetings when I realized it would be a better use of my time than staring at my phone, waiting to hear from you." As soon as the words leave my mouth, I cringe. Hopefully she thinks I'm that invested in buying the property, even though it sounded as if I've been pining, just waiting to hear her voice again.

To be honest, it's a little of both.

"I don't think it will do any good. She's not wavering, even after I threw some unpleasant projections for our future at her. And you and I being seen together isn't going to make her change her mind."

My mind is racing, trying to work the problem of the Gamble house. Step one is making sure Cara doesn't give up. Without her, I have almost no chance. "Do you have appointments this afternoon?"

"It *was* a full day, but one of my clients rescheduled because her baby's sick—her human baby, I mean—so now I get a lunch break."

"I'll be back in town before lunchtime. Is that diner about five miles out of town still open?"

"Last I knew."

"Gin thinks you're at work, so if we meet there for a quick lunch, nobody will know."

When there's only silence from the other end, but I can see the call timer still running on the screen, I assume she's getting ready to tell me no—that it's over.

"Okay."

Once again, Cara surprises me. She must *really* want out of that house. I do some quick navigational math. "I can be there for noon, if that works for you."

"Closer to twelve-thirty would be better. My last client before lunch is a talker and sometimes I have trouble getting her out the door."

"The dog or the human?"

Her soft laughter comes through my speakers, and if I wasn't navigating a particularly nasty highway interchange, I'd close my eyes to savor the sound. "The human. She's single and works from home, so when she gets a chance for live and in-person interaction, she takes it. I won't have a lot of time, but twelve-thirty at the diner?"

"I'll be there."

After we disconnect, I reach over and stroke Penny's back. I've got just enough time to drop her and my bags at my mother's house before heading to lunch with Cara. Luckily, Mom's at work, so I won't have to answer any nosy questions and Penelope will have the house to herself.

When we pull into Colleen's driveway and Penny sees where we are, she gives me a dramatic sigh. The accompanying look lets me know if she could talk, I'd be getting quite the earful right now.

I'm running early, so once I have Penny settled, I change into jeans and a T-shirt. The entire time, I'm trying to come up with advice for Cara on how to soften Gin toward our cause.

I'm not coming up with much.

At this point, I have to admit my ego caused me to make a mistake it'll be hard to recover from. Cara wasn't wrong when she said I should have made the offer in a way that obscured my identity. Getting her to sell would still have been a challenge because of the promise Gin made to Marcus, but at least the Reilly name wouldn't have been in the mix.

But it's too late now. There's no way, if I drop the offer and then another offer comes in from a different entity, that Gin doesn't figure that out. For the moment, it looks as if the only way to achieve my goal is to keep pushing forward and try to wear the woman down with the reality of her situation.

When I pull into the parking lot of the old diner, Cara's getting out of her car, giving me a glimpse of her with her guard down. She's still so pretty, with her dark hair in a messy bun and worn jeans hugging her curves, but I can see that she's exhausted. Maybe even defeated.

I *have* to get her out of that house somehow.

By quickening my steps, I'm able to beat her to the door so I can hold it open for her. The smile she gives me as she steps inside doesn't reach her eyes, but we're quiet until the hostess seats us at a quiet booth toward the back of the old-fashioned dining car.

"I think I got most of the dog hair off," she says as she slides across the vinyl seat, looking down at herself. "I change in the garage when I get home because Gin's allergic to dogs, but I forgot to replace the clean set of clothes I had at the shop for mid-day appointments or errands."

"Your mom is allergic to dogs so you made dog fur your actual job?" I chuckle as I pull two menus from the rack at the end of the table and hand her one. "I guess that's one way to keep her from visiting you at work."

"To be honest, I'm not sure the allergy is even real. She doesn't like dogs and dogs don't like her, so claiming she's allergic to them keeps people from looking at her sideways, wondering what's wrong with her that even a black Lab doesn't want to go anywhere near her."

Whether or not dogs can tell Gin Gamble isn't a good person isn't a topic I'm wading into. The woman's feelings about me are entirely mutual, but I can't lose sight of the fact she's Cara's mother. "Speaking of Gin, she's not budging, huh?"

"Not even a little." She looks at me over the top of her menu and sighs. "I think it's a dead end road."

I don't believe in dead ends—there's always a way around them—but our server steps up to the booth to take our orders. Cara orders a BLT on wheat toast with fries, and I decide on a turkey sandwich. Quick to make and easy to eat because we don't have a lot of time. Both of us get coffee and she asks for a glass of water to go with it.

Once we're alone again, I lean forward, resting my forearms on the table. "Did you explain to her that it's already in bad enough shape so it won't pass the inspections needed for a mortgage? Most people couldn't buy it even if she was looking to sell."

"I did tell her that, and I also told her I don't know if it'll cave in or get taken for back taxes first, but either way, we'll have nothing."

The taxes are current on the property for now. It was one of the first things I looked into. "I didn't realize she hates my family that much."

"Oh, she does. But I think it's the promise she made to my dad to keep it in the family that's the real problem. Even if you had made the offer under another name, I don't think she'd sell it."

"Unless there's a fortune hidden under the floorboards, I think that's a promise she's going to have to break. And the sooner she realizes that, the sooner she can get on with her life. And, more importantly, the sooner *you* can move on."

She takes a sip of her coffee and winces. I'm not surprised—it's pretty bitter. "I told her how it is and how it's only going to get worse with every passing year, but she's convinced I'll marry some guy from Sumac Falls and he'll fix the house up and she'll live with us and...it's quite the fairy tale. But the bottom line is that her only plan for that house is that it becomes my problem—more than it already is, I mean. Like a *my name on the deed* kind of problem."

And there's that detour around the dead end I'm looking for.

"Cara Gamble?" I look her right in the eye and smile. "You should marry me."

Chapter Fifteen

CARA

I should *marry* him?

Did Hayden Reilly seriously just semi-propose to me in this ancient diner with the shitty coffee?

I laugh at him, because there's no way he's being serious right now. "I guess sending my mother to an early grave would solve a lot of my problems, but it's certainly not Plan A."

"If you marry me, we both get what we want."

"Oh sure, I woke up this morning wishing I could marry the man who hurt and humiliated me and then disappeared for seventeen years." He has to be joking, but then he reaches out and covers my hand with his. The contact jolts through me, and I take a breath that's shallow and shaky rather than the deep, steadying breath I was going for.

"I can't change what I did to you in the past," he says in a low voice. "But I have a chance to try to make amends by making your future better."

He *is* serious. I should say something—or at least pull my hand away—but I'm frozen, staring into his eyes. Hayden Reilly actually believes the way to solve this problem is to marry me.

72

And while there may have been a day the idea of him being my husband made me giddy, that day came and went a very long time ago.

I'm starting to wonder if he found an old treasure map and there's an X marked on our basement or something. He *really* wants our house.

The server arrives with our lunch and Hayden has to let go of my hand so she can set the plates down. The loss of his touch and the presence of the server gives me a minute to shake off the sense I live in a snow globe that Hayden just gave a hearty shake.

Marriage.

To Hayden.

It's going to take me more than a minute to wrap my head around this, but that's all I get. After I assure our server I don't need anything else without even checking I got the right food, she walks away and we're alone again.

"I know it sounds out there," he says, and I snort because that's an understatement, "but it would be temporary. We get married. She sells the house to us and moves into something more manageable for her, and then we get divorced and I buy you out of the house."

Even while that level of deception is making my stomach hurt, hope it could actually work flares up inside of me. I try to ignore it because me marrying Hayden isn't going to happen. "I'm not comfortable manipulating my mother like that."

"That's too bad because she doesn't seem to have any problem with manipulating *you*."

I throw a stern look his way. "Rude."

"But still true."

I deliberately take a huge bite of my BLT so I have a reason not to talk for a few seconds. Somehow, he's going to have an answer for whatever objection I offer, and I get the impression Hayden's a man who's accustomed to getting what he wants. And he wants our house.

The fact he's keeping the focus on how the deal would benefit *my* life isn't lost on me. It's true, of course, but the man didn't ride back into Sumac Falls to rescue a damsel in distress he ghosted almost two decades ago. He came back for the sole purpose of buying my parents' home and, honestly, that still doesn't make a lot of sense to me. Sure, it was a beautiful home once—a shining example of its style to showcase the Gamble wealth—but my gut says there's more to it than a desire to restore it. I mean, he's willing to get *married* to get his hands on it? That's extreme.

"Tell me the real reason you want to buy our house," I tell him.

Oh, *now* look who's taking a big bite of his sandwich.

Hayden chews slowly. Swallows. Wipes his mouth with his napkin. Takes a long drink of coffee. Wipes his mouth again. He's obviously trying to figure out what he wants to say, and I just wait, ignoring my food and watching him.

"That house has been almost as much a part of my family history as it's been a part of yours," he finally says. "For an entirely different reason, of course. For my great-great grandfather, it was a symbol of everything Jonas Gamble took from him. But I thought it was beautiful and it drove me to want more in my life. Now that I *have* more, seeing it slide into disrepair feels wrong to me, and I want it to *be* that beautiful house again."

It's a nice little speech, though I my gut tells me there's still more. He's holding something back, but a chime from my phone lets me know I have to be pulling out of the parking lot in a few minutes if I don't want to be late for my afternoon appointment. I need to focus on the conversational highlights here.

Like the part where he said I should marry him.

"Hayden, there's no way she's going to accept any of this— and not only because of your last name. You roll into town and try to buy our house, which I've been urging her to consider sell- ing, but she says no because it has to stay in the family. And then, out of the blue, you and I decide to get married? That's such an obvious ruse, I'd be ashamed to even try it."

"You might be surprised what people are willing to believe if it fills a deep subconscious need. I know Gin can be stubborn and I know I'm a Reilly, but I think she'd jump at the offer if it wasn't for your dad. Us getting married allows her to keep that promise *and* get out of that house, and there's a good chance she won't think too much about it. She'll *want* to believe us."

I wince. "Doesn't that make it worse, though? Lying to my mom is bad enough, but manipulating her emotional weaknesses feels like something a loving daughter wouldn't even consider."

"I know you have to go, but think about it, okay? And while you're thinking about whether it's right or wrong to manipulate an emotional weakness of hers, think about whether she offers you the same consideration or if she's been manipulating *your* emotional weaknesses for years."

"Ouch." He's not wrong, but I still can't meet his eyes as I take a last sip of water. "I'll think about it, but I still don't think it will work and I'm the one who'll have to live with the fallout—and the humiliation—for the rest of my life. This town never forgets."

"Tell me about it." He stands as I slide out of the booth, the uneaten portion of my BLT wrapped in my napkin. "I'll get the bill, and I appreciate you driving out here to meet with me."

"Thank you. And I'll be in touch, though don't get your hopes up."

I manage to walk out of the diner without looking back. But as I'm getting into my car, I look up and I can see Hayden in the window. He's definitely watching me, but I ignore him and hope he can't see the instant flush in my cheeks.

But as I put my car in reverse, I can't help looking again and this time we make eye contact. He smiles. I drive away without returning it.

Cara Gamble? You should marry me.

I confess I scribbled *Cara Reilly* and *Mrs. Hayden Reilly* on a notebook page when I should have been doing homework more than once, but that was a very long time ago. I'm a grown woman now, with very little imagination left.

Marrying Hayden isn't going to happen.

Chapter Sixteen

HAYDEN

After leaving the diner, I'm not in the mood to go to my mother's house. I'll have to soon, of course, because Penny's there. But on the off-chance my mom's home early, I need a few minutes of walking in the fresh air alone to process the hard left-turn my plan took today.

You don't get to be as successful as I am in business without mastering the ability to pivot, but asking Cara Gamble to marry me was one hell of a pivot. Or telling her she should, actually. It isn't going to go down as one of the more romantic proposals ever put out there.

I spent the entire drive from the diner to the main street of Sumac Falls trying to come to terms with my own audacity—marrying a woman in order to facilitate taking possession of her family home *should* feel wrong. The fact it doesn't makes me worry about myself a little.

By the time I find a parking spot, my spinning thoughts are starting to slow to the point I can sort through them. After locking my car, I set out down the sidewalk at a slow pace with my hands in my pockets and my gaze roaming over the windows and signs around me. Some are familiar, having been there for decades. Others are new, including a surprising number of tanning and nail salons. I've yet to see any extra-tan people with impeccable manicures walking around, so I'm not sure how Sumac Falls sustains them all.

Once I'm calmer, I let my mind wander back to Cara. I assume the reason the suggestion of marriage doesn't feel wrong to me is that I'm not hiding my motivation from her. Letting her believe I was in love with her and wanted her to be my wife until death do us part, and then divorcing her once I have the deed? *That* would be wrong.

But if she's in on it from the start, I'm not deceiving her.

I pop into the market to pick up some fresh fruit for my mom's house, and I'm already through the door and fully inside when I realize my mistake.

I mostly kept to myself when I was young, and I rarely visit town when I come to see the family. The residents of Sumac Falls who *do* know me either give me a wide berth or they want to tell me everything that's happened in their lives over the last seventeen years.

I'm not in the mood for either right now, but Shawna Carpenter is manning the cash register—as she's been doing for as long as I can remember—and the way her whole body perks up tells me I'm going to be here a while.

I always liked her when I was growing up. While Shawna's a notorious gossip, she never chooses sides and treats all of her customers—basically the population of Sumac Falls—the same. She never looked down on my family, even during the really tough times after we lost my dad.

Once I've chosen the fruit I want, Shawna gives me a warm smile and plunks the bananas on the scale. "I hear you've been in and out of town quite a bit lately."

I think *quite a bit* is an exaggeration, but considering how seldom I visit Sumac Falls, I can understand why people have noticed. "Just felt like getting out of the city, but I've still got a lot going on in the office, so I'll be going back and forth for a while."

She gives me a sideways look without losing her orange-scanning rhythm, and I know I'm busted. Shawna might not have as many details as she'd like, but she either knows about the offer on the Gamble house or my dinner with Cara.

Maybe both.

If Cara had accepted my proposal, this would be a perfect opportunity to sow the seeds of our deception. And I *think* she's going to accept it in the very near future, but I'm not sure enough to risk her being gossip fodder for no reason.

Like the best gossip collectors, Shawna doesn't ask any pointed questions. She just waits, hoping I'll fill the silence with the kind of social small talk that offers up all kinds of personal tidbits if one's paying attention.

Unfortunately for her, I'm comfortable with silence—babbling in boardrooms never ends well—so she surrenders and by the time I run my card through the reader to pay, I know a lot about the stray cat she adopted.

Not wanting to risk running into anybody else I know while I'm in limbo, not knowing exactly what the gossip is and not being able to confirm or deny anything they've heard, I walk straight to my car, putting the bag of fruit into Penny's booster seat.

When I pull into my mother's driveway, her car is still gone, but my brother's is parked in her spot. I wasn't expecting to see him so soon, and I hadn't really thought about what, if anything, I was going to tell him about Cara. I didn't tell my mom I was having dinner with her because of her reaction to Penny seeing her professionally, but I don't know if Cara told anybody. As far as I know, nobody else knows about our lunch today, though.

As I walk in the door, he's clearly on his way out. "Hayden, I didn't know you were back. I mean, I did once I got here because your dog is here, but before that, I mean."

"I was going to shoot you a text later, but I had to drop her and run." Aaron's brow furrows, no doubt because he's trying to figure out what urgent thing I might have going on in this town I don't live in. I hold up the bag. "Still fighting the battle to convince Mom fruit tastes better fresh than from a can."

"She likes those little half-cherries they put in the canned stuff. And just so you know, if Penny's weird about me for a while, it's because I didn't know she was here and caught a glimpse of pale fur skittering under the table."

I'm next to her in seconds, running my hand over her body. She doesn't look hurt, but I pin my brother with an icy glare. "You didn't throw anything at her, did you?"

"No, I didn't throw anything." Aaron's face reddens and he won't meet my gaze. "But the scream I let out might haunt her dreams forever."

I laugh so hard, Penny sidles away from me, but I can't help it. "Like the raccoon in the trash barrel when you were...what? Ten?"

"Yeah, but maybe this scream was louder because this was in a house. On some level, we know there's always a chance of raccoons in the garbage cans. It was lower-pitched this time, of course, because I'm a grown man now."

By the time I get my second round of laughter under control, Aaron's annoyed and Penny has left the room entirely. "I didn't know you'd be here or I would have sent you a text."

"I'm running a clean shirt to Hope because she changed into the one she keeps at the office after a nervous kid lost his oatmeal. But then she spilled coffee on that one and even though her fancy orthodontist lab coat covers it, it also keeps it from drying." He waves a hand. "Or something like that. Anyway, she told Mom I was on my way so Mom asked me to grab the spare fob to her car because she thinks the battery's dying in the one she uses every day."

"I'll grab batteries for both while I'm in town."

"Sounds good." Aaron starts toward the door, but then he stops and turns back. "Speaking of you not communicating with your only brother—I didn't hear it from you, but I *did* hear you went on a date with Cara Gamble last weekend."

For a second, I think we were spotted at lunch today, but then the *last weekend* catches in my mind. "It was more like a meeting, but at a restaurant, so there was dinner and wine."

Aaron tips his head, giving me a wry look. "Like a date."

"Monday night, I had dinner at a restaurant with the CEO of an international hotel group and we even shared a bottle of wine. I can't speak for him, but I'm fairly certain it wasn't a date."

"Were you totally in love with that CEO in high school?" My brother points a finger at me. "You have a history with Cara, so don't try to tell me it was just like any other business meeting held over dinner."

Totally in love.

He isn't wrong, but when I think about high school, I always focus on Marcus and Gin Gamble, but not Cara. It hurts too much to remember my short-lived romance with her, but thinking about her parents fuels my ambition.

Along with some nasty threats, they told me I wasn't good enough to stand on their front porch. Now I'm going to *own* that front porch, even if I have to use Cara to get the sale done.

Luckily, she's as motivated to see me close on the property as I am because she'll be free to live her own life. If she has to lie to her mother to make it happen, that's on Gin. It's her own fault her daughter's willing to grab on to the life ring I'm throwing in order to keep from being dragged down by the sinking ship that's the Gamble house.

But if she agrees to my proposal, I don't want to have argued too hard against the connection between us. I don't like lying to my family, but it's necessary to protect the entire endeavor. And I may as well start now.

"Okay, it was something like a date," I concede. "It didn't start that way, but it didn't take long for it to feel almost like old times."

I expect gloating or maybe even outright laughter, but Aaron looks skeptical. "For both of you, or just you? Because last I knew that woman wasn't your biggest fan. And for good reason, I might add."

I'm glad he's walking out the door as he finishes talking, so he can't see the expression on my face. His words hurt, but Aaron doesn't know *why* I broke Cara's heart. And I don't ever want him to know because it's too late to change anything. He'll just feel guilty about something that wasn't his fault.

And now the ghost of Marcus Gamble is living in my head again, the past pushing the present out of my mind and hardening my resolve. I'm going to get this done.

I'm going to marry the man's daughter.

And then I'm going to take his house.

Chapter Seventeen

CARA

On Monday afternoon, I find out my supplier has raised the prices on two products I can't run my business without. Five minutes later, I get a text message from Hayden.

HAYDEN

Are you still thinking?

If he'd sent the message any other day between his ridiculous proposal and me sitting with pen and paper, trying to calculate how to tighten my financial belt another notch, it would have been an easy text to answer. But he caught me in a weak moment and my thumbs hover over the keyboard for a few seconds, itching to grab the lifeline he's throwing me.

CARA

No matter how much I think about it, I don't think it can work.

It isn't a yes, but it also isn't a definitive no. The idea of telling Gin I'm marrying Hayden Reilly makes my stomach hurt, and no matter what he says, I don't see the ruse playing out the way he's so certain it will. And yet, I can't bring myself to reject the proposal out of hand.

I thought about Hayden yesterday, while I was standing next to my mother in the cemetery for our annual Father's Day visit to my dad's grave. The Gambles have a private, fenced area within the larger grounds, which seems unnecessarily showy to me. I don't like these visits for his birthday and other important dates, preferring to remember my dad in small, happy ways—remembering his laugh, or seeing a tractor and remembering how obsessed he was with them. But my mother insists and it feels like a thing a good daughter would do, so I go.

Yesterday, though, there was anger. Anger at my dad for putting us in this position. Anger at my mother for keeping us in it. I'd looked around, trying to get my emotions under control, and saw the area by the outer fence where members of the Reilly family were laid to rest. Hayden's father is there, having been killed in a workplace accident sometime right before he'd started middle school. And once I'd thought of Hayden, his proposal popped back into my head and lingered there while Gin talked to the slab of marble with my father's name engraved on it.

HAYDEN

I'm in Boston, but I'm coming back tomorrow afternoon. Let's meet for dinner.

His text drags me back to the present, where I'm staring at numbers that don't add up. I buy specific shampoos that are best for the animals in my community and I don't want to switch to a more generic, all-purpose shampoo. But maybe I can shop around for a disinfectant that's still as effective, but perhaps cheaper.

First, though, I need to make Hayden stop dangling his wild ideas in front of me, distracting me and making me hope things could be better.

CARA

> Maybe. I'm still trying to figure out if it's
> brilliant or the worst idea I've ever heard.

HAYDEN

> Two things can be true at the same time.

I laugh at the message, feeling lighter. Then another text comes through on the heels of the first.

HAYDEN

> I'm going into a meeting, but I'm leaving
> dinner open all week so we can get together
> whenever works for you.

I don't bother to respond, since he's going into a meeting, but the invitation stays with me as I make a note of which products I need to research and go through the process of closing up the shop for the day.

During my walk home, I know I should be considering the feasibility of the marriage idea, but all I can think about is having dinner with Hayden again. While lunch was rushed and ended on a strange note—*Cara Gamble, you should marry me*—I really enjoyed both of our meals together. There were moments the past crept in, reminding me that once upon a time, he really hurt me. But it was a long time ago, and this grown version of him has all the traits I fell for then, but with added confidence and broader shoulders.

And seeing him with Penelope didn't do me any favors when it comes to reminding myself he's a heartless jerk.

No, I absolutely should *not* have dinner with him again, I decide as I walk up my front steps. The marriage thing is a non-starter, as far as I can see, and spending time with Hayden just makes me yearn for things I can't have. A fresh start. A life of my own.

Him.

By the following evening, I'm feeling steady again. I've

managed to juggle the price increases without sacrificing quality, and Gin's in a better mood. She thinks the matter is closed, so the iciness between us has thawed. And Hayden hasn't popped up on my phone.

Maybe life isn't good, but it's stable again and that's probably the best I can hope for. It's what I'm used to and, as my mother said, we'll find a way. Probably. We always have.

And then I get in the shower.

Not only is the water just a bit hotter than lukewarm, but it's starting to run cooler as I rush through rinsing the last of the conditioner out of my hair. Even though I keep turning the cold water lower and lower, there's no hot water left by the time I hit the button to turn off the overhead spray. Frigid water swirls around my feet as I turn the faucet off.

After wrapping my hair in a threadbare towel, I wrap another around my body and step out onto the bathmat. Then I just stand there, letting the chilled water run down my skin while I try not to cry.

I can handle putting plastic over some of the windows to keep the draft out in the winter. Every summer, we keep the curtains closed while the sun is shining and rely on breezes and fans to move the evening and night air. I've put up with trying to sleep in stifling humidity. I clean our gutters and mow the massive lawn we don't use. I've even patched a small section of the garage roof.

But not being able to take a shower?

Gin yells my name and lets me know supper's on the table. Since I'm hungry enough to table the total emotional breakdown for later—although I guess there won't be any more crying jags in the shower for a while—I towel dry my hair and then walk to my bedroom in a towel that's so small and worn, it's barely a nod to not actually walking around naked.

By the time I get downstairs, wearing a T-shirt with no bra and cotton boxers because we're a house of women, my mother's already halfway through the leftover tuna casserole on her plate.

It's one of my least favorite meals, but it's cheap and two people can make it stretch.

"I think the hot water heater's about to shit the bed," I say as I slide into my chair.

She nods. "We might have to get one of those shampoo-and-conditioner-in-one products, and maybe get wet, shut the water off while we lather up, and then rinse off really quick."

"That might buy us a little time, but I think once they start to go bad, they go fast."

"I'll ask around and see if anybody's selling one," she tells me, as if people replace perfectly good hot water heaters and sell the used ones for cheap every day in Sumac Falls. "If we have to, we'll heat water for dishes and baths until we find one."

My fork hits my plate with a clatter, startling us both. I didn't mean to drop it, but the idea of toting buckets of boiling water up the stairs like this house is a sixteenth century castle is so mind-blowing, my fingers forgot how to hold a utensil.

I wait for her to laugh, but she's either serious or she's been practicing her poker face. "We can't...that's not really a viable option, Mom."

"It's more viable than buying a new hot water heater."

I pick up my fork, but only to move my food around on the plate so I have something to look at. My delayed emotional break-down is joining forces with my rising anger to build a perfect storm, and my mother might not like my expression at the moment.

"We'll get through it, Carolina," she says in a much softer tone. She might not be able to see my eyes, but she knows. "We always do."

I swallow hard, determined to keep my voice as level as possible. "We can't do this for the rest of our lives, Mom. Do you really see us catching water from the leaky roof in metal pails we then boil on the stove so we can take baths? What are we going to do when the stove dies?"

"There's nothing wrong with the roof."

"Yet." I knock my knuckles lightly on the wooden table. "But I don't remember when that roof was last done, which means it was a *very* long time ago. And you get the point I'm making."

"Maybe Sherry can give me more hours at the flower shop."

Even if she doubled Gin's hours and gave her a raise, it wouldn't be enough. "Or we could consider Hayden's offer."

"No." Gin slaps both palms on the table, making me jump. "I promised your father I would keep this house in the family."

"Dad's gone," I say quietly—almost a whisper. "But you and I are still here and I don't think he would want us to struggle like this. Do you really think Dad would have wanted this for us?"

"Leave it alone," she tells me, her voice thick with threatening tears.

"I can't anymore." I can't do *any* of it.

"I'm not selling this house. Not to that Reilly boy and not to anybody else. And that's my final word." She's pushed back the tears and given way to anger. "I don't want to hear any more about this."

I take a bite of tuna casserole, hating the texture in my mouth almost as much as I hate cold showers. And drafty windows and wet basements. Except for Pampered Pets, I hate everything about my life.

But now I know how I can change it. All I have to do is marry Hayden Reilly.

Chapter Eighteen

HAYDEN

My phone chimes while I'm doing a deep dive on a financial statement Taylor, my assistant, dumped in my inbox with an urgent flag. Usually being interrupted while I'm working would annoy me, even if it's a Tuesday evening, but there's a reason I didn't put my phone in Do Not Disturb mode. And that reason has sent me a text message.

CARA

Can we meet? Someplace private, preferably.

I've already eaten and Penny's annoyed with the traveling back and forth between Boston and Sumac Falls, so I'd rather not go out tonight. I will if she insists, of course. But if she's realized marrying me is her only way out, I'd rather *not* have that conversation in a restaurant.

HAYDEN

My mother's at her bingo game and won't be home for hours. You can come here if you park down the street and wear dark sunglasses and a ball cap.

I smile as I type it, but there's only one reason I could see her wanting to meet and, if I'm right, her being seen at my mother's house will make sense to everybody very soon.

CARA

It's too bad I threw away the Cher wig my mom wore for Halloween when I was a kid after the chipmunks turned it into a birthing center. I'll be there soon.

By the time I make notations of where I left off in the financial statement and put the work away, I estimate I only have a few minutes before Cara arrives. I make a quick trip to the bathroom and then let Penny out to do the same. She's very particular about where she pees and by the time she finds a patch of worthy grass, I'm out of time.

The doorbell rings and Penny barks. I'm never quite sure if she's being protective of me, or if she's just that annoyed at having her peace disturbed, but nobody ever sneaks up on me. I blow out a breath and then open the door.

She looks like she's had a rough day—after a rough night and a rougher day before that. The messy bun isn't even trying to contain her hair, there are bags under her eyes, and she's so tense, I'm afraid she'll shatter if I touch her.

"Come on in," I say, stepping out of the way. As soon as she sees who was at the door, Penny stops barking and even looks pleased to see our visitor.

Cara sits on the edge of the couch with her hands on her lap and one leg bouncing. She's clearly nervous, but then she takes a deep breath and settles more comfortably on the cushion.

To my astonishment, Penny jumps onto the couch and then climbs in her lap. After giving me a rather smug look, my dog rolls onto her side, shamelessly inviting Cara to rub her belly.

"My mother is being unreasonable," Cara says, not looking at me. She keeps her gaze on her hand, which is gently stroking my traitorous dog. "More than usual, I mean."

"Is she even considering my offer, or is she rejecting it out of hand?"

"If your offer was standing on our front steps, the door would splinter from being slammed so hard in its face."

I blow out a sigh of frustration. "While slamming her own fingers in the door."

"And mine with them."

I should feel the initial stirrings of imminent victory at the bitterness in those two words, but there's defeat there, too. I don't like hearing that.

Then she raises her gaze to mine and I see a spark of anger. "She's not even pretending to include me in the equation."

"I'm sorry," I say, and I mean it. Though I set an objective for myself and I intend to meet it, navigating mothers is hard on a good day. And it doesn't sound as if Cara and Gin have many good days.

She shakes her head, her fingers still lazily stroking Penny's hair. "Walk me through it."

"We get married and she sells the house to us. Once she's settled in a new place, free from obligation to an old house and a promise she shouldn't have made, she'll be happy. When it feels right, we divorce and I buy you out of the house. Then you're free to live your own life."

Her brow furrows. "Buying the house twice doesn't sound fair to you."

"In the settlement, half of the value at the time won't be the same as my offer to Gin."

"But still." She's shaking her head.

"Do you think your mother's going to take a chunk of that money and give it to you for all the work, worry and money you've put into it all these years?"

She snorts. "I'd like to think so, but probably not."

"Then let me worry about what's fair to me and you focus on what's fair to yourself." I want to push and get her to agree, but I let her think about it while Penny enjoys Cara soothing her nerves by loving on her.

Then Cara looks up at me, her eyes sad. "When I sign the house over to you, there's a good chance it'll destroy my relationship with my mother forever. I'm angry with her right now, and I can see where somebody on the outside—like you—might think she deserves it, but she's my mom. And forever is a long time."

"That *is* a possibility," I say quietly. "There's also a possibility that having a fresh start will allow her to distance herself from the property and she won't care as much as you think. Or you can make me the villain—tell Gin and everybody else I tricked you out of the house. Almost everybody in this town will believe that in a heartbeat."

She laughs sharply, startling Penny. "And you think everybody believing you cheated the Gambles out of their family home will be a picnic?"

I don't care what people think. The important thing is that I *own* it. "Not a picnic, but also not something that will keep me up at night."

"What about Colleen and Aaron and his family?"

"Their place in this community is pretty solid. All they have to do is shake their heads and make sad sounds when they hear my name for a while and they'll be fine." I want to move away from what people will think—I don't really care—and back to details. "There will be a basic prenup, along with an NDA. We both have assets to protect."

She snorts. "I think we have different definitions of assets."

"You have a business you built from nothing and that's able to support you if you aren't also supporting your mother and her property," I say. "It's most certainly an asset."

I like the way her cheeks blush, and I *really* like the way her lips almost curve into a smile. She should smile more often and if I have my way, she'll have good reason to smile because she'll be able to set down her family's baggage and walk away.

"There will also be a clause regarding Penelope Louise," I add.

She laughs at me. "You think I'll try to take your dog in the divorce?"

"Who *wouldn't* want to take Penny if given the chance?"

"That's fair." She makes a kissing sound at my dog, who preens. "But no, I wouldn't fight you for Penelope Louise. She clearly adores you."

"She also adores *you*, and she hates everybody."

"Most dogs love me, which is good considering my job." She breathes deeply, then gives me a look that says she can't believe she's doing this. "When would this happen?"

"Ideally as soon as possible," I say, and she makes a low distressed sound that has Penny licking her hand in comfort. I pull up the calendar on my phone. "The best way to preserve family relationships and fend off legal challenges is to really sell a whirlwind reunion romance. After all these years, we can't live another day without each other, and all that. We need a little time to plan the wedding. Saturday the twenty-ninth? That's a week and a half."

"A week and a half," she repeats, sounding numb. "You're kidding about an actual wedding, right? We could just visit the courthouse and get it over with."

"Flattering, but no. We have to really sell it if it's going to work." And I'm not about to miss out on the satisfaction of seeing the look on everybody's faces when a Gamble vows to be a Reilly by marriage until death do we part.

"Nobody's going to believe it."

"Your mother is the only person who has to believe it. Admittedly, it'll be an easier sell if half the town isn't planting doubts in her mind, but we can't control that."

"It'll be more than half the town doubting it."

Of course it will, because nobody will believe a Gamble would fall for a Reilly. And it doesn't matter that the house is deteriorating along with the family fortune—the dynamics of a small town are pretty much carved in granite.

The Gambles are too good for Reillys. Everybody believes it. Some even say it out loud.

So yes, I want them to watch Cara Gamble stand in front of the people of this town and vow to be my wife.

My wife.

"Okay," she says, and then she puts her hand over her mouth as if she can't believe she said it. "I'll marry you."

Chapter Nineteen

CARA

Did I just agree to marry Hayden freakin' Reilly?

I think I did, and though I'm utterly shocked at myself, I don't think I'm sorry.

Maybe I should have talked to Mel first.

Actually, there's no *maybe* about it. I absolutely should have told my best friend that marrying Hayden was a thing that might happen. And I *definitely* should have talked to her before coming over here tonight and accepting his proposal. She's the only person in my life who's one hundred percent Team Cara, and I can't believe I'm doing this without her input.

But I also know why I *didn't* text her.

There's no way Mel would have agreed with this plan. As my best friend, it would be her job to remind me I can't trust Hayden, and that the entire idea is so ridiculous I should have laughed while blocking his number in my phone.

She would have talked me out of it.

I should have let her, but then I would have lost my best chance to live a life that doesn't include boiling water to fill the bathtub and tuna casserole three nights in a row. I wouldn't even be able to cry about it in the shower.

And that's why I don't take the words back now. Instead, I just let them hang out there while I run my hand down Penelope's soft hair over and over. She doesn't really need soothing, but I do.

Okay. I'll marry you.

Hayden is quiet, watching me pet his dog, and I appreciate that. He doesn't push or start burying me with details. I'm not sure it's possible to process what's happening right now, but at least he's giving me the space to try.

Somewhere in this house is an analog clock, and I listen to the very faint ticking of the second hand moving around the face.

"I don't *want* to do this," I clarify once the ticking of the clock starts to feel like pressure. "Going into a fraudulent marriage I know will end in divorce isn't exactly something I've dreamed about. And I don't want to do this to my mother."

"I understand that, Cara. I really do."

"But if I continue living like this, my relationship with Gin is going to blow up eventually, anyway, but neither of us will have any way out when it does." I exhale a shaky breath and then look him in the eye. "So let's nail down some of the details."

Hayden sits back in his chair and not looking smug is probably taking a huge effort on his part. "Well, we picked the date."

"*You* picked the date," I point out, and my pulse quickens again at the thought of marrying him in a week and a half.

"The less time our families have to really think about the situation and come up with hard questions, the better." He pauses until I nod my agreement. "What's next?"

With my mind racing the way it is, it's hard to grasp a single thought to share. "You know how gossip gets around this town, and I don't want this to be any harder for Gin than it'll already be, so you can't tell *anybody* until I've told her."

"Do you want us to tell her together?"

My burst of shocked laughter startles Penny, and I rub her

belly in apology. "Absolutely not. I'll tell her first, and then let you know when it's done so you can tell Colleen and your brother."

"Okay. Speaking of gossip, even though the relationship won't be real, it *will* be exclusive." His voice is low, but there's no give in his expression. He's *very* serious about this. "As long as you're my wife, no matter the reason, there can't be anybody else in your life."

I want to laugh at the idea of me dating *anybody* right now, but my mouth is too dry and I'm not sure I'm breathing correctly. It's hard to tell with the way my heart is pounding, and Penny wiggles to remind me I should be petting her. I must have stopped when the heat rushed through my body, sapping all the strength from my muscles.

My wife.

Sure, it's all fake. But the way those two little words, said in his deliciously deep voice, have been seared into my mind is very real.

"That applies to both of us, of course," he says, and I hope he mistook my inability to form words for outrage at a perceived double standard.

I clear my throat as discreetly as I can, praying my voice will work. "Of course."

"We'll maintain separate finances," he continues. "Anything that's necessary to maintain the pretense, I'll pay for. Dinners out and that sort of thing. And the wedding, of course."

My cheeks feel hotter with every word he says, but I can't exactly disagree on that point. I can't afford to. "Okay."

"I mentioned the prenup and NDA earlier. Taylor—my assistant—will send me all of the documents we need. We can go over them together and if you have concerns, I'll pay for a lawyer of your choice to go over them with you. There's a time crunch, but it's doable."

I don't know the first thing about lawyers. There's one in Sumac Falls, and he's been doing the town's divorces, wills, and property line disputes for as long as I can remember. Since I definitely wouldn't use a local, I'll keep my fingers crossed Hayden's assistant sends those documents in plain language.

I've been so hung up on the outrageousness of the entire situation, I haven't really thought about the logistics. But now questions start popping into my head.

"What happens if Gin decides—after the wedding—that she doesn't want to sell us the house after all?" I ask. "There has to be some kind of expiration date if this doesn't work out."

His eyebrow arches. "Do you think that's a possibility?"

"It's Gin. She's irrational when it comes to that house, so anything's a possibility." It's hard to talk so frankly about my mom, but I gave her every chance to be reasonable about selling the house. I don't have a choice anymore.

"Six months?"

I blink, the reality of being Mrs. Hayden Reilly for half a year beginning to settle in. This is a bit of a long game, and I'm not sure I have the nerves for it.

"If, after two months, we're not making any progress on the Gin front, we can start showing some cracks in the marriage. I'll start spending more time in Boston and, especially with the hasty wedding, nobody will be surprised when we split up after six months."

"That'll definitely give Sumac Falls something to talk about," I mutter.

Hayden laughs softly, and Penny shifts her body so she can see him without taking away my belly rub access. "There's no way through this without gossip, Cara. We both know that. All I can say is that I'm willing to be the bad guy if it goes sideways on us, and you're the only one who can decide if it's worth it to you."

"It is," I say quickly before the doubts can speak for me. I know it's worth it, and that's why I'm here. "So where are we going to live? Gin's not going to give us the deed to the house as a wedding present, and don't forget her dream of a mother-in-law suite."

"That's not going to happen," he says in what's probably his Boss of the Boardroom voice.

"So where exactly are we going to be doing the happily married couple thing for at least two months and possibly up to six?"

A single bark from Penny is the only warning we get before Colleen Reilly walks through the front door. She drops her keys on a side table and takes a few more steps before she looks up and her gaze lands directly on me.

She freezes.

I'm already frozen, so if it wasn't for Hayden standing up, it would seem as if time had been stopped in the Reilly living room.

I can hear that damn clock ticking again, though. Time's definitely still moving.

"Hi, Mom," Hayden says in an upbeat, casual way, as if it's totally unremarkable that Colleen just came home to find a Gamble sitting on her couch. "I thought you'd be at bingo tonight."

"Clearly."

"I found a leash in my shop and thought it might be Penelope's, and I was going by and stopped to ask Hayden if it was hers and then I was just...petting Penny, I guess." I know I'm babbling, but I need to say *something* as I get to my feet. As much as my shot nerves want me to make a run for it, she's between me and the front door. I'm sure there's a back door, but I don't know where it is and this situation won't be made less awkward by me running around her house trying to find another way out.

When Colleen's gaze shifts from her son back to me, I can see he got his icy blue eyes from her. She looks at me for what's probably a few seconds, but feels like months, and if I could look away from her, I'm afraid I'd see frost crawling across the floor and up the walls.

"Somebody didn't notice they were missing their leash when they left?" she asks finally, and through the corner of my eye, I see Hayden opening his mouth to speak.

99

"Usually," I say quickly. "But I remembered that Hayden was carrying Penny, so maybe we wouldn't have noticed."

Colleen snorts, but her expression softens as she turns to her son. "Of course Penny wouldn't have to walk on her own."

Hayden laughs and walks over to scoop Penny off the couch, managing to brush his hand along my back as he passes behind me. I stiffen and hope Colleen doesn't notice.

"I'll touch base with you soon about those details, Cara," Hayden says, and I wince when Colleen's eyes narrow.

"I should go home and start calling around to see who's missing a leash," I say very quickly, doubling down on my weak excuse for being in her house. "It was nice to see you, Mrs. Reilly."

She gives me a tight smile and moves out of my way. "Thank you for thinking of Penelope."

As I do my best not to look like I'm fleeing as I go out the door, it's not lost on me that she didn't say it was nice to see *me*, and she didn't wish me a good night or anything. After all these years, it must have been quite a shock for her to find a Gamble in her home.

Just wait until she finds out I'm going to be her daughter-in-law.

Chapter Twenty

CARA

I wake up on Wednesday morning an engaged woman.

I'm marrying Hayden Reilly, and while teenage me would have been spinning in circles and squealing with joy, adult me stares at the ceiling and wonders what the hell I've done.

Do whatever it takes. There's my sister's voice in my head again, but I don't think this is exactly what Georgia had in mind. I groan and pull the sheet over my head. I have to tell Georgia what I've done. I have to tell Mel. I have to tell her parents.

And I have to tell *my* mother.

Many times over the years, I've wished for a tiny kitchenette in my room. Just a Keurig and a mini-fridge so I could have a cup of coffee before facing my mother. Today, I've never wished for it more. Coffee wouldn't make breaking the news any easier, but at least I'd be fully caffeinated.

Pampered Pets has a full schedule today, but the first appointment isn't until nine. Plenty of time to drink coffee and maybe have some toast while I blow up our lives. The appointment will be a good excuse to escape the emotional rubble for the day.

It also adds a ticking clock element, so I have no choice but to force myself out of bed and get it over with.

Just to make it worse, it's a Crock-Pot oatmeal morning. I have no idea where Gin got the recipe, so I don't know if it's Gin, the recipe creator or our ancient Crock-Pot that's to blame, but the stuff is nasty. I'd planned to nibble on some toast out of deference to the nerves making a mess of my stomach, but she's already dumped a ladleful of the slop into a bowl for me. There's going to be enough fighting without adding a breakfast battle into the mix.

Her bowl is empty and I still have a few spoonfuls hardening into cement in mine when I realize she's about to leave the table and I can't put it off anymore. Not if I want a few minutes to hash it out before I have to leave.

"So, Mom," I say before pausing to clear my throat. Then I have to take a sip of coffee because my mouth's suddenly dry. "You know I've seen Hayden."

"I thought I made myself clear. I don't want to hear that Reilly boy's name in this house again."

Her tone does the trick, triggering the defiance I need to get through this and save myself. "I'm marrying him."

For a long time, there's no sound in the house except the old mantel clock ticking in the living room, my heart pounding in my ears, and the occasional car passing on the street.

"No," she finally says, her expression blank. Her lips don't even have that pinched look, and I can only assume she's in shock.

"Yes. It's happening. He asked me to marry him and I accepted."

"You barely know him, but we know his family and...just no. You're not marrying a Reilly. *Any* Reilly at all, but especially that one."

That catches in my mind again—why does Gin seem to have a grudge against Hayden in particular? It doesn't make any sense. But now is not the time to go off on tangents.

"*You* barely know him. I know him very well." I used to, anyway. "I grew up with him and we dated in high school."

"First of all, high school was a long time ago. And secondly, you didn't date. He asked you to homecoming and then stood you up."

And there's that familiar pang of hurt and humiliation. *Thanks, Mom.* "He asked me to homecoming because we'd been seeing each other for months. I think you can figure out why I didn't tell you about it. And we reconnected online a while back. This isn't out of the blue, Mom."

Her eyes narrow at my lie. "He started talking to you on the internet *before* he tried to buy my house?"

And there's the suspicion I was afraid of. "He knows I don't want to leave you alone here, so he thought if he buys the house, you can get something small and cute, and I'd be free to move to Boston. I don't want to live in Boston, though. I love this house when it's not draining the life out of me."

"You can't marry him."

"You said you wanted me to marry some guy from Sumac Falls. Hayden is a guy from Sumac Falls."

Her cheeks are hot, and I'm afraid she's going to bend the spoon in her hand if she doesn't put it down. "Carolina Marie Gamble, I'm not going to tell you again—I promised your father I would keep this house in the family."

I already know there's no sense in telling her again that no reasonable man would expect two women he loved to let a house fall down around their ears. But I've learned the hard and exhausting way that Gin won't see reason.

Instead, I have to lean into Hayden's ridiculous plan.

"If you sell it to Hayden and me, the house *does* stay in the family because I'm your daughter."

"If you marry that Reilly boy, you'll be a Reilly."

"And yet, still your daughter." Her mother's attachment to the house was almost as ridiculous as the family feud. "I won't change my name. A lot of women don't these days, you know. I'll still be Cara Gamble and this will be my house."

"That's not—"

"And my house will have a hot water heater. You'll have kept your promise to Dad, and you can get a fresh start and everybody wins."

"For now. But when you have a child, it'll be a Reilly and that'll be the end of it."

Oh, for the love of— "That would be an issue no matter who I married. But we'll hyphenate the kid's name to Gamble-Reilly and maybe *that* can be the end of this feud crap."

She stands, her chair scraping so harshly against the old linoleum, I wince. Then she practically throws her bowl into the sink, and I'm surprised it doesn't shatter. "This is the most ridiculous conversation we've ever had."

It's certainly ridiculous, but any more than the conversations we've been having lately? I don't think so. "I think it's more ridiculous for us to stay on this sinking ship until we drown because you made a promise to a man who's no longer with us."

"Not just a man, Carolina. My husband. Your father. While you may not care about honoring your father, *I* certainly care about honoring him."

I can't even speak for a long moment. Angry and hateful words want to fly out of my mouth, but I clench my jaw tight until I can't stand it anymore.

"I don't care about honoring my father?" As much as I don't want to throw fuel on this fire, there's a limit to how much of this crap I can tolerate. "I'm the one who's *been* honoring him, you know. If not for me, you would have had to break that promise years ago."

"Do *not* speak to me like that."

"We're getting married," I say firmly. "And then you can sell the house to us. It stays in the family and Hayden can restore it so it's beautiful for your grandchildren and future Gamble generations to come."

"Absolutely not."

"Fine. We'll get married and I'll move to Boston with him and you can keep your promise and this house all to yourself."

It's an empty threat. I'm pretty sure everybody in my family —probably everybody in Sumac Falls—has figured out I won't leave her. But this time it might land for Gin because it's the first time I've said I'll be leaving for a very handsome man with a cute dog and a lot of money. That's a little more believable, if still a lie.

I'll only go through with this if my mother surrenders to the fact she's selling her house to Hayden Reilly because our marriage and my name on the paperwork fulfills the promise she made to my dad. Sure, I want to get out from under this house, but the only reason I'll let that man put a ring on my finger is making sure my mom is taken care of and able to live on her own—or has the foundation to do so. Her choices after that will be her own, because I can't take the pressure anymore.

"You're not moving to Boston," she says finally, and then she turns to leave.

"Do you want an invitation to the wedding?"

She whirls back to face me. "Of course I do. I'm not missing my own daughter's wedding."

Then she's gone and I'm surprised I don't melt right out of the chair into a puddle on the floor. Telling me I'm not moving to Boston and accepting there will be a wedding is as close as I'll get to knowing the plan will probably work.

I'm getting married.

I ignore the lump of oatmeal turning in my stomach and send a text to Mel first.

CARA

Stop by the shop if you get a chance today.

MEL

I'm not free until six. Are you working late?

I hadn't planned to, but I'm not facing Gin again until I've talked to Mel. I'll spend the time cleaning, and hope my mother's too angry to tell anybody before then.

CARA

I'll be here.

And then I text Hayden and I'm not surprised my fingers are trembling.

CARA

It's done. There's no going back now.

Chapter Twenty-One

HAYDEN

"Cara and I are getting married."

I asked Aaron to stop by after dinner—the usual Wednesday night dinner at his house was canceled due to Hope and Daisy being under the weather—so he and our mother are sitting on the couch. I'm standing across the room, facing them, and I'm glad I tucked Penny into her bed upstairs before dropping this bomb. I don't want her upset by the fallout.

I'm braced for an angry tirade or maybe even tears, but after opening and closing her mouth a couple of times, Colleen just shakes her head. It appears she's speechless, which is interesting. I've always wondered what it would take.

"No," she finally manages to say, as if I might misinterpret her shaking her head hard enough to loosen a few strands of hair from the messy bun it's mostly gathered into.

I wait for more, but it seems the one word is all she has. "I wasn't so much asking you as letting you know."

"Hayden William Reilly, I am not sharing grandchildren with that woman."

I pinch the bridge of my nose, annoyed at not having foreseen my mother's brain shooting right past the marriage to the babies. Babies I'd neglected to consider while concocting a plan to get my hands on the deed to the Gamble house.

I wonder if hypothetical children have crossed Cara's mind yet, and how much of an obstacle they'll be when Gin considers them. Colleen has Daisy and AJ, but does Gin want a grandchild more than she hates me? Not that she'll actually get one, but she doesn't know that.

I can only put out one fire at a time, though, so I focus on *my* mom.

"If we have children—" it would mean we had sex, which I can't think about right now "—we'll split holidays so you don't have to pass a Gamble any mashed potatoes."

She gives me one of those maternal looks that says she'd like to throw a shoe at my head right about now, but my focus shifts to Aaron. My brother hasn't said a word, and the husband of an orthodontist should know better than to clench his jaw that hard.

The eye contact with him seems to shake words loose. "I know you can be ruthless when it comes to business, but this is... I didn't think you'd sink this low."

The disgust in my brother's voice is reflected in his eyes, and I'm tempted to break my own rule right off the bat and tell him what's actually going on. But I made Cara swear she wouldn't tell anybody the truth—not even her sister or best friend—so I have to stick by the story.

"This isn't about business. You know we dated in high school."

"You did?" Colleen throws her hands up. "What the hell is going on?"

"Yes, we dated for a few months in high school." Then I was forced to break up with Cara and I handled it poorly, but I don't want to get into it. "We crossed paths online recently and started talking. Since I've been back, we've spent some time together, and we don't want to be apart again."

"Is this a joke? Did you hide cameras somewhere?" She looks around as though she might spot a lens. "It's not funny, Hayden."

"It's not a joke, Mom. Cara and I are getting married, and we really hope our families will be happy for us."

She stares at me, her eyes narrowed and her breath coming fast, and then she spins and storms out of the room. I hear a cupboard door slam in the kitchen and then the clanking of ice cubes tumbling into a glass. Whether she's adding water or vodka to the ice is anybody's guess.

Now I'm alone with Aaron, and he stands, folding his arms across his chest. "You reconnected online? Funny how you didn't mention that when we talked about there being no way Gin will sell you that house, or after I told you I knew you'd gone to dinner."

"We were keeping it low-key. You know how this town is."

"I'm your brother."

"And our mother, who works for your wife, is the primary person I didn't want in the loop." He snorts, but doesn't deny it would have been a tough thing to keep from Hope. And from there, it would have spread.

"You being Cara's husband, which means Gin selling you the house keeps it in her family, doesn't factor into it at all, huh?"

I hate lying to my brother, but luckily I have years of hiding my thoughts during business discussions. "The feelings between Cara and I rekindling is the important part, but yes, it will enable Gin to sell the house to me—for Cara and me to live in—without breaking her deathbed promise to her husband."

I know Aaron wants to push harder, but Colleen reenters the room. "When is this wedding supposed to happen?"

And now for round two. "The twenty-ninth."

She blinks. "Of?"

"June." I watch her struggling, and then do the math for her. "Nine days."

I'm horrified to see tears welling in her eyes. "This has to be a joke. If you're pranking me, Hayden, please stop now. It's not funny."

I expected my mother to be angry and to yell—and maybe *actually* throw a shoe at me—but I didn't want to make her cry. I can't cave, though. *There's no going back now.* I can't put Cara in that position. "Mom, please be happy for me. You've been after me to get married for years."

"Not to a Gamble!" She's mad again, and the tears are angrily swiped away.

Penny's nails clack on the stairs as she joins the party. I thought she'd avoid the noise, but maybe she doesn't want to miss her human getting lectured by his mother. She looks around, taking in the situation, and then curls up in the furry bed kept tucked in the corner whenever we're here.

"That's not fair," I say quietly. "Whatever's gone on between this family and hers, she's never done anything wrong. She's a good daughter, and a local business owner. She's smart and funny and kind, and—in a week and a half—she's going to be my wife."

"I have to go," Aaron says, heading for the door. "Congratulations, I guess."

"Wait," I call after him, just as he opens the door. "You're going to be my best man, right?"

"Of course I am, you asshole. I'm your brother." He slams the door closed behind him.

My mom sinks onto the couch, then lowers her face to her hands for a moment. "I left my water in the kitchen."

"I'll get it."

By the time I return with the glass of ice water she'd poured, she seems to have gotten her initial emotional response under control. She doesn't look happy, but it feels safe to hand her a glass of very cold liquid I'd rather not wear.

"You'll stay in Sumac Falls?" she asks. "After, I mean? What about your company?"

"We're still working out the details," I hedge. "The plan is for

Gin to sell the house to Cara and me, and find a small retirement home somewhere."

"Somewhere far away?" she asks hopefully, making me chuckle.

"Probably not, but it won't matter. Cara and I will restore the house and probably split time between here, with me working remotely, and Boston. But we'll be here for holidays and random family dinners."

She takes a long drink of water and then sighs before leaning back against the cushions. "I need to process this. And where are you getting married? Nine days, Hayden?"

"You don't have to worry about a thing. Once we have the final details figured out, all you have to do is show up and smile."

Her eyes narrow. "You're definitely going to want a bride's side and a groom's side for the seating, with a really wide aisle between them."

Even though that sounds ominous, relief floods through me. She's accepted there will be a wedding, at least. "Noted."

"Okay, my show's going to start. Leave me alone to watch it while I process all this." I bend low to kiss her cheek, but she grabs my face between her hands. "Will this make you happy?"

Owning the Gamble house will make me *very* happy. "Yes. Cara makes me happy, Mom."

She looks like she sucked a lemon, but at least she manages a weak smile. "Then I'll be happy for you."

"Thank you. I'm going for a drive while you watch your show," I say. I need to get out of this house for a few minutes, and driving calms me. "Penny, you want to go for a ride?"

My faithful sidekick just nestles further into her bed, squeezes her eyes shut and pretends she didn't hear me.

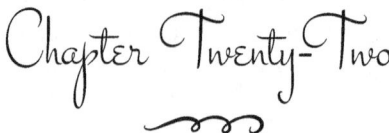

Chapter Twenty-Two

CARA

"Look, I've wrestled bigger dogs than you and won." Mocha, a mixed-breed rescue no bigger than a loaf of bread, doesn't even blink. "You'll feel so much better when I get that tangle out."

She sits perfectly still, just staring at me, and I'm not sure if she's trying to pretend she's invisible or if she's attempting some kind of mind control. Mocha's my last appointment of the day, and I don't know if there's something in the air or if it's the way my morning started, but every one of them has been a challenge.

So far I've won them all, but I'm tempted to put down the de-matting comb and go straight for the scissors.

I dislike bribing my furry clients, but the clock's ticking, so I grab a lick mat and load it with all-natural peanut butter—all of my customers list food approvals and allergies during intro visits—and a few tiny treats. The mat has suction cups to hold it to the grooming table, and by the time Mocha's gotten every speck of peanut butter out of the maze, I've detangled her without cutting out chunks of her hair.

Mocha's mom is thrilled, tipping generously, and then I'm finally alone. I have almost an hour before Mel's supposed to arrive, so I throw myself into cleaning. While I wash and sanitize the lick mat, I practice what I'm going to say to her. By the time I'm finished sanitizing the rest of the equipment and vacuuming and mopping the floor, I'm still not sure.

I can't tell her the truth. I want to, of course, and it would certainly be easier than lying to my best friend. But there's a lot at stake, and I promised Hayden. If he has to lie to his mother and brother, I have to lie to Mel.

It's not really a skill I'm great at, but now that there's a glimmer of hope I can get out from under that house, it's become something I want so desperately, I'll do whatever I have to do.

Dammit, I still haven't talked to Georgia.

A few minutes before six, Mel walks in. "I'm actually early. Put it on your calendar!"

I laugh, feeling better for a few seconds. Her bouncy blonde ponytail, warm brown eyes, and easy smile always cheer me up. But then I remember why I asked her to come and my amusement fades away. She sets the tote on the grooming table and pulls out a massive bottle of white wine before unwrapping two wine glasses.

"You brought wine?"

Mel shrugs. "I know you wouldn't have had me come over if it wasn't urgent. And I know Hayden Reilly's still hanging around town. And you have Gin for a mother. I'm not sure what's going on, but whatever it is merits alcohol."

I look at the bottle, nodding. "It's an all of the above situation, so it's probably good we both walked here. Crack it open."

She pours us each a drink—none of that inch in the bottom of the glass nonsense for Mel—and hands me one. I'm still trying to find the words to give her the news, and I'm still coming up blank.

"How about a toast?" I say, thinking it'll be a fun way to tell my best friend I'm getting married. I'll pretend I'm happy and then take a very, very long sip.

Her face lights up and she raises her glass. "Is she selling him the house?"

That's the part she's going to cheer for, but only that, and I imagine her glass shattering on the floor, splashing wine everywhere. "Actually, maybe put the glasses down for a minute."

"She's *not* selling him the house?" Mel, clearly confused, sets down her wine and crosses her arms. "Are we celebrating or not?"

"We are," I say quickly. "I'm getting married!"

Her head tilts in the exact same way as one of my favorite four-legged clients, and I have to fight down a nervous giggle. "*Married?* To who?"

"Hayden."

She barks out a laugh. "I haven't even had a drink yet, so this wine must put off some potent fumes. I swear it sounded like you said you're marrying Hayden freakin' Reilly."

"That's the second time you've called him that. You know that's not actually his middle name, right?"

"The only thing I know is that I should have brought a bottle of vodka instead of wine." It doesn't stop her from downing a third of her glass in one shot. "This is a joke, right?"

"It's not a joke." A fraud? Yes. A bad idea? Probably. But a joke, it's not. That would require, among other things, for the situation I'm in to be funny. "You know I've always thought about him."

"I've thought about the guy who taught me how to sneak out of my house without getting caught once or twice over the years, too, but if he shows up in Sumac Falls, I'm not going to marry him because we dated in high school."

"I'm sure your husband appreciates that."

We've both emptied our glasses already, and this time I do the pouring. She's not wrong about this conversation pairing better with vodka, but I'll take whatever help I can get right now.

"Cara, you better tell me everything."

I tell her the same story we're telling everybody—we'd always pined for each other and we reconnected online. Then, when he showed up in town, we realized we're still in love and don't want to be apart anymore.

"Bullshit. The only pining was you wishing you could take a pine two-by-four to the side of his head," Mel declares when I'm done, and I take a long drink of wine because lying makes my mouth so dry.

The way my best friend is looking at me isn't helping. I hate this and it's *so* tempting to tell her the truth. I can just swear her to secrecy.

Maybe more wine will help.

"If you were talking to Hayden online, you would have told me. You tell me everything."

I knew this was coming. "Maybe I knew you would tell me it's a bad idea and remind me he broke my heart once."

"Because it's a bad idea and, oh yeah, he broke your heart once." She reaches for the wine bottle.

"I didn't want to hear it."

We argue for a while—drinking wine the entire time—about her being my best friend and doing her job. My rebuttal that I knew she wouldn't let go of the past and I didn't want to lose out on a future with him because of a mistake he made seventeen years ago didn't seem to impress her.

At some point we ended up sitting on the floor, our backs against the wall and the almost empty wine bottle between us.

"How come you don't have a couch?" Mel asks as she divides the last of the wine between our glasses.

"Because this is my work, not my house. If I had a couch here, the dogs would just sleep on it and then people wouldn't pay me."

"How come you don't have any snacks?"

"Because the dogs would eat them."

These questions are easier to answer than why I'm marrying Hayden. Plus, I don't have to lie. Letting dogs lounge around on couches, eating snacks, is no way to run a grooming business.

My glass is empty again. Have I eaten anything since the PB&J that I brought for lunch. I don't think so. The wine bottle's empty, too. I'm about to ask her why she didn't bring one for each of us when the door opens.

Uh-oh. I probably shouldn't have any customers right now. I imagine what a doggy haircut given in my current condition would look like and can't hold back the giggle.

Well, *that's* not professional.

Then I realize it's Hayden and feel all hot and melty inside. He's so freakin' hot—even hotter than when we were in high school.

And I'm going to be his wife.

Mel makes an exaggerated gagging sound I find hilarious. "I should have locked the door."

Chapter Twenty-Three

HAYDEN

I look at the two women sitting on the floor of the shop with their backs against the wall. There's an empty bottle of wine lying on its side, and Mel still has a little in her glass, but Cara's is empty. They're probably going to be sorry tomorrow—especially if Cara didn't eat anything after work.

She probably didn't, based on the way she keeps looking at me and giggling. And Mel looks like she just realized she sat in a pile of shit left by a four-legged customer.

At least Cara looks happy to see me.

"I was driving past and saw the lights on." I say, shoving my hands in my pockets and feeling awkward. It's not something I'm used to. "It's late, so I—well, I was afraid maybe you were staying here because Gin threw you out or something."

Mel laughs, holding up her glass. "That's actually sweet, even though you're still an asshole. But Gin can't throw Cara out. She'd starve."

It's been a long time since somebody other than my brother has called me an asshole to my face, but I let it go. Mel was Cara's best friend in high school, so I would expect her to hate me even more than the Gamble family does. Holding grudges is in the best friend job description.

"She wouldn't starve," Cara says, frowning. "But she'd probably freeze during the winter."

I'm not sure what Cara has told Mel, but I'm guessing since the two of them have knocked down a giant bottle of wine sitting on the floor of a dog salon, our upcoming wedding's probably not a secret. I hope she's sober enough to remember *everybody* in our lives has to be told the whirlwind reunion lie. No exceptions. And not only because Gin has to believe it.

I didn't really stress the legal aspect to Cara, but if Gin decides to come after me for taking her house by fraudulent methods after the divorce and buyout, I need for everybody from my brother to Cara's best friend to be able to swear under oath we married for love. I'm going to take Marcus Gamble's house, and I don't want his widow to have any grounds for taking it back.

"My car's out front. Let me drive you both home so I don't have to worry about you."

Cara sits up straighter, her face lighting up. My ego swells, enjoying her reaction to the idea of spending even a few minutes with me. Sure, we'll also have Mel with us, but I'll take what I can get.

"Is Penny in the car?" she asks, and my ego deflates like a popped balloon.

"She's at my mom's. I asked her if she wanted to go for a ride, but she'd found a comfy spot in her bed and didn't want to leave it."

Mel nods. "The doggy equivalent of *dammit, I just took my bra off.*"

"Yes." Cara looks at her friend as if she's said something incredibly wise. "Penny had put her comfy jammies on and wanted to be left alone."

"Men never understand."

I hold up my hands. "I just asked her if she wanted to go for a ride. She usually *likes* going in the car with me."

"Read the room," Mel snaps. "She just took her bra off, Hayden."

Cara giggles and tries to take a sip of wine from her empty glass.

They're well past the point of me leaving them here to walk home. Sumac Falls is a small town and they've lived here their entire lives, so I don't think they'll get lost. But I also grew up here, so I know if they hurt themselves or decide to do something rash, they'll be the talk of the town for who knows how long.

"The wine's gone, so let me take you home, sweetheart." The endearment makes her eyes widen, but I'm hoping it'll remind her that, as far as everybody else is concerned, we're wildly in love. "We're going to town hall for the marriage license in the morning, remember?"

"Tomorrow?" Mel looks at Cara, holding up her hand in a sloppy *what the hell* gesture. "You *just* got engaged."

"We wasted *so* many years," Cara says dramatically, as though she's performing Shakespeare on stage, and I wince. "We don't want to waste another single day together."

Mel snorts. "Are you knocked up?"

"No!" Cara looks shocked. "If I was pregnant, would I do this?"

Then she tries to drink more wine from her empty glass.

"Time to go home, ladies," I declare, because somebody has to take charge and it certainly can't be either of them.

"Are there snacks in your car?" Mel asks.

"Only Penelope's doggy snacks."

She considers that for a few seconds. "Are they peanut butter flavored?"

"Cheese, I think."

"Ooh, *cheese*," both women say at the same time, and I see I've made a crucial mistake.

Two weeks ago, I was a boring but successful businessman with a plan to execute a real estate transaction. Now I'm a guy who's got to get two very drunk women—one of whom I'm marrying in nine days—into my car and home while fending off their attempts to eat my dog's artificial cheese snacks.

I see a roll of doggie waste bags and take a couple in case one of them throws up. It's not a perfect system, but being proactive can't hurt. I slip them into my pocket just in case.

"Cara, he's stealing your poop bags," Mel says in a really loud whisper.

"Once we get married, they'll be *our* poop bags," Cara replies in a ridiculously dreamy voice.

"See!" Mel elbows Cara, who falls over. "He's only marrying you for your poop bags. I knew it!"

"Do you have video cameras in here?" I ask Cara as she pushes herself back to a wobbly version of upright. I hope she does, because I'd love to have a copy of this video.

"Why?" Mel's eyes narrows. "We don't need video. I'll testify against you in court. And everybody will believe you stole the poop bags because you're a *Reilly*."

Ouch. She's probably not wrong, but it's not a pleasant thing to hear. I don't bother explaining the video question because she's probably too drunk to listen. And I don't tell them I want the poop bags in case they vomit because I don't want to manifest that mess.

Luckily, I'm parked right outside the shop. Mel makes me carefully wrap the empty wineglasses before putting them in her tote. Based on their giggles and difficulty navigating the act of standing up and looking natural, I'm surprised to find only the one empty wine bottle. I'm guessing neither drinks very often.

I end up putting them in the back seat together rather than having Cara sit in front with me. One, Penny's car seat is still buckled into the shotgun seat and two, if anybody's going to be sick, I'd rather not have the wine's reappearance splashed on my dash and center console.

"Drop Cara off first," Mel commands as I pull away from the curb, poking the back of my shoulder.

"You live closer."

"She has to pee."

I sigh, digging deep for patience. "We literally just left her shop."

"I didn't have to go then," Cara says.

I surrender because it's easier than arguing with two intoxicated women. It's not as though I'd be having quality conversation with Cara anyway. She's currently telling Mel all about my dog and how gorgeous Penelope Louise is.

"We should steal her as payment for the poop bags," Mel says, again in that really loud whisper.

"I can't. It's in the prenup," Cara says, and when my eyes flick to the rearview mirror, I see her put her finger over her lips.

"Prenup?" Mel shrieks, just as I pull up to the curb in front of the Gamble house.

"I have to protect my ass," Cara says. "No, wait. My *assets*. Okay, have to pee. Love you, Mel. Thank you for the ride, Hayden. Five stars."

I manage to get out and around my car in time to help her climb out of the backseat thanks to her fumbling with the seatbelt release. I make sure she navigates the curb and the sidewalk okay, but I can't bring myself to step onto the property. I wait until she's on the porch and going through the front door before I turn back, hoping Mel isn't stealing my car or rummaging through my glove box for doggy snacks.

She's snoring, which is best case scenario as far as I'm concerned. I drive back into town and pull into her driveway. I see a man I vaguely remember looking out the window and wave him out. After a brief re-introduction and an explanation of the night's events, I leave it to Lucas to shake his wife awake and get her into the house.

As I'm looping the handle of her tote over his free arm, I see the little bag of doggy snacks tucked in between the wrapped wine glasses.

I just wave and get in the car. As I back out onto the street, I imagine her finding them in the morning and smile. A little payback for the crack about the waste bags in my pocket.

Chapter Twenty-Four

CARA

I hesitate at the entrance of town hall, the remains of my hangover making me miserable, and look at Hayden. He's holding the door open for me, Penny cradled in his other arm, but suddenly crossing the threshold seems like a *very* big deal. Once we sign our names to the official paperwork, there's no turning back.

Do whatever you have to do.

With my sister's voice echoing through my mind—and dammit, I *still* haven't updated her—I take a deep breath and step into the gloomy town hall. It's all brick on the outside and dark wood on the inside, and it smells like a box of old books stored too long in a basement.

Debbie Fitzwilliam has served as the town clerk in Sumac Falls for almost five years, having taken over from her mother when she retired. Debbie's also a distant cousin of mine, I guess, since we share a great-great grandmother. Not a Gamble grandmother, thankfully, but on a maternal side, so they have nothing to do with the feud. That's a good thing, because it's all ridiculous enough without dragging the town administration into it.

I stare at the notices on the bulletin board and Hayden keeps busy reading emails on his phone, turned away from the counter with Penny tucked in one arm, while a man tries to register a vehicle he doesn't have a title for. Despite a prominent sign detailing the cutoff years for vehicles requiring titles, he's refusing to take no for an answer. When hostility creeps into the guy's tone, Hayden stiffens and lowers his phone, but Debbie sends the upset man on his way with a smile and a promise to research the issue and get in touch with him before the end of the business day.

When it's finally our turn, Debbie's welcoming smile freezes when she realizes the man standing at my side is not only Hayden Reilly, but he's with me. The frozen, overly toothy smile and wide eyes are a little scary, and I'm afraid of what words might come out of her mouth.

"Hi Debbie," I say, trying to snap her out of her shock and also head her off at the conversational pass. "We'd like to apply for a marriage license, please."

She laughs, and I can't say that I blame her. The entire thing is laughable, and yet here I am, asking for the document that will allow me to become Hayden's wife.

His wife.

A distressed sound escapes before I can stop it, and I press my fingers to my mouth. I couldn't speak right now if I had to, so I glance at Hayden, hoping he'll take over. But he only waits, one eyebrow arched, while our town clerk gets her amusement under control.

It takes a minute.

"Wait." Debbie's face rearranges into a frown, her gaze bouncing from me to Hayden and back as if watching a very close-quarters tennis match, before it finally lands on me. "You're serious."

"Very serious," Hayden says, smiling, and the arm that's not cradling Penny slides around my waist. "We'll also need an application for a permit to use the town gazebo on June twenty-ninth."

"Oh, that soon?" Her gaze flicks down to my abdomen.

Hayden clears his throat, reclaiming her attention. "I can't wait any longer than that to be her husband.

If Debbie was looking at me right now, she might have noticed the way my smile freezes and my skin flushes hot all over, but her attention's focused fully on Hayden's romantic declaration. "Oh. I'll just get the...okay."

When she walks to the ancient wooden filing cabinet to get the forms we need, I take a step sideways and Hayden lets his arm fall away. I know it's important that we sell this couple thing, but a little warning would have been nice.

Even though my body is still tingling from the contact and Hayden smells incredibly good, I'm able to get myself under control by the time Debbie returns with the form. She snaps it under the clip of a battered wooden clipboard, along with a pen, and hands it to me.

"You can use that little table over there to fill it out, and I'll need your birth certificates and a government-issued ID, and if either of you—well, Hayden—has a name change or divorce, you'll need the documentation for that."

I follow Hayden and Penny to the table that has two wooden chairs tucked under it, and take the clipboard as he settles the dog on his lap. I skim the fields we have to fill out, and then glance over my shoulder to see if Debbie's staring at us. Luckily, the phone rings and there's nobody but her to answer it.

"We have to indicate what name we'll use after," I whisper to Hayden.

"I hate to say it, but it might be easier for Gin if you choose to keep your name."

"Why do you hate to say it?" I blurt the question out without thought.

He looks at me for a few seconds, some kind of ferocity in his eyes, and I can't tell what he's thinking. Then he blinks and it's gone. "Just a saying. I don't know."

"Okay. The whole head-over-heels thing might be more believable if we both hyphenated, though."

He taps the end of the pen on the paper a few times, considering. "Changing my name would be a paperwork nightmare, business-wise."

"Funny how women are expected to do it, though," I mutter. "We'll just keep our own names and if anybody has an opinion, there's always the family feud to fall back on. Getting married is one thing. Calling myself a Reilly? I think not."

I meant it as a joke, but the way his jaw tenses tells me he didn't think it was very funny. With the name issue settled, we fill out the rest of the paperwork and take it back to Debbie.

She gives a guilty start when we step back to the counter, and I catch her sliding her phone under a stack of papers. "All done?"

That didn't take long, I think as I hand her the clipboard and pen, and she gives me a weak smile as she slides them out. "I'll just photocopy these documents real quick. Be right back."

"She was texting somebody the news," I whisper once the copy machine's racket will cover my voice. "It'll be all over town."

"That's the plan," he whispers back, and since he's right, I shut my mouth and give Penny a little scratch under her chin.

Ten minutes later, we step out into the sunshine with the document we need to become man and wife.

Hayden pauses once the door closes behind us, setting Penny on the sidewalk. She sighs and sits down. "Do you have time for ice cream?"

"Is that a trick question? This is clearly a trap."

His chuckle is low and makes me smile. "Technically, Debbie isn't supposed to gossip about any business residents conduct at town hall, but you and I both know she might literally explode if she isn't the first to tell everybody in her contacts we're getting married."

"You said that was the plan." I think of Debbie hiding her phone and guess at least a half-dozen people knew before we were even done filling out the application. "And that involves ice cream how?"

"If we're going to sell this reunion love story, we should probably be seen enjoying each other's company. Ice cream always made you smile, so maybe you'll stop scowling at me."

The reference to what was still the best summer of my life, even with the way it all turned out, throws me. And the way he's looking at me right now—all soft eyes and endearing smile—is the same way he *used* to look at me.

Back then, we couldn't be seen together, of course. Hayden would get the ice cream because he had a bike and could get to our secret spot by the river faster than I could. We'd sit on the flat rock by the shore, in the shade of the trees, and eat rapidly melting ice cream while we watched the water run and talked about anything and everything...except our families.

My parents would never have let me date him. His mother would have hated him dating me. And so we were our own little secret—right up until we were going to go public at homecoming and he stood me up instead.

"We can get some ice cream and sit on the bench in the town square," he says. "People will probably drive laps around it, thinking we look like a happy little family in the making, so *of course* we should be getting married."

Why does having an ice cream date in the park feel so much more intimate to me than actually marrying the man? Part of me wants to bolt—to run in the opposite direction of his blue eyes, delicious smell and adorable dog.

But I've come this far—Debbie's made sure everybody knows by now—and backing out would not only be embarrassing, but cost me the chance to be free of the financial and emotional burden of the house.

"Fine," I snap, wanting him to know I'm not happy about it. "We can go look romantic in public, but you're paying for the ice cream."

Chapter Twenty-Five

HAYDEN

Because I'm paying but the only place to buy soft-serve ice cream is in the cafe, I leave Penny outside with Cara to wait for me. Usually Penny would be upset by this turn of events, but she doesn't seem to mind.

I don't know the young woman running the counter, but I vaguely recognize two of the women sitting at a table as old acquaintances of Gin Gamble. I smile a greeting at them, getting arched eyebrows and tight smiles in return. Word that Hayden Reilly bought ice cream for two will spread before we're done with our cones.

Cara scowls when I walk out the door. She really needs to stop frowning at me all the time because she doesn't exactly look like a woman who's so swept off her feet by love for me, she has to marry me immediately. She looks more like a woman waiting for me to turn my back so she can smack me upside the head with a cast iron skillet.

"Why didn't you get chocolate?" she asks as I hand her one of the vanilla cones.

A small thing like Cara remembering chocolate ice cream is

my favorite shouldn't make my heart pound like this. "Because dogs can't have chocolate and Miss Penny here doesn't follow pesky rules like not giving dogs ice cream. In the city, we try to frequent places that have frozen doggy treats, but when ice cream is the only option, I get vanilla so I can share."

The scowl fades away as Cara gives Penny a sweet smile. I wish she'd look at *me* like that. I'm the one eating the vanilla ice cream. "She could have had some of mine."

"We don't like to be presumptuous," I say, and she snorts.

It's a short walk to the bench in the town square, and we walk quickly, both of us licking around the edges of our ice cream. By the time we sit, Penny's practically dancing, waiting for her share. I use a plastic spoon to take some of mine and put it in the paper bowl I'd asked for. As soon as I set it on the ground, she buries her face in it.

I turn my body toward Cara, hoping a lot of nosy people are watching. "So Cara is short for Carolina and your sister's name is Georgia. Is that some kind of *state you were conceived in* thing?"

"It's more of a weird family quirk, I guess—like an inside joke. My great-aunt's name is Tennessee, but everybody calls her Tess. My grandfather—her brother—then married a woman named Arizona, so my dad's aunt and mother were both named for states. And then my dad fell in love with Gin, which is short for Virginia. It's almost like he *had* to name us after states at that point."

"So we can have daughters and name them...I don't know, Nebraska and Idaho?"

I've never seen anybody choke on soft-serve ice cream before, but Cara does her best. Once she recovers, she gives me a cranky look. "We won't be having children because we won't be sharing a bed."

I wish she didn't sound so definitive about that. "Is a marriage even legal if it's not consummated?"

"I don't know. Is it 1845 right now?" she snaps back.

I laugh, but I know under the humor lurks a conversation we need to have. "Speaking of having sex."

She snorts. "I think you mean speaking of *not* having sex, because we won't be."

This is a tough conversation to be having while her tongue keeps flicking out to lick her ice cream. "So, our wedding night—"

"Will be as fake as our marriage," she says without hesitation.

I keep going because this part of the plan is important. "Considering how much this quaint little hometown of ours loves to gossip, I doubt it will go unnoticed if you and I leave our wedding reception in separate cars to return to separate homes."

She considers my words, scowling again. "I guess that *would* be an interesting choice for two people who've supposedly fallen head over heels back in love after being reunited."

Back in love. I catch that very important word, but I don't react to it as I drop more ice cream into Penny's dish. It's important to keep Cara focused on the path ahead. Maybe she loved me once, but that was a long time ago and taking a detour through our painful past won't serve either of us.

I can't try to explain homecoming without telling her what really happened that night, and I don't want to do that. The only way I can make up for breaking her heart is by getting her mother to sell me the house.

"I have a suggestion for dealing with that issue," I tell her instead. "When we leave the reception, we can go to my apartment in Boston."

"I have appointments on Monday. The first is at ten o'clock, I think." She sighs. "I know that probably doesn't seem very important to you in the grander scheme of things, but I can't take a time out from my life for this thing."

This thing being our marriage. "I've never downplayed your business, Cara, and I never will. We can drive down in my car. I'll have a car service bring you home in time for your first appointment on Monday because I need to handle a few things in the office. There's no reason everybody shouldn't accept that two people with busy lives and existing obligations wouldn't sneak a weekend away, but put off a proper honeymoon until later."

"You're very good at scheming," she says, and I'm not sure if she means it as a compliment or not. "And does your apartment have a guest room or will you be sleeping on the couch?"

"I have a guest room, but I can reserve a hotel room for you if you'd be more comfortable."

As expected, her nose wrinkles. "That would be a huge waste of money."

"It's a very comfortable guestroom. And then, as I said, the fact we both have preexisting obligations is a very believable story because it's the truth."

"Fine. That's what we'll go with, then. But what about after?"

"After what?"

"After...you know." She rolls her eyes. "It's going to take a little while to get the house sale sorted and find Gin a place to live and we never finished that discussion because your mother came home."

"And you ran out of there like your ass was on fire." When I chuckle, she rolls her eyes, but the corners of her lips quirk into an *almost* smile.

"What's the plan for us?" she asks. "As a married couple, I mean."

"I've been thinking about that because, as the shock fades, our mothers are going to want the answer. I think we lean in on me going back and forth to Boston quite a lot. I have a nice space at my mom's, with a sitting room and its own bathroom so when I'm in Sumac Falls, it would make sense for you to stay with me there. Maybe being in the house alone those nights and keeping us apart the others will put some pressure on Gin."

"I don't love the idea of staying at Colleen's."

"It'll be fine. Once she gets to know you for yourself, apart from the Gamble family—"

"*My* family."

"She'll love you."

Cara doesn't look convinced, which is fair considering the generations of Reillys who have decidedly *not* loved Gambles. "That's kind of sloppy, as plans go."

"It is, but not having everything figured out goes well with the whirlwind wedding."

"I guess so," she says, sounding unsure.

We're not doing a good job of looking like a couple madly in love, so I tilt my body her way and rest my arm along the back of the bench. The contact makes her stiffen for a second, but when she relaxes without shrugging me off, I breathe a sigh of relief.

I don't think it would help relax her if I told her it's not easy for me, either. Every time I touch her, it's not enough. I want to haul her into my arms and kiss her until all of the history between us fades into nothingness. I think about her constantly when I'm awake, and I dream about her when I finally sleep.

This morning I woke up with the memory of heartache filling my senses and my hand splayed across the tattoo on my chest.

No, telling Cara any of that would definitely *not* help her relax.

Before I can think of something that *might* reassure her, a ringing sound from the area of her back pocket means I have to move again so she can pull out her phone. I can tell by her expression when she sees the screen, it's not a happy call. Maybe Gin already heard Cara's sitting right in the middle of town with that Reilly boy and can't wait until she gets home to vent her anger.

"It's my sister," she says. "Somebody must have told her."

"*You* haven't told her yet?"

"I was going to tell her after I told Mel, but I didn't realize there would be so much wine involved. And it's hard for my sister to grab time for calls, so..." She sighs and then gives me an apologetic look before accepting the call. "Hi, Georgia."

I can only hear Cara's side of the conversation, even though she's sitting close to me, so at least her sister doesn't seem to be yelling.

"I didn't want to tell you by text, so I was going to call but things keep coming up. But yes, it's true. We're getting married on the twenty-ninth. I know it's short notice, but I hope you and Tony can make it."

There's a long silence on Cara's part, and I really want to lean closer and see if I can make out what Georgia's saying. I don't, though, focusing instead on eating my ice cream.

"No, it's not that. I swear," Cara says. "Of course I love him. I always have."

My pulse quickens as heat runs through my veins, but then Cara turns to me and rolls her eyes. The reminder she's lying is like an emotional ice bath, and I say nothing as she tells her sister she has to run and promises to call her back later.

She's quiet for a bit after the call, and I let her be while we—with some help from Penny—finish our cones. Once she's done, she gives me a sad look. "I was so worried about lying to my mother, I didn't really stop to think about how it would feel to lie to Mel and Georgia."

I hate seeing the uncertainty in her eyes, but I can't let her off the hook. Even if we said we'd realized we were being reckless and called it off, she'd be the subject of gossip and Gin would be even *less* likely to sell me the house. "I know it's hard, but keep your eye on the goal—your mother being able to take care of her own life so you can live yours."

She draws in a deep breath, steadying herself. "I know. What's the next step?"

"I have to go back to Boston tomorrow for some meetings I can't do remotely. I was thinking if you have space in your morning, we could drop in at the flower shop together before I go."

She laughs. "I actually do have a cancellation I haven't filled yet."

I toss our napkins in the nearby trash can. "You seem to deal with cancellations a lot."

"Sometimes." She shrugs. "We usually schedule the next appointment before they leave and a lot can change in six to eight weeks. When people are juggling jobs, school, kids, doctor appointments and more, the family dog getting a bath and haircut is the easiest thing to bump, so I've learned to be flexible. My customers appreciate it."

"So we'll get the flowers sorted tomorrow, then."

She shakes her head. "I don't think you want to do that."

"I don't want to help choose the flowers for my wedding?"

"My mother will be in the shop tomorrow morning. She helps Sherry out part-time and Friday mornings are one of the times she's there."

I don't tell her I already know that. Gin and I are going to have to cross paths at some point before she becomes my mother-in-law, and I'd prefer it to be on neutral ground. "It'll be fine, Cara."

"Okay." She doesn't look like she believes me. "But I want to be on record saying this is a bad idea."

I reach out and swipe a small bit of ice cream from the corner of her mouth, and she doesn't flinch away. "So noted."

Chapter Twenty-Six

CARA

My first afternoon client is a Great Dane who loves being groomed and shows his appreciation with copious amounts of slobber.

Despite the mess, Boris is one of my favorites and after the morning I had, it's a blessing not to have to wrestle a wet dog into submission. Boris happily does anything I ask of him, and all I have to do is accept really slimy kisses in return.

It's worth it.

About two minutes after Boris is picked up, the door opens and Emily and Bob Pearson walk in. Mel's parents often stop by and say hello when they're doing errands in town, but this is the first time I've seen them since the wedding engagement I haven't told them about.

When Emily puts her hands on her hips and her eyebrow arches, I know she's heard the gossip. "What is this we hear about you marrying Hayden Reilly on Saturday?"

My cheeks flame and I can't look her in the eye, so I make a big deal out of trying to brush dog hair off of my shirt. "I was going to call to invite you. Hayden and I...we connected a while ago and he came to town and— I know it's all happening fast, but we don't want to wait."

I know I'm talking too fast because I'm uncomfortable lying to the Pearsons and I just want to get the words out. I really did intend to call them, but lying to them felt even harder than lying to my mother, and I hadn't worked up the courage yet.

I don't know if Mel told them or if they heard about our trip to town hall, but they hadn't heard the news from me and they should have.

"I'm sorry I didn't call you right away."

I'm relieved when Emily laughs and waves her hand as if to say it doesn't matter. "You're caught up in a whirlwind romance, my girl. And we're happy for you."

When she moves in for a hug, I hold up my hand. "Before you hug me, you should know I'm covered in Great Dane slime."

"Boris?" When I nod, Emily laughs again and gives me a hug anyway, though she's careful to leave plenty of daylight between us. "I stopped by there to drop off a casserole when they had pneumonia and the smell got Boris's mouth watering. He shook his head and the slime splattered all over me. But he's a good boy."

"And Em makes a great casserole," Bob says. "You can hardly blame the dog for slobbering."

Emily beams at her husband before turning back to me. "How is Gin taking the news?"

"I'll let you know after she starts speaking to me again." I wanted it to come out like a joke, but neither of them laugh.

"I'm sure this is hard for her, him being a Reilly and all," Bob says.

"And because she'll have to share you with somebody else," Emily adds sharply.

"Em." Bob gives his wife one of those married couple looks, even though it's no secret Emily isn't Gin's biggest fan.

They've always been friendly, if not actual friends, but in the years since my father passed away, Emily and Bob have struggled with keeping their opinions about Gin's dependency on me to themselves.

"Is there anything we can do to help you with the wedding?" Emily asks, smoothly pivoting back to what she thinks is a happier subject.

"I think we're all set. We're keeping it simple, and Hayden's assistant is handling some of the details. We're going to the flower shop in the morning to order the arrangements."

Emily frowns. "Doesn't Gin work Friday mornings?"

"I warned him." I hold up my hands and shrug. "He's very much a rip-the-bandage-off guy."

"And who's walking you down the aisle? I don't see Gin volunteering to give you away."

"I'm going to walk by myself." And I'll be praying the entire time I don't trip while everybody is staring at me. That's the kind of thing this town would talk about forever, and thanks to cell-phones, they'd have photos and videos to go with the story.

Emily sighs. "I've heard that's a popular thing to do now—brides walking down the aisle alone."

I almost turn to Bob and ask him to do it. The idea of walking down the aisle alone, with everybody staring at me, is terrifying. If I ask Bob, at least I'd have somebody holding my arm, making sure I don't fall on my face. And he's always been like a second dad to me, especially after I lost my *actual* dad. If this wedding wasn't a scam, I wouldn't hesitate to ask him.

But I know how much it means for a bride to ask a man to walk her down the aisle. Bob would feel so honored, and I can't bring myself to make a special memory with him I know up front is tainted.

"We won't keep you," Emily said. "We just wanted to stop by and congratulate you since we were in town."

Bob gives me a light hug, mindful of the Great Dane slobber. "I know you'll be busy getting ready for the wedding, but you'll have to bring him for dinner after."

Tears prick my eyes, not only because I really hate lying to the

Pearsons, but because they always give me the kind of love and support I wish I could get from my actual mother.

"We'd love that." I get another hug from Emily and then they're gone with a reminder to call them if I need anything at all.

Guilt weighs heavily on me as I prep the shop for my next client. I'd focused so much on Gin while making the choice to become Hayden's co-conspirator, I hadn't really considered how it would feel to lie to everybody else in my life.

But I can't back out now. And I told Georgia I'd do whatever it took to get Gin to sell the house to Hayden. There's no way she meant to marry the guy, but that's what it's going to take.

All I can do is have faith that the people who love me and really matter to me—Mel and her parents—will understand why I had to do it.

I don't know if Gin will *ever* truly understand, but this is my only chance to live my own life and I have to take it. Even if it hurts the people I love.

Chapter Twenty-Seven

CARA

"Are you sure you want to do this?" I ask Hayden for the third or fourth time. I'm not sure if it's for his benefit or mine, but I keep hoping he'll change his mind. I've been so hopeful he'd back out, in fact, I didn't tell my mother we were coming.

Now that we're standing outside the flower shop, I wish I had. Not so she'd be prepared when Hayden walks through the door, but so she could have told Sherry she couldn't make it in today at all. I'm sure that's what she would have done because she hasn't said another word about him or the wedding to me, and I think she's hoping if she ignores it, it'll all go away.

Denial isn't going to work on Hayden any better than it does a dying water heater.

"Of course we're going to do this." His hand is on the door now. "We need flowers for our wedding, sweetheart."

My teeth clench, and I have to make a conscious effort to relax my jaw as he steps aside and gestures for me to go first. I hear the soft chime as I step through, and then I have to blink at the transition from bright sun to Sherry's cool, softly lit flower shop. I hear my mother's sharp intake of breath before I even realize it's her behind the counter and not Sherry.

"Hi, Mom," I say because I can't think of anything else.

"Hello, Gin," Hayden says from beside me, and then his hand is on the small of my back. It's even harder to think once he's touching me, but I realize he's trying to gently nudge me forward, away from the door, so he can get in. "It's good to see you again."

My mother's mouth is pinched and her eyes narrow at the casual use of her first name, but she's not yelling or throwing the vase of flowers by the cash register at him. That's a small win, but I'll take it.

"Welcome," Sherry says in a bright voice as she emerges from the back room. "I heard the happy news. Congratulations to both of you!"

"Thank you," Hayden and I say in unison.

Gin still hasn't said a word.

She's taking turns, staring at each of us, and every time her gaze lands on me, it feels a few degrees hotter in the room. Maybe that *setting people on fire with her eyeballs* thing is starting to work for her. Then I see her mentally gather herself, blow out a hard breath, and paste a very fake smile on her face.

"Yes, congratulations," she says finally. "It's good to see you, too, Hayden. I guess you'll be needing floral arrangements for the wedding."

Relief saps the tension out of my muscles, and Hayden must feel it because his hand makes two small circles on my back. I know I should probably take the lead in this endeavor, but my mind is suddenly blank. I need a bouquet, at the very least, but I don't know what I want. Some flowers with a ribbon, I guess.

Hayden comes to my rescue again. "We're not really sure what we want, so if you have any ideas, we'd love to have your input."

I watch Gin thaw slightly, which seems like a miracle, and then she nods. "Let me run out back and grab a few things to show you."

She's gone before Sherry can say a word, but I don't kid

myself. It's not a sudden enthusiasm for her daughter's wedding planning. She needs a few minutes to process and get her head on straight, and then she'll be back. Hopefully with some flower ideas, because I still don't have any. I like flowers in a general sense, but I don't know a lot about them.

Hopefully she won't emerge with Harry 8.0. Sherry keeps the Harry lookalikes in the back room in case Mel's dad wanders in, and a prickly cactus as a Reilly wedding arrangement might amuse her enough to try the joke.

Hayden glances at the display on his smartwatch and frowns before sliding his phone out of his pocket. "I'm sorry, but I need to step out and take this."

I nod, and as soon as the door closes behind him, Sherry leans across the counter. She looks like she's going to tell me a secret, but there's nobody else in the shop and Mom's out back, so the closeness feels unnecessary. "What's going on, Cara?"

"He gets a lot of business calls. I don't think he'll be very long."

She blows out an annoyed breath. "Like I care about his phone calls. The last time I saw you—which was maybe last week—you weren't dating anybody and now you're in here picking out a bouquet to hold while you walk down the aisle with a Reilly?"

"We reconnected online and have been talking for a while," I say, wishing I didn't have to lie to this woman, who'd been an honorary aunt for most of my life. At least repeating the lie multiple times is making it roll a little more smoothly off my tongue. "It's not as sudden as it appears."

She makes a sound that's a little bit of agreement mixed with a whole lot of skepticism. The way she's staring at me makes me squirm, but I can't look away and I just hope my cheeks don't look as warm as they feel.

Then she laughs. "Honestly? I don't care one way or the other, as long as you know what you're doing and whatever that is gets her out of that overblown money pit."

The words stun me, and the realization I'm not alone in knowing my mother needs to be set free of the house she's lived in since her marriage almost brings tears to my eyes. Even though I can't tell her the truth, I appreciate having an ally in Gin's best friend.

She goes on, seemingly oblivious to my reaction. "I keep telling her there's a house right up the road from me coming up for sale soon, and it would be perfect for her. And your future husband has the means to repair your house, so it's a win for everybody."

Sherry moved into the fairly new 55+ community on the outskirts of Sumac Falls after her divorce. The houses are small, but cute, and the idea of having a property management company doing all the groundskeeping and maintenance for my mother that I'm currently struggling with makes my knees weak.

"I don't know how many times I've told her she'd be so much happier there," I say.

"Mmhmm. But her excuse is that she can't sell the only home you've ever known out from under you."

I'd bang my head against the counter, but it's glass and I can't afford to replace it. "She actually says that out loud?"

"Every time I bring it up." Sherry shrugs. "And, of course, the promise she made to Marcus."

"Right. That."

"Unfortunately, she told everybody about it in the days after he died, so I think that, not only would she feel like she let Marcus down, but everybody in town would know it." She shakes her head. "Trust me, I've tried. But it doesn't matter now because she'll be able to sell the house to you and your husband, so it'll stay in the family. Promise kept and problem solved."

I'm saved from having to respond to that by the door chime going off. Hayden's back, and a moment later, Gin appears from the back room. She's carrying a few long stem roses in a variety of shades and a bunch of baby's breath, but nothing else. It's not exactly original, but she might have been going for classic.

"I didn't ask if you have a venue yet. I know you live in Boston," she says to Hayden, somehow managing to drown the name of the city in disdain, "but I assume you'll be getting married here in Sumac Falls since your families are here."

"We're getting married here, Mom," I say tersely, because there's no chance Gin hasn't already heard we got the marriage license and she just wanted to take a dig at Hayden for choosing city life. "At the gazebo in the square."

"Perfect," Sherry says, pulling a binder out from under the counter and flipping through laminated pages before turning it to face them. "We have a standard arrangement for weddings at the town gazebo. If you like it, you can just individualize the flowers."

I look down at the photo and a tingling sensation spreads over my body. It's gorgeous—splashes of colorful flowers in baskets on the three wooden steps. A basket hanging in the center of the archway, with smaller baskets in each corner. Flowery vines connect each of the baskets and then trail down the wooden supports. All the way around the gazebo, there's a basket centered between each upright with the same flowers trailing down over the white wood.

It's beautiful and somehow seeing these very-wedding-flowers photos makes this real in a way the official document from town hall didn't. I'm really doing this. I need a dress. And a bouquet. And Mel needs a dress.

A wedding cake.

Champagne.

Are we feeding our guests? We don't even have a real guest list, just a list of family members who hate each other.

"Cara? Do you like them?" His hands move to my waist, holding my body against his while he rests his chin on my shoulder to look at the photo. It probably looks to Gin and Sherry like he's being affectionate, but I suspect he's trying to keep me from sliding to the ground and putting my head between my knees. I nod.

"You can swap more formal—elegant, I guess—flowers in, but

most people who get married at the gazebo are looking for summer joy," Sherry says.

"We like this look." He pauses, maybe waiting for me to say something, before forging on. "Can you make a bouquet to match?"

"Of course. And a boutonniere for you?"

"Yes. I'll be wearing a suit, not a tux, and it'll be pinned." He lets go of me then, his fingers trailing over my waist for a moment, and a second later hands Sherry a credit card. "You can put this on file, for anything the bride and her mother want."

"I think small corsages for me and—" Gin pauses just long enough for the hesitation to be noticeable. "Colleen."

Hayden smiles. "That sounds lovely."

It *does* sound lovely, but I'm going to have to reach out to Sherry privately and have her keep an eye on those corsages because the mother of the bride wearing a corsage that matches my bouquet and the mother of the groom having wilted poison ivy pinned to her dress is no way to blend a family.

Sherry hands Hayden back his credit card. "I think that's all we need for now, then. We'll get started on it right away because it's right around the corner."

"Thank you." Then Hayden turns his considerable charm on my mother. "Gin, I'd love for our families to get together for a dinner before the wedding. It would be nice to have everybody together before the big day."

Smart guy, I think. Hit her with the idea of sharing a meal with the enemy while she has an audience. Sure, the audience is her best friend, but she's not going to make a scene in the flower shop.

"That sounds lovely," she echoes back at him, sprinkling the same amount of fake sweetener over the words.

"We should go," I say before this can get any worse. On top of all the things I belatedly realized I need to make happen in a little over a week, the Gambles and Reillys are going to share a meal?

Finger sandwiches maybe. I'm not giving Gin and Colleen cutlery. "Hayden has to head back to Boston for a bit."

"We'll get on that dinner, though," Hayden assures Gin. "Cara can let you know the plan."

"Lovely," Gin says, losing the battle to not look and sound as if she just smelled something horribly disgusting.

Once we're outside and have moved far enough down the sidewalk so we can't be seen through the flower shop windows, I stop and lean against the cool brick wall. "I can't believe you did that."

"We can't get married without flowers."

I narrow my eyes and poke his shoulder with my finger. "You know I'm talking about the dinner."

He grasps my wrist, gently, my pulse pounding under his curled fingers. "We have to have them in a room together *before* the ceremony. I'd rather have them throwing mashed potatoes at each other than our wedding cake."

"True." Why am I not pulling my hand away? I really should. "I was already thinking finger sandwiches so there are no knives and forks on the table."

His fingers slide down my wrist to *my* fingers, and he brings my hand to his mouth. His breath is warm against my skin, and then the kiss he plants there is so hot every nerve in my body sizzles. "It's going to be okay, Cara. Everything's going according to plan."

My reaction to his mouth on my skin is *not* part of the plan. It's just a show for any of the citizens of Sumac Falls looking our way. He's just a means to an end for me, and I'm absolutely not going to fall for this man *again*.

I *mean* it.

He lowers our hands, though his fingers stay tangled with mine. "Trust me."

Trusting him is what got me into this mess in the first place.

145

Chapter Twenty-Eight

HAYDEN

Since Cara has a grooming appointment to get to, we part ways on the sidewalk. I would have liked to spend more time with her and maybe talk through some more of the details, but we both have to get to work. I pick up Penelope and my bags, and head back to Boston.

I ignore the business calls that come in during the drive, which is unlike me. But I have a lot to get done and dictating task lists into my phone calms me. Although, they're not so much tasks as things I need to run by Cara later.

Things like what she's going to wear and what kind of cake she'd like and what kind of reception she wants to have. I'd said a simple wedding, but there isn't anything simple about it, I guess.

I already have Penny and my laptop with me, so I skip my apartment and drive straight to the tall, shiny building my company offices are in. We have an underground garage and private elevator, so in no time, I'm waving to the Reilly Financial receptionists and heading down the hushed hallways with Penny at my side.

There's an office between the hallway and mine, and it's the domain of Taylor Sullivan. Executive Assistant doesn't even begin to cover her role in my life. Shortly after I opened my own financial firm, I poached her from her previous boss. He kept asking her questions and then speaking over her answers, though it was obvious she knew more about what was going on than he did. I respect her, I pay her well, and she helped me make my company what it is. I know her next birthday will be her sixtieth and I dread the day she tells me she's ready to retire.

While I appreciate her playing the dragon guarding the mouth of my cave for the most part, it also means I can't sneak into my office.

"Good afternoon," she says pleasantly enough, bending to give Penny her customary chin rub. It's always struck me as less Penny looking for affection, and more as her tolerating the greeting due her as the boss's dog.

"Good afternoon," I respond. I'm not surprised that when I open the door and follow Penny into my office, Taylor's right behind us.

Her closing the door behind us doesn't bode well for me. I set my computer bag on the desk and hit the button to open the shades. My office is best described as austere. Steel. Glass. Leather chairs. Other than Penny's bed, this room isn't designed for comfort. If somebody wants to lounge on a couch, they can go home and do it. I'm here to work.

"It's unlike you to be out of the office so much," Taylor says.

It's more than a simple observation. There's something else she wants to say, and whatever it is, it's making her uncomfortable. I know she's not carrying news of some kind of hostile takeover of my company. Every person in my company who has the power to even think about it is somebody I trust implicitly. But there's something going on.

"Just say it," I urge, giving her a smile to remind her she's free to speak her mind in this office. I pull my phone out of my pocket and toss it on my desk before settling into my chair.

"I'm not sure *exactly* what you're doing back in New Hampshire, but I know it's personal." She shrugs. "The people who don't know what little I *do* know are afraid you're sick. Or that somebody in your family is sick. And some are concerned you're thinking about moving the company up there."

I hadn't considered that. "Nobody's sick, and I don't want them worrying about their jobs. Not only is that bad for morale, but I don't want them hunting for new jobs with some other firm."

"That was my thought, yes. But I can't lay those concerns to rest without giving them *something*."

"I'm getting married."

She laughs for a moment, but when I don't laugh with her, her amusement dies off pretty quickly. "Are you really?"

"I am." I lean back in my chair. "I'll be marrying Cara Gamble on the twenty-ninth of this month, in Sumac Falls."

She sits in the leather chair across from me without invitation. "Cara Gamble. Like the Gamble property? Hayden, what the hell are you doing?"

Taylor is probably the only person in the world who can speak to me like that in this office and get away with it. She's also one of the few people who know one of the goals I set for myself was buying that house.

"I know it looks bad," I say, holding up my hands. "But we dated in high school and we went to dinner and sparks reignited and...we're getting married."

"Must have been quite the dinner."

I ignore that and try to shift the focus back to the business at hand. "I'll probably be splitting time between here and New Hampshire for a while, but you can reassure everybody that neither this company nor their jobs are going anywhere."

"Good." She looks at me for a few seconds, then smiles and shakes her head. "Married. I know you well enough to know this isn't like you and you're probably up to something. But you also told me about the girl you left behind once, so maybe I'm wrong."

I neither confirm nor deny. "It'll be a private ceremony in our hometown, if anybody asks. I don't want it to be a whole thing around here, though of course I want you and your husband to be there."

"Understood. Will you be needing my assistance with the planning?"

"Definitely." I break down the basic terms of the prenup and NDA, and ask her to draft the documents in the simplest terms possible, so Cara can understand them. "Obviously, I need those ASAP."

"So this wedding won't be changing your intention to buy the house?"

"No." The word sounds curt, even to my own ears, so I force a smile. "Gin will be selling the house to Cara and me, as a married couple."

Her eyebrow shoots up. "But you want it in the prenup that you'll pay her half the value of the house you'll have already given her mother full, fair value for?"

More than the fair value, actually, but I zip it. Taylor already doesn't believe me.

I look her in the eye. "*We* will be buying her mother's house, so obviously in a divorce, it would be joint property. But hopefully the prenup will never be relevant, and I'll be a married man with a house and a company to run and the best dog ever."

Taylor looks at Penny, who's lying on her bed watching us. "And what does Penelope Louise think of the other woman in your life?"

"Believe it or not, she loves Cara. She even chooses to curl up with her over me sometimes."

"Really?" Taylor smiles, and for the first time, she relaxes and looks genuinely happy for me. "Isn't that interesting."

Chapter Twenty-Nine

CARA

Mel calls me Saturday afternoon, just as I'm closing up the shop. When the phone rings, I think it might be Hayden, who has sent me *many* emails from Boston, and I squash the pang of disappointment when I see my best friend's name on the screen.

"What are you planning to wear?" she says as soon as I answer. "Are you and Gin going wedding dress shopping? If you are, I want to go."

I almost tell her I'm just going to dig something out of the back of my closet, but I remember just in time I'm supposed to be swept up in a whirlwind romance. "There's no chance Gin wants to help me find something to wear to a Reilly wedding, even if I'm the bride. Maybe *especially* if I'm the bride. She did okay at the flower shop, but I'd like to involve her as little as possible."

"Since I'm your maid of honor, I'm going with you." There's a pause. "Wait, I am, right? Did you ask me to be your maid of honor?"

"I don't remember. There was a lot of wine. But also, we might have just assumed because of course you are."

"Okay, good. Now what kind of dress are you thinking?"

Honestly, I've been trying not to think about it at all because it's overwhelming and I can't keep hyperventilating while I'm working. It makes the dogs nervous. "I'm not sure."

"Are you done for the day? Let's go to Concord and find a dress."

"Right now?" I'm not sure any dress I can afford will be worth the cost of the gas to run to the city. "I was planning to mow the lawn before it gets dark. It's supposed to be hot and humid tomorrow."

"Mowing the lawn," she repeats in a voice that's so flat, she almost sounds angry. "You are getting married a week from today and you don't have anything to wear. You know, some brides would be panicking a little."

A week from today. Okay, now that panic's starting to kick in. "There's a box of Gin's old dresses in the garage, from back when she and my dad were young. I can probably find something cute and retro in there."

"As your maid of honor, I have to tell you that every time you talk, you're making the situation worse. We're not rummaging through boxes that would have been rejected by donation centers back before we even started school, looking for something you can wear to your wedding. I'm coming to pick you up now, and we'll go to Concord, find a dress, and then binge on fast food."

"We can look, I guess," I say, because it actually does sound fun.

"Wait. How hairy are you right now?"

"I don't think it matters if I've shaved my legs just to try dresses on, Mel. I'll shave them before the big day."

"I meant dog hair, but good to know."

We laugh together, and then I tell her I'm good. For whatever reason, other than a cat, I had low-allergy dogs today and very little fur flew. She promises to be here soon and disconnects. I finish the cleaning and sanitizing, and I'm just locking the door when her SUV pulls up to the curb.

"This is going to be so fun," she says once we're on the road.

I nod, hoping it's true. I took a peek at my banking app after she called, just to confirm it was as bleak as I remember. I'll try things on and make her happy, but unless I find something very deeply discounted—and then an additional 75% off the lowest clearance price—I won't be buying a dress tonight. Just the trip through a fast food drive-thru will hurt.

"Back to being hairy but promising you'll shave your legs before your wedding day," Mel continues, and I groan. "Are you and Hayden not doing anything razor-worthy or what?"

"I..." *Dammit.* I remember an arcade game I played once as a kid that was about jumping over pits and avoiding quicksand, and my engagement is starting to feel a lot like that game. I wasn't good at that one, either. "Hayden doesn't care about a little peach fuzz on my legs."

"Mmmhmm."

"Also, I live with my mother and he's staying with Colleen, so we don't exactly have a lot of alone time." I *can* offer her up a small truth, though. "Trust me, the spark is still there, even after all this time."

"Have you talked about the wedding? Like the actual planning, I mean?"

I guess it depends on her definition of talking, but exchanging emails is talking, I think. "Yeah, we kind of have to since it's in a week."

"Everybody knows you picked your flowers, but what about a reception? Cake? Music? An officiant? All that stuff."

"He hired Debbie to be the officiant, since the town hall is closed every other Saturday and she's free. Hayden wanted somebody from somewhere other than Sumac Falls, for obvious reasons, but it was too short notice. And I have pictures of possible cakes." I start to pull out my phone, then realize having her look at cake photos while driving is probably a bad idea. "I'll show them to you while we're eating. We're just going to use a Bluetooth speaker and do the music ourselves."

"You're not doing food and everything, are you?"

"No, because we don't really have time to plan all of that, other than a champagne toast and the cake. Plus, we decided we want to keep it moving. People hanging around, socializing and eating, is when gossip starts and we'd like to keep the amount of time our families are together and on display to a minimum."

"That's probably a good idea." She snickers. "Less exciting for the guests, of course, but still a good idea."

We're deep into a debate about cake flavors when she pulls into a parking lot. It's not exactly a high-end clothing store, but it's several steps up from where I usually shop. I'm about to object when she holds up her hand.

"We're just looking," she says. "This is the best place to find a variety of summer dresses, so we can get an idea of what you want."

In my jeans and T-shirt, I feel too underdressed to even walk through the door, but Mel sails through the entrance looking like she owns the place. I follow along as she heads straight for the dresses and starts rummaging through the racks.

I pull one out and hold it up, but she makes a face and takes it away, putting it back. I laugh and stand back, letting my maid of honor work her magic. The fourth one she draped over her arm, I vetoed. The jewel tone floral pattern is gorgeous, but it's a little loud for a wedding dress.

Once she's chosen half a dozen, we head for the dressing rooms. I'm not surprised at all when she pushes her way in with me.

"You might need help with zippers or buttons," she says.

"You're afraid I'll just say I hate them all because they're expensive."

"I'm not *afraid* you'll do that. I *know* you will. Now strip."

The first one is a little too cutesy, with its embroidered edges and shirring around the bodice. "I'm pretty sure I had this exact dress when I was six."

The second isn't flattering to my curves, and I go from looking like a six-year-old to knowing people would look at me

153

and assume mine's a shotgun wedding. The third is pretty, but the pale lemon tint doesn't work well with my skin tone. The fourth makes me look as though I should be standing on a prairie, waiting for Ma and Pa to come over the horizon in a covered wagon.

I'm pretty sure the fifth dress I try on is the priciest of the bunch, but I step into it, looping my arms through the spaghetti straps before pulling up the side zipper.

The fabric is soft and slightly shimmery, in a pale blush color. The spaghetti straps, scooped neckline and slightly fitted bodice flaring into a knee-length skirt are all so simple, but on me, it looks elegant.

Bridal.

"That's the one, Cara." She presses her fingertips to her mouth, and tears are actually welling up in her eyes. "It's perfection."

It *is* perfect. It's beautiful and I can see myself at the top of the gazebo steps, framed by joyful summer flowers, as I become Hayden's wife. I want it so much, but I also saw the price tag before I stepped into it and I can't. I'm nodding, my eyes also tearing up even as I'm whispering that it's too much.

When I reach for the zipper, Mel grabs my arm. "This is the one, and I'm buying it for you."

"No." Mel and Lucas don't live on as tight a budget as mine, but I can't let her do this. "You're not buying this dress, Mel. It's too much."

She grabs her purse off the bench and unzips it. Then she pulls out a white envelope and hands it to me. There's a note on the front, and it's in her husband's handwriting. *Happy bridal shower, Cara. Let your maid of honor spoil you. (Save some for the french fries.)* And inside there are what looks like two hundred dollars' worth of twenties.

I'm actually crying now, and Mel snatches up my T-shirt, which she presses to my entire face. "Don't you dare cry on that dress, Carolina Gamble."

I can't accept this. Not when it's all a lie and I'm just trying to get Gin to sell Hayden the house. It's one thing to stand on a gazebo and recite some vows we both know we don't really mean, but accepting money for my wedding dress from Mel and Lucas is a fraudulent step too far.

I cry into my T-shirt while Mel unzips the dress and guides me through stepping out of it. I hear the hanger rattle and then she wraps her arm around me.

"You're not a happy crier, so something's up," she says. "Maybe Gin and your sister are buying this—and Georgia actually gets a pass because she's not actually here—but I know you're lying."

I'm thankful I have the balled up T-shirt so she can't see my face. But I can't bring myself to say anything, even with my eyes hidden from her searching gaze. I'm not sure I can convince Mel I'm telling the truth. Even if my heart was in it, she knows me too well—probably better than Georgia does and definitely better than Gin.

"I've given it a lot of thought," she continues, either not noticing or not caring that I didn't deny her accusation. "There's no chance you started talking to Hayden Reilly online without ever telling me."

"Maybe I hid it because I knew you'd give me hell after what he put me through in high school," I mumble into the T-shirt. It's not really a lie, since it's a hypothetical. Then I give my face a good swipe and look up. I can't hide in there forever, and I also have to wear the shirt out of here, which is going to be interesting. And damp.

"After you went to dinner with him, you said you just want him to buy the house." She points her finger at me, bouncing on her toes as if she just scored a point against me in tennis. "And it's no secret that Gin made some sacred vow she wouldn't let the house go to anybody outside the family. Two plus Hayden being her son-in-law equals four."

I sigh, backed into a conversational corner. Hayden said he

wasn't even going to tell his own brother the truth, even though he and Aaron are close, so telling Mel she's right doesn't seem fair. Saying nothing is the best I can do.

She shakes her head. "Part of me thinks I should lock you in my trunk until you come to your senses because this is not okay."

"You have an SUV," I point out. "I'll climb over the backseat and open the liftgate."

She waves that away, not caring. When I point out plot holes in movies, she does the same thing. Mel doesn't let reality ruin her entertainment.

"But the other part of me," she continues, "knows that this might be the only way you get to live your life because if Gin lives to be really, really old, it might be too late for you."

Her voice cracks toward the end, and tears well up in my eyes in response. Mel is the only person I've ever said the hard things out loud to.

Is this what Prince Charles felt like, having to wait until his mother passed away before he could do anything with his life?

Every time I spend a little bit of money on something that just makes me happy, something in the house breaks, so I don't spend money on fun stuff anymore.

What if she outlives me, Mel? What will happen to her? I'll have devoted my entire life to taking care of the house and it will still fall down around her. It'll all be for nothing.

"I'm going to go along with this," Mel says quietly, as if she's talking to herself instead of to me. "And if anybody asks me if I knew you were talking to him online, I'm going to say yes even though it's a lie. I'll say that of course I knew all along and didn't say a word because I'm Cara's best friend and I love her like she's my sister."

"I love you, too," I say because if nothing else, *that* is an undeniable truth.

"Let us buy you this dress," she says softly. "You're going to look so beautiful on Saturday. And I'm also going to look beautiful, but I'll downplay it a bit so nobody looks at me."

I laugh, and then throw my arms around her neck. "Thank you."

"Do *not* fall in love with your husband." It's such a ridiculous thing to say, we both laugh some more. "Now, let's buy this dress and go find some very salty french fries."

Chapter Thirty

HAYDEN

I really can't stand this town. I'm on my second lap of the main street, looking for a parking space, and why are there so many cars clogging up the town square right now? Did everybody decide to get a spray tan and manicure on the same day?

It's a town also sadly lacking in lodging. It occurred to me over the weekend that the gossipy citizens of Sumac Falls aren't seeing Cara and I together enough to convince them we're in love. While they might buy our inability to spend nights together thanks to the family feud and our mothers loathing each other, if the town had a motel, we could at least give the appearance we can't stand to be apart.

As far as I know, there's still only one bed and breakfast in town, and that's not an option. It was the second grandest home, after the Gamble house, and it's not in much better shape now—probably because it never has guests. Mrs. Barlow just registered it as a B&B after her husband died so she could use it as a tax write-off, or so the story goes.

The lack of places to stay is probably for the best. As much as two lovers hiding away in an inn because they're desperate to be alone looks good for the tale we're spinning, being alone with Cara in a room with a bed might *actually* kill me.

I finally find a parking space and make the short walk to Pampered Pets Grooming. Because Cara told me she might still be working with a dog, I left Penelope at my mother's house. She mostly ignores other dogs, but I don't want to upset any of Cara's four-legged clients.

I peer through the glass door and see that she's in the process of lifting a fairly large brown dog—some kind of mixed breed, I guess—down from the table. I wait until she's secured it in a fenced-in area decorated to look like a barn stall before I push the door open.

The dog barks the alarm until Cara snaps her fingers. "Kevin, be quiet."

"Kevin?"

"Yes, his name is Kevin. I don't ask." She brushes some hair from her shirt and walks over to her small counter. After shifting an appointment book out of the way, she hands me a sheaf of papers. "You should give them a quick look and make sure I initialed and signed everywhere I was supposed to."

I take the prenup and NDA documents and start flipping through them. "And you were okay with everything? Nothing you want to talk through?"

She shrugs one shoulder before turning to clean the grooming table. "I understood everything, and we'd already talked about the basics—we leave with the assets we came with, I keep my mouth shut about the plan, and I can't have Penny in the divorce."

I smile and take out my phone. After setting the papers on the counter, I open my scanner app and start scanning each page, one at a time. Cara was able to print them, but when she asked how best to scan them to return them to Taylor, I told her it would be easier for me to stop by. My scans go straight to a cloud folder Taylor has access to.

It also gave me an excuse to see her. "Any chance you want to grab something to eat at the diner? It wouldn't hurt to be seen together around town."

She laughs. "Trying to get a decent meal into me before our big family dinner tomorrow?"

"I had to promise an entire weekend of babysitting Daisy and AJ so Aaron and Hope can go away somewhere before they'd agree to host the dinner. But asking either of our mothers to host the other would have been a disaster. Aaron's last name might be Reilly, but they're the closest to neutral ground we have."

"Tell me again why we can't just go to a restaurant?

I've asked myself that same question several times, so I give Cara the answer I've given myself. "Because there's a fifty-fifty chance the dinner ends with my mother and your mother throwing glassware at each other, and that gets expensive fast in a restaurant."

She laughs. "I'm not sure your sister-in-law would consider her home the best food fight backup plan. And I'd say it's more like a ten percent chance it goes that far. I mean, wrecking a meal over an old family grudge is far-fetched."

I glance sideways at her. "Whatever is between our mothers is personal—beyond their last names, I mean. I don't know what, but I think something happened in high school that caused problems of their own."

"A sub-grudge?" she says, and I snort. "But why? My mother wasn't even a Gamble until she married my father."

"Sometimes it has nothing to do with great-great-grandparents or blue-ribbon pickles. It's just two teenage girls who hate each other."

Kevin—who's had his front paws on the top of the gate, blatantly eavesdropping—lets out a deep woofing sound.

"I know, buddy," Cara says in a soft voice. "Your mama always runs late, so you should be used to it by now. I hope she hurries up, though, because that guy over there is going to buy me a burger and fries tonight, and I'm starving."

Cara Gamble's going on a date with me.

No, I remind myself sternly. Not a date. Dating is for real relationships. Our meal will essentially be a business dinner—a strategic performance to further our story.

Since I'm finished scanning the documents, I slide my phone back in my pocket and the papers back into the manilla envelope Cara had kept them in. I set it on the counter for now, but I'll take these physical papers with me and give them to Taylor, who'll send final versions to Cara. I don't want stray copies floating around.

I do need to make sure we're on the same page before we go eat, though. "While we're at the diner, you know everybody that'll be there has to believe we're in love, right? We don't people out there gossiping about how we look like awkward strangers having a meal together."

"Awkward strangers?" She raises an eyebrow at me, the corners of her mouth tilting up. "So no stabbing you in the leg with a fork under the table?"

"I prefer that *nobody* stab me with a fork, but especially not the woman I'm marrying in a few days." I step closer to her, moving into her personal space to see how she'll react. "I was talking more about how your cheeks flush when I'm this close to you, as if you're not used to me being near."

Cara doesn't back up. Instead, she tips her head so I can see the mischievous curve of her mouth. When she trails her fingertips up my forearm, I suck in a breath. "How about the way the muscles in your jaw flex when I touch you?"

I'd hoped I was doing a better job of hiding my reaction to her touch, but it appears even my usually considerable control isn't up to the challenge. My self-discipline is currently being burned through in an effort not to haul her into my arms and kiss her like a *real* fiancé would.

Cara's eyes widen. "If you look at me like that in public, you won't have any trouble selling the story. And I don't think anybody expects us to be making out in the middle of a family diner or anything."

SHANNON STACEY

I *can't* let my mind get sidetracked with savoring the idea of making out with Cara, so I try to get myself back on topic. Sliding my hand into my pocket, I pull out the small box, and open it to reveal a diamond ring. It's not particularly flashy, but the diamond set in platinum is classically elegant. "I was hoping for a quiet moment to give you this."

"Oh." Cara starts to reach for it, but then pauses with her hand in the air, fingers curling. "It's huge, Hayden. It's fake, right? Tell me it's fake."

"It is *not* fake." I take her hand and slide the ring onto her finger. "I'm a little offended you would even ask me that."

"I can't be responsible for this," she hisses, but she hasn't taken her eyes off the way it catches the light. "The marriage is fake, so the ring should be fake, too."

"Cara, you need to stop saying that out loud, even when we're alone because you'll be more likely to say it when we're *not* alone."

"I know. I just need to..." She sighs, eyes still on the ring. "I know."

You just need to what? Why does she need to keep reinforcing to herself that our engagement is fake? I don't ask, though, because the door opens and Kevin loses his mind.

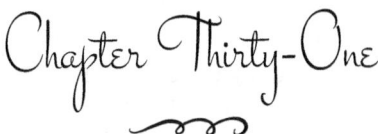

Chapter Thirty-One

CARA

Kevin gets about thirty seconds of his human's attention before she notices Hayden. Liz Mayfield's eyes light up with recognition, and I brace myself for whatever's about to come out of her mouth.

"Hayden Reilly! Look at you, all grown up!" Then, before he has a chance to react, she rushes forward and pulls him into a hug.

I try to hide how much I enjoy Hayden's discomfort, but he gives me a look over her shoulder letting me know my acting skills aren't exactly on par. I'm able to keep from actually laughing out loud, though, which I'll take as a win.

"Oh, gosh," Liz says, stepping backward. "I'm sorry. You probably don't even remember me."

"Mrs. Mayfield—of course I remember you," he says with a warm smile. "It's good to see you again."

Her relief is obvious, and then she turns to me. "My husband and Hayden's dad worked together and were good friends. There were a lot of backyard barbecues back in those days."

"Those were good times," he says with a genuine smile. "How have you been?"

"Oh, good. We're good." She's practically beaming now. "Downright boring compared to you two. Congratulations on your engagement!"

"Thank—"

"And your upcoming wedding, of course," Liz continues. "You're certainly in a rush."

She doesn't do the nosy glance at my midsection this time. We covered that when she dropped Kevin off for his appointment. Having already congratulated me, Liz keeps all of her attention on Hayden.

"When you know it's right, why wait?" he responds. It doesn't sound rehearsed at all, and I envy his ability to deliver lies so smoothly.

It's also a good reminder to *me* that Hayden is a smooth liar. While we're both getting something out of this arrangement, I *have* to remember nothing he says or does is real, no matter how warm and fuzzy his words make me feel.

"We're not doing invitations because we don't want to wait long enough for printers and RSVPs and all of that," he continues. "But everybody's welcome to come down to the gazebo on Saturday afternoon and celebrate with us."

Liz's cheeks actually flush with pleasure. "We might just do that."

Kevin's had enough of the small talk and starts howling for his human to hurry up. Liz leaves me an extraordinarily generous tip, and when I give her a questioning look, she winks and tells me it's for the wedding.

By the time they leave and I'm finished cleaning up, all I can think about is a bacon cheeseburger with a side of extra-salty french fries. I've earned them.

On second thought, maybe I should stick to the regular amount of salt on my fries because I have a wedding dress to wear in a few days.

A *wedding dress.*

Honestly, that sounds like a great reason for *extra* salt, not less. And extra dessert, too. A thick slab of hot apple pie with ice cream oozing into all the nooks and crannies. Maybe a mountain of whipped cream on top, too.

"I'm going to drop this in my car," Hayden says, interrupting my dessert fantasies by holding up the envelope of documents I'd signed. "Where's your car parked?"

"I walked today. The weather's gorgeous and if I walk, I don't have to find a parking space."

"It's still gorgeous out there. Should we leave my car and walk to the diner?"

"Sure." It sounds less awkward than getting in his car and being reminded of my last time riding in it. I am *never* splitting a bottle of wine with Mel in my shop after hours again. Especially if I haven't eaten anything.

After he leaves the paperwork in his car—not tossing them on the passenger seat like I would, but securing them in a locked briefcase in his trunk—we head toward the diner.

I've taken maybe three steps when his pinky hooks mine and I look up at him. Hayden is smiling at me, one eyebrow quirked, and I roll my eyes before threading my fingers through his.

Our hands being clasped presses the band of the engagement ring against my skin, making me conscious of the ring he'd slipped on my finger.

I really wish the diamond was as fake as our engagement because I don't need another thing to stress about. Worrying about taking care of the rock on my hand will be high on the list.

But I'm proud of myself as we stroll down the sidewalk hand-in-hand, showing off what a loving couple we are to others out on the street or anybody peeking through a window. My heart's not racing, my breathing's normal, and I don't think my cheeks are even a little pink.

As long as I don't think too much about that moment in my shop when I'm *very* sure he was about to kiss me, I'll be fine.

When we reach the diner, he lets go of my hand to open the door for me. My thumb immediately pokes at the base of my ring finger, making sure the ring is still there. I absolutely *can't* lose this ring because there's no chance I can replace it. There aren't enough shaggy dogs in Sumac Falls for that, even in spring when the skunks are feisty.

Because it's a Monday night, the diner's barely half-full, but it feels like I just stepped on to a stage at sold-out Gilette Stadium when every single person stops eating—or pouring coffee—to watch us. I want to turn on my heel and leave, but Hayden rests his hand at the small of my back and I forget anybody else is even in the room.

How, so many years later, does Hayden's touch still make my heart rate soar and my skin flush?

He guides me to an empty booth, ignoring the quiet ones in the back. Of course he has to choose one along the front wall, right in the midst of the other diners, and where everybody out on the street can see us through the window.

When Lorene steps out from behind the coffee counter to approach our table before the college kid who works summer shifts can greet us first, I know Hayden's plan for us to be seen and talked about is a winner. Lorene has owned the diner for as long as I can remember, and she's one of the most standoffish people in Sumac Falls. Gin says she's super sweet, but deliberately chooses not to be at work so she doesn't spend all of her time listening to her customers share every detail of their lives. That was for therapists and bartenders, according to Lorene.

But a Reilly and a Gamble sitting down to share a meal in her diner only days after getting a marriage license must be enough to break through Lorene's shell because she's all smiles.

"I hear congratulations are in order," she says in possibly the friendliest tone I've ever heard her use. Word must be getting around that if I'm expecting, I'm not showing yet because she doesn't try to peek over the table to see my midsection. People assuming this is a shotgun wedding situation and glancing— whether surreptitiously or blatantly—at my stomach wasn't something I'd foreseen happening. And it's especially annoying when I'm about to make questionable food choices.

"Thank you," Hayden says smoothly, shifting his gaze from Lorene to me. "We're so happy."

That's my cue to make sure I'm beaming with joy when Lorene also turns her attention to me. Thinking about the french fries I'm about to order definitely helps, though I'm not as smooth a liar as Hayden. Hopefully anybody who notices it will chalk my wavering smile up to pre-wedding jitters.

"Incredibly happy," I say when it becomes obvious Lorene expects me to chime in. I don't really know what else to say.

Hayden comes to my rescue—*again*. "Wedding planning really works up an appetite, though. Thinking about your burgers and fries was the only thing that got us through picking a cake flavor."

"Had dessert first, did you?"

He chuckled, shaking his head. "Just the debate without the tasting, unfortunately. Or maybe *fortunately*, since we have plenty of room for fries now."

Once Lorene has taken our orders, I can relax my face a little, but I'm still conscious that half the people in the diner are talking about us. And I'm also aware I can't accidentally say *anything* that might give us away—especially a snarky comment about how good Hayden is at working cons.

It's a lot of pressure, so I don't say anything at all while Lorene drops off our sodas and moves on. But when I reach for my straw, the diamond on my finger catches the light, mesmerizing me.

My breath catches in my chest when Hayden's fingers brush mine, his fingertips skimming over my knuckles in a way I don't *think* should be exceptionally sensual. And yet a shiver runs down my spine before he pulls his hand back.

"Relax," he whispers, handing me my straw.

That's easy for him to say. He's not the one sitting with the knowledge our hands touching is enough to make me squirm in my seat, and craving salty french fries is one thing. I can't be craving Hayden, too.

"I'm not used to getting so much attention," I say in a low voice because it's the truth, but would also make sense to anybody who might overhear me.

"All the attention will be on you Saturday."

"Great," I say with overly exaggerated excitement. "That helps so much!"

He laughs and relaxes against the booth. "What song should we play for our first dance?"

I freeze in the act of sucking soda through the straw and it's a good thing it hadn't reached my mouth yet, because I probably would have choked.

I'm still struggling to wrap my head around the fact I'm marrying Hayden at all. That he'll be taking me in his arms and holding me close, swaying to music, while everybody watches hadn't even occurred to me.

It's too much.

My expression probably gives away my thoughts on the matter because Hayden shakes his head. "Even with a scaled-down reception, there are milestones we don't want to skip. And our first dance as man and wife is one of them."

"Fine. But no songs from high school." Almost every love song made back then was a song I cried to in my room. We didn't have an "our song" because most of our time together was spent by the river, rather than at dances or in cars with radios, but it was a solid six months—at least—after homecoming night before I could listen to any song about love or heartbreak without crying.

"Challenge accepted," he says, pulling out his phone. After a list of popular wedding songs is on his screen, he turns it so I can see.

I skim the list and laugh. "I'm absolutely here for the 'Chicken Dance' being our first dance as a married couple."

"I should probably specify first dance songs."

"Less fun, but sure."

We spend thirty minutes going through song lists, and it actually is fun. We laugh together over some of the most frequently listed songs, many of which were probably contenders for our grandparents' first dances.

"Just surprise me with something," I finally tell him, because reading lyrics about love and marriage when I'm only getting the marriage part is starting to give me a headache.

"Okay, how about this," he says, dragging a fry through the puddle of ketchup on his plate. "Let's see what favorite movies we have in common and maybe one of them has a song we can use."

Not a bad idea, but Hayden has terrible taste in movies, and I spend more time laughing at his choices than coming up with any of my own.

"Wait. Did you see *Armageddon*?" he asks.

"Only eleven or twelve times."

"That's a good song."

I wrinkle my nose, taking a sip of my drink while I think about it. The song is good, and I think it had fallen off the charts by the time I went through my heartbreak playlist phase. And, honestly, there's a good chance I won't even notice the song when he's holding me close.

"Of course, the bride and groom doing the 'Chicken Dance' would also be memorable," he teases.

Just like that, Aerosmith's "I Don't Want to Miss a Thing" becomes our official wedding song.

The whole evening is like a dream—a perfect date as daydreamed by my teenage self—and I really wish it didn't have to come to an end.

Of course it has to, though, and as we step out onto the sidewalk and Hayden turns back toward the direction of his car, the dreaminess gives way to panic. Of course he's going to insist on driving me home.

And if I were Hayden, I'd probably assume Gin will peek out her window and, if she did, she would expect to see him kiss me goodnight.

In this moment, there's literally nothing I want more than to feel Hayden's mouth on mine.

But I can't.

I'm already having a hard enough time maintaining that boundary between the way young me felt about Hayden and the absolute lie that our relationship is now. I do *not* want to end a date to the diner—something we never got to do before—by kissing in his car.

"I'm closer to home than I am to your car," I tell him. "I'll just walk."

"I can drop you off."

But I'm already pulling my hand from his. "Thanks for the burger."

"Cara, wait. We should—"

"See you tomorrow for dinner." Before he can say anything else, I turn and practically speed-walk up the sidewalk in the opposite direction without looking back. I know it's childish, but my heart just can't take any more games tonight.

When I get home, Gin's sitting in her recliner in front of the television, and she barely acknowledges me when I call out a greeting to her.

I leave her alone. She's been forced to accept that not only will she have to give up the house, but her daughter is marrying a Reilly, so it's no surprise she's wallowing in misery. I know this is hard for her.

And I also know tomorrow, when she has to walk into Aaron's house and share a meal with Colleen Reilly, is going to be even harder. I just hope everybody is pleasant—no matter how hard they have to fake it—and there aren't any food fights.

And nobody gets stabbed with a fork.

Chapter Thirty-Two

CARA

I swear, I'm about two seconds from doing a Google search on whether you can be adopted by some other family at my age.

"Mom, we're going to be late!" It's the third time I've called up the stairs to her, and I'm starting to wonder if she's going to back out of this Gamble-Reilly family dinner in protest.

Having to text Hayden last minute and tell him we're not coming wouldn't bode well for family harmony on Saturday. And not just Gamble-Reilly harmony. I might actually disinvite my mother.

My phone chimes and I sigh, expecting a *where are you* text from Hayden, but it's a message from my sister.

GEORGIA

Are you there yet?

CARA

I'm still waiting for Mom. And if I was there, I wouldn't answer. I don't think being on my phone the whole time would make a good impression on my future mother-in-law.

Just typing the words—my *mother-in-law*—into my phone makes my stomach hurt.

GEORGIA

> Just call me and set your phone down
> somewhere. I'll mute my end and listen in.
> Maybe I'll even pop some popcorn.

There's zero chance of that happening. Knowing my luck, she'd accidentally unmute herself and laugh at a bad time. The evening was going to be awkward enough without trying to explain that.

I'd texted her an invite to the dinner because she's my sister and I wanted to keep her in the loop. But I knew she wouldn't be able to make it on such short notice, so maybe I should have skipped inviting her in the first place. Georgia's enjoying this—from a safe distance—way too much.

CARA

> I'll text you tomorrow and let you know how it
> went.

GEORGIA

> I want ALL the juicy details.

I send her a thumbs-up emoji, but I hope there's nothing juicy about tonight. Dry. Boring. Uneventful. That's the goal.

When Gin *finally* comes down the stairs, I'm relieved to see that she's dressed nicely. It wouldn't have surprised me if she put on raggedy old sweats in protest or—on the flip side—wore her funeral dress, complete with her pearls. But she's wearing jeans and a nice blouse, while I'm in jeans and a tank with a summery cardigan over it.

The relief is short lived, though, because she's carrying a small gift bag and nothing about this situation points to my mother going into this dinner with *that* much goodwill.

"What's in the bag?" I ask, trying for more casual curiosity and less dread.

"One doesn't show up for a dinner invitation without a token gift for the hostess, Carolina. You know that."

The way she smiles makes me think I should take a peek in that bag before she hands it over to a member of the Reilly family. Gin's not a fan of anything that slithers, creeps, or crawls, so whatever's in there probably doesn't bite, but she looks too pleased with herself for my liking.

It'll be a battle, though, and we don't have time for that. Plus, if I make her too mad, she might refuse to go. I need Gin and Colleen in the same room tonight because I have enough on my plate without worrying about them coming face to face for the first time at my actual wedding.

"Do you want to drive?" I ask as we walk out to the cars. If she's driving, it would make sense for me to hold the gift bag and I'm sure I can sneak a peek inside.

"I'm not in the mood." She makes sure I get her point by yanking my passenger door open so hard it's a miracle the handle doesn't come off in her hand.

Okay then.

By the time I slide into the driver's seat, Gin already has her seatbelt on and she's holding the bag on her lap with both hands. The bag hasn't moved and there are no ticking sounds or unpleasant odors coming from it, so all I can do at this point is cross my fingers my mother's playing nice.

The silence between us barely has a chance to grow uncomfortable before I pull into Aaron's driveway. I've noticed this house before because it's a beautiful Colonial with a big lawn and a horseshoe driveway, and if nothing else, I'll get to see the inside tonight.

As I park near the front door, Gin sniffs. "None of these new houses have any character at all."

Sure, because windows that don't close right anymore and

floors that are no longer level are what makes a house a home. "Be nice, please."

She heaves a put-upon sigh that Penny would be proud of, and then manages to undo her seatbelt without shifting the gift bag enough for me to justify holding it for her. I give up and get out, and then we walk up the front steps together.

That's when I see that my mother is not the only person being tempted by pettiness tonight. In front of Aaron's door is a rectangular spot outlined by a faint line of dirt.

One of the Reillys actually took up their *welcome* mat.

Hoping Gin doesn't notice—and maybe trying to keep myself from turning and running off into the woods—I take a deep breath and press the doorbell.

Chapter Thirty-Three

HAYDEN

When the doorbell chimes, the tension in my brother's home spikes, which is saying something considering it's been sky high since Colleen and I arrived.

"I'll get it," I say, heading toward the door. Since I forced this night on my family, Cara and her mother definitely qualify as *my* guests.

My mother holds up her hand. "I'll get it."

I try to head her off because I don't want Colleen's face to be the first one Gin sees when the door opens, but Hope cuts in front of both of us with the speed and aggression of a Boston commuter.

"I'll answer my own door, thank you very much," my sister-in-law says with an uncharacteristic edge to her tone.

She pins us each with a warning look usually reserved for her children, and then pulls open the door. "Welcome! Please, come in."

There's a moment after Cara moves toward me when Gin hesitates. Just when I'm convinced Cara's mother is either unwilling or unable to cross a Reilly threshold, she steps inside.

No alarms go off and nobody bursts into flames, so maybe this will be okay.

That's when I notice the gift bag Gin is holding.

When Cara reaches me, I pull her into my arms. Knowing it will look like I'm kissing my fiancé's cheek, I press my lips close to her ear. "What's in the bag?"

"She wouldn't tell me," she whispers back, and every muscle in my body tenses.

Cara moves out of my arms, but she doesn't go far. With her side pressed against mine, she reaches down and threads our fingers together. I give her a hand a reassuring squeeze as Gin passes the gift to Hope.

At least she didn't hand it to my mother. While Gin might enjoy watching my mother stick her hand into some disgusting surprise, she wouldn't do that to Hope. I don't think.

"I brought you a little thank you gift," Gin says. "For inviting us into your home."

I hold my breath as my sister-in-law reaches into the bag, and I'm pretty sure Cara's doing the same.

"Pickles." Hope looks slightly confused by the unusual hostess gift, but my mother doesn't. She might actually need help unclenching her jaw if she doesn't relax it soon. "Thank you."

"I wasn't sure if you drink wine," Gin says, "so I brought you some homemade pickles. It was my mother-in-law's recipe, and she won a blue ribbon at the fair."

Cara's clenching my hand so hard, my fingers are throbbing, but I keep the smile on my face as I try to take my mother's emotional temperature.

Colleen is watching me now, not her pickle-toting nemesis, and I can't tell what she's thinking. With our hands entwined and Cara's body turned close to mine, I know we look like a couple. But sometimes mothers see more than we'd like.

"Thank you so much," I hear Hope saying. "We love pickles in this house, so we'll definitely enjoy them. You know everybody right?"

My mother's eyes lock with mine for the space of a few heart-beats, and then she smiles—it almost looks real—and turns to Cara's mother. "Hello, Gin. I hope you like lasagna."

"Hello, Colleen. I do, and it smells delicious."

That went well, I think as Daisy and AJ come down the stairs. Cara must think so too, because her hand is relaxing, allowing the restoration of blood flow to my fingertips.

Before Aaron or Hope can say anything, Colleen steps forward. "These are my grandchildren, Daisy and Aaron Junior—or simply AJ, as we usually call him."

"It's nice to meet you both," Gin says, managing a smile for the kids. After they murmur greetings, she turns back to Colleen. "You have beautiful grandchildren."

"Thank you. It's great to see the next generation carrying on the Reilly name," Colleen says, and then she casts a pointed look at me while Gin's hands curl into fists at her side. Cara's fingers are strangling mine again.

"We'll be hyphenating our kids' names," I say quickly, before Gin can respond to the dig. "Gamble-Reilly, so our children will continue the legacy of both families. Together."

"Dinner's about ready," Hope says abruptly, her cheeriness sounding more forced by the second. "Let's eat."

Chapter Thirty-Four

CARA

Saved by the lasagna, I think, as most of the Reillys head toward the dining room. Hayden starts to go, but his fingers are still laced through mine and I haven't moved, so he has to stop or else jerk me forward.

When he gives me a questioning look, I reluctantly let go of his hand. I like the way they fit together so well. "We'll be right in. I just want to say hi to Penny really quick. I see her peeking out at me."

He smiles and heads for the kitchen, while I sit on the edge of the sofa. Penny immediately comes out of hiding and jumps up to rest her front paws on my knee so I can lift her onto my lap. Stroking my hand over her back makes my ring refract the light, and Gin shakes her head.

"Such an impractical ring," she says. Then, after tightening her lips for a few seconds, she gives me a tight smile. "It's very pretty, though."

"I'm so glad you came tonight. It's important to us both that our families are here—and will be at the wedding—to celebrate us."

"I'm not going to miss my daughter's wedding," she says, and then she sniffs. "I could do without jabs about the names, though."

"It was probably payback for the pickles," I tell her, and the smirk she can't hold back confirms she mentioned that blue ribbon deliberately. "Let's go join them. We don't want to be rude."

"Speak for yourself," she mutters.

After setting Penny down so she can resume hiding, I lead the way into the dining room, mostly as a warning that Gin's about to enter. It's probably a good thing I did because some fierce whispering between Colleen and Hayden ceases immediately. They're both smiling by the time my mother turns the corner, but I'm sure he got an earful about pickles, blue ribbons and surname hyphenations.

I'm not sure whether the Reilly family spent time charting the seating arrangement or we just got lucky, but Gin and Colleen will be out of arm's reach and also not in each other's direct sightline.

It puts me at the foot of the table, which I don't love, but I'll have Hayden on my right and my mother on my left. Next to Hayden is Daisy and then Colleen. AJ is sitting between Gin and Hope. Aaron, of course, is at the head of the table.

I can tell they added a leaf to the table because the ends show some wear and the center panel is shiny and flawless, but it means plenty of room and zero chance either Gin or Colleen can reach the other one's thigh with a fork or sharp knife.

Thankfully, Hayden takes the lead in making dinner conversation, keeping it focused on the wedding plans for the most part. Yes, he ordered the cake in Boston and his assistant and her husband will be bringing it with them. No, we are not doing dinner with the reception. Penelope Louise will not be in attendance because it would stress her out, so she'll be staying in Boston with her dog sitter.

Hope's the one asking most of the questions because Gin and

Colleen seem determined to survive this night by not talking. And Daisy and AJ are adorable and chatty, so they fill any gaps in the conversation.

Until Colleen decides to take it up a notch.

"I don't understand why you can't wait and have an autumn ceremony," she says. "Then we'd have time to plan a proper wedding, and the fall foliage is a gorgeous background for photos."

"I agree with Colleen," Gin says, and I wonder if all the Reillys and Gambles buried in Sumac Falls rolling over in their graves at the same time would show up on the Richter scale.

They want time to change our minds. I get that. But there's no way Hayden and I can keep up the pretense of being engaged over months. The only way this lie works is if we're so swept away by love, we have to get married *right now*.

Hayden threads his fingers through mine, holding my hand right there on the table between us. "We're not waiting. We've waited long enough."

"Three weeks?" Colleen's tone is almost as arched as her eyebrows, and the temperature in the room might have dropped a few degrees.

"As I explained to you," Hayden says in a tone that matches his mother's, "we've been back in each other's lives for longer than three weeks. And we've known each other our entire lives."

"If getting married is the right thing now, it'll still be the right thing in September," Colleen insists.

"Sherry makes the most beautiful fall flower arrangements in the shop," Gin adds.

Because my mom rejoining the conversation stops it from being a tense moment between mother and son, I jump back in. "We've already chosen the flowers, Mom. They're gorgeous, as you know, and everybody else will see them when we get married on *Saturday*."

"Name one good reason why you can't wait just a few months," Colleen demands.

"Because we don't want to," Hayden and I say at the same time.

"Where are you planning to live?" Colleen throws the question out like a grenade. "Hayden, you said you'd be splitting your time, but that you'd be here for holidays and other things."

"The plan has always been for our house to stay in the family for the next generation," I say, hoping to make a point without going into too much details. "My mom will be able to find something more comfortable, maybe in that new community."

I can tell by her breathing that Gin's had just about enough of this conversation, but Colleen isn't ready to give up yet. "That takes time. What's going to happen in the meantime. Are you going to live in *her* house, Hayden?"

"We're still figuring stuff out, Mom," Hayden says.

"You'd have time to figure it all out if you put off the wedding," Colleen pointed out. "But that's fine. I just hope that old house doesn't finally collapse while you're in it."

Gin's muscles bunch as she prepares to stand. I'm not sure if she intends to dump her drink over Colleen's head or storm out the door, but I'd prefer neither happens. I nudge her ankle with my foot and give her a pleading look. She looks as angry as I've seen her in a long time, but she relaxes back into her seat.

"AJ, did you tell Uncle Hayden you found out who your kindergarten teacher will be next year?" Hope interjects in a voice that gets more forcefully cheery as the night goes on.

The boy's mother chose her question wisely—AJ has a *lot* to say about kindergarten, and he talks so fast, nobody else can get a word in even if they wanted to. Every time his excited chatter starts to flag, somebody prompts him and off he goes again. Daisy jumps in with her own kindergarten stories, and the two kids manage to get them through to the end of the meal.

Luckily, there's no mention of dessert. Even if something had been planned, it was obvious Hope's nerves were shot and, while nobody was attacked with cutlery or flying dinner rolls, prolonging the evening doesn't seem like a great idea.

Especially when Daisy and AJ are dismissed from the table and we lose our adorable conversational buffers.

There's not much else to do. Gin and I offer to help clean up, but Hope waves us off. Sitting in the living room, trying to think of neutral things to talk about will either lead to awkward silence or more verbal sparring. We've done what we set out to do, which was test whether Colleen Reilly and Gin Gamble could tolerate each other's presence enough for them to attend the wedding.

And it went okay...ish.

The goodbyes are stilted, but neither of our mothers takes a verbal shot at the other. After thanking Hope and Aaron, I say goodbye to Colleen—my future mother-in-law, which is surreal—and then I accept a kiss on the cheek from Hayden.

He was aiming for my mouth, and he chuckles against my face when I turn at the last second. It just feels strange to kiss in front of both of our mothers, even with the story we're selling them. And maybe, thanks to the angles, they can't tell he missed my mouth.

Gin and I drive home in tense silence. I know I should say something, but nothing I say is going to make her okay with what I asked of her tonight. Instead, I let her stew, knowing if she wants to talk about it, she won't be shy.

After being in Aaron's big new house, with its open spaces and high end finishes, our house looks extra shabby, but I try not to wallow in the comparison. I remember, when I was in elementary school, some of the kids thought my family was rich because we lived in the big Gamble house—the only mansion in town. I knew, even then, that my family had been rich once, but we certainly weren't anymore. What a life looks like from the outside never tells the whole story. Or a *true* story.

Gin goes straight to the kitchen to set up the auto brew on the coffeemaker so it'll be ready to drink when we get up in the morning. I'm braced for a torrent of anti-Reilly rhetoric, but she simply finishes her task and then fills the tumbler she keeps next to her bed with fresh water.

I can't stand the silence anymore. "Thanks again for tonight, Mom. It wasn't so bad, was it?"

"They were friendly enough, I suppose, but I have a headache and I'm going to read in my room for a while." She starts walking in that direction, but can't resist a final shot over her shoulder. "The lasagna was too runny, though."

I want to push back—the lasagna was excellent, actually—but I let her go. If being civil in the presence of the Reilly family and then trash-talking them behind closed doors is how my mother's going to get through this, I'll let it be.

The next time Gin and Colleen will be in the same place will be my wedding. *Saturday.* Four more sleeps and a wake-up, and Hayden and I will be standing in front of our friends and families, vowing to love each other until death do we part.

I lift my hand so the ridiculously large and utterly gorgeous ring on my finger catches the light, and I remember the way he looked at me when I went into his arms to say goodbye.

I knew in that moment he wanted to kiss me, and I also knew I wanted him to.

This plan of Hayden's to buy our house better be worth it because there's a good chance I'm going to get my heart broken—again—in the process.

Chapter Thirty-Five

HAYDEN

Besides babysitting, another of my punishments for inflicting Gin Gamble on my mother and a surprise dinner hosting on Hope is kitchen cleanup duty.

It's not too bad. They have a top of the line dishwasher, so it's mostly just solving the puzzle of how to make everything fit. I've had a lot of practice with my own dishwasher, of course, but it's not hard to make space in an appliance for a single plate and fork.

I hear my mother saying goodbye to the others in the living room, followed by the sound of the front door closing. I'm not surprised she didn't come and say goodbye to me. Her sitting down to share a meal with Gin Gamble was a big ask, so I'm not her favorite person right now. I'll probably get an earful about blue ribbon pickles when I get home, though.

I've got the plates and glasses sorted, and I'm working on the cutlery when Aaron walks into the kitchen. He doesn't help, but instead leans against the island and folds his arms. "That went pretty well, all things considered."

"Mom and Gin both came close to blowing up, but I'm sure

it was understood that anybody causing a problem would be uninvited from the wedding."

"That helped, I'm sure." Aaron chuckles. "Saturday. In a few days, you'll be a married man."

"I should have talked her into eloping." It was a lie. I was looking forward to the entire town witnessing the fact I am, in fact, good enough for the Gambles. One of them, anyway. But the lie keeps the conversation light.

My brother laughs. "Tracking you down would really have brought Mom and Gin together."

"We would have been home before they were done arguing about who was going to drive."

"Don't be mad, but I honestly thought you were just scamming Cara out of her family home. I didn't want to think you were capable of using a woman's heart to do it, but that's what it looked like to me." He sighs while I focus on making sure all of the knives are point-down in the silverware basket. "But now that I've seen you together, it's clear you guys are the real deal."

For obvious reasons, his words make me uncomfortable, and I'm thankful I'm bent over the dishwasher. Fussing with the silverware keeps me from having to look my brother in the eye.

But there's a less obvious reason for my discomfort, too, and it's the one that's making it hard for me to think. Neither Cara nor I have much in the way of acting skills, so why was one dinner with us enough to change the mind of the man who knows me better than anybody?

Because we actually are the real deal?

No. I can't let myself believe that. Not today. Not while we're standing at the altar. And definitely not while we're acting out our roles as man and wife, waiting for Gin to sign the paperwork that will make the house mine.

"Aaron," Hope calls from the living room. "Daisy and AJ are squabbling over something upstairs and I'm not dealing with it because you owe me for life after tonight."

"I don't think we settled on *life*," he calls back, and then he points at me. "Don't forget you'll be watching my kids for a weekend. Maybe even a *long* weekend, if Hope can work it into her schedule."

"I'm looking forward to it."

By the time he's done refereeing his kids, I've finished cleaning the dining room and kitchen, and the dishwasher's running. Hope's on the couch with her feet up on the coffee table, watching rich housewives yell at each other on the TV, while Aaron's doing his best not to nod off.

"I should get Penny," I say. "She's sensitive to tension. And Mom's probably pacing, waiting to give me hell when I walk through the door. The sooner we get it over with, the sooner Penny can relax."

"Have fun with that," Aaron says smugly from his position of being the son who married a woman Colleen adores and gave her grandchildren, and not the son who made her share a meal with Gambles.

I go upstairs to say goodbye to Daisy and AJ, and then I thank Hope again for dinner. Unfortunately, it just doesn't take that long to walk to my mother's house, so I don't get a lot of decompression time before I have to go through the door.

Penny's happy to be back to her fluffy bed, at least, and I take my time putting her harness and leash away before making eye contact with Colleen. She's watching the same show Hope was, but she mutes it when I sink onto the couch next to her.

"Thank you, Mom," I tell her. "I know that was hard for you, but it meant a lot to Cara and me."

"It *was* hard." She puts her hand on mine, surprising me. I was expecting anger. "But seeing you two together... I wish she wasn't a Gamble, but I want you to be happy."

I nod, letting her words sink in. The goal is to convince our friends and family we're head-over-heels in love with each other, but it's a little alarming how easily the two people who know me best have accepted it.

Before I can think of a response, she pats my hand twice and then pushes herself to her feet. "It was a long day, so I'm going to go read in bed for a while. If I fall asleep before I come back down, I'll see you in the morning."

Once she's gone, I grab the television remote and start flipping through the channels, looking for something that might offer distraction without requiring concentration. Since we're alone, Penny abandons her bed and relaxes into her favorite position—stretched out beside me so her entire body is pressed along the length of my thigh.

I want to call Cara, but I don't want to interrupt anything if Gin didn't take the evening as well as Colleen did. Plus, on the telephone, her mother might not be able to hear me, but she'd be able to hear Cara's end of the conversation. A text conversation, though, is not only private, but Cara can ignore it if she's in the middle of something or just not in the mood to talk about it.

HAYDEN

How are things at your house?

CARA

My mom claimed a headache and went to her room to be alone.

HAYDEN

Same with my mom, more or less. Let's blame the lasagna.

She sends back a laughing emoji, which makes me smile. I really want to hear her voice, but I also don't want to be pushy. Showing up in town and getting her to marry me so I can have her house is probably pushy enough.

HAYDEN

Do you have any free time tomorrow?

CARA

I'm booked up solid the next two days. A bug went around the elementary school and I'm trying to get the rescheduled appointments out of the way this week. And I need to get Gin to commit to what she's wearing Saturday.

That's disappointing, but I'll be patient. After Saturday, everything will be different.

Chapter Thirty-Six

CARA

By the time my last furry client walks out the door on Thursday afternoon with a little less fur, I'm exhausted. Word about my upcoming nuptials—and *how* is my wedding only two days away? —has gotten around and leaked into my refuge from the world.

Every human who walked into Pampered Pets Grooming today congratulated me. I appreciate the well-wishes, even the clumsily disguised attempts at digging for fresh gossip, but every reminder twisted the knot of anxiety and guilt in my stomach.

I want to go home, climb into bed and pull the covers over my head, but Gin sends me a text letting me know we're out of butter. That's her way of asking me to stop at the market on my way home without actually asking me for a favor, and I'm tempted to pretend I didn't see it. I don't know what she's making for dinner tonight, though, and I assume it's something that tastes better with butter because what doesn't?

It should have added two minutes to my walk, but a line has formed while Shawna and a customer debate whether the discounted price of a buy-two special applies if a person only buys one of the item in question. But even while Shawna argues the entire point of a buy-two special is that the customer buys *two*, I can see her gaze flicking to me.

Shawna—who is about Gin's age—is a notorious gossip. Since almost everybody in Sumac Falls makes at least one trip through the market each week, she has the perfect job for collecting tidbits of information and piecing them together like a puzzle.

By the time I set the tub of butter—along with the chips and the package of candy bars I'm splurging on—down on the belt, she's practically glowing. "You're the talk of the town this week. Congratulations."

"Thanks. I'm very excited," I say for the sixth or seventh time today, trying not to sound like I *really* don't want to hear it.

"And I hear there was a family dinner? I thought there was a better chance of me winning the lottery than Colleen Reilly and Gin Gamble sitting down at the same table to share a meal." She's quiet for a moment, and then chuckles. "There was a time we thought only one of them was going to make it out of high school."

This is my opportunity to get a little more insight into the grudge that feels deeper than an old family feud. Most of her attention is on the groceries she's scanning, so it shouldn't be hard to keep her talking.

"My mom doesn't talk about high school a lot," I say casually. "So she and Colleen really hated each other, huh?"

"I've never seen two people hate each other more. It all started with a boy, of course. They both had crushes on a new kid in school—I don't even remember his name because he wasn't here very long before his dad got a better job and they moved again. They were never friends, but both of them wanting that boy turned them mean. I remember there being an *accident* with Gin's science fair project." She actually stops scanning to put air quotes around the word.

"Mom's a tyrant about good grades. That must have set her off."

Shawna sighs and her mouth turns down slightly at the corners before she ducks her head back to the task, clearly uncomfortable. "One day in...I guess it was sophomore year, Colleen got her period and bled through her pants in Algebra II class. Pretty badly, I heard, and she was wearing light pink pants, too."

I wince in sympathy. I don't miss worrying about that in class, and I know it's traumatic for every girl it happens to. And you know it was bad when even the town's most notorious gossip isn't comfortable talking about it.

"Later on during lunch, Gin found a can somewhere and went around the cafeteria and hallways, asking for donations for Colleen, saying the Reilly family was too poor to buy tampons for her."

I actually gasp out loud, and my cheeks burn even though it's not my shame to bear. I know teen girls can be as hostile as feral cats sometimes and Gin certainly has a mean streak she didn't totally outgrow, but it's painful to hear my mother was capable of being so cruel.

Shawna seems to shake off the memories and gives me the kind of smile that says she's trying too hard. "But that was a long time ago, and it's all water under a very old bridge. Now you'll all be one big happy family."

To my credit, I don't laugh in her face—or burst into tears. Either was a possibility, really, but I paste on a big smile and nod with a lot more enthusiasm than I feel.

As soon as the machine says my transaction's approved and I can have my card back, I slide it in my back pocket and grab my bag. I give Shawna a big, fake smile when she says she hopes I'll have pictures next time I come in and then make my escape. But as I walk through the exit door, I lock eyes with Aaron Reilly, who's on his way in. I'm so over this day.

Aaron stops in his tracks.

There's a very awkward moment—usually Gambles pretend

Reillys are invisible and vice versa—and then we both seem to remember we're about to be in-laws and smile at the same time.

"Thank you again for hosting dinner," I say as we step out of the way of other customers. "And I'm sorry about the whole pickle thing."

When he grins, he looks a lot like his brother. "Hey, those pickles are amazing. I'll deny it to the grave if you tell my mother, but I would have given them a blue ribbon if I was judging them at the fair."

"Your secret is safe with me. Trust me, the last thing I want in my life is more drama."

"For two people who don't want drama, you and Hayden really know how to stir it up."

Just wait until we get divorced, I think, but I don't say it out loud, of course. "I'm glad I ran into you so I could thank you again, but my mom's waiting for this butter, so I'd better go."

"It was our pleasure, and I'll see you on Saturday, I guess."

I'm afraid if I open my mouth some truly unhinged laughter will come out, so I just smile and nod and start walking. Luckily, I make it home without running into anybody else who wants to talk about the Gamble-Reilly wedding, which gives me a few minutes to center myself before seeing my mom.

After changing my clothes in the garage, I take the butter out of the bag before stowing my chips and candy behind an old box of who-knows-what. Maybe it's petty and there's a good chance I'll end up sharing with my mom anyway, but for right now, I want to keep the treats all to myself.

Gin's just setting pork chops and white rice down on the table when I walk in, and I'm glad I stopped at the market. I don't love plain rice. I *really* don't love it dry. But at least we have some homemade chunky applesauce to go with it, left over from Gin and Sherry's last canning kick.

"Aunt Tess called me today," Gin says just as I've taken my first bite. "Somebody in this town likes to gossip and she heard you're marrying a Reilly."

Somebody in this town likes to gossip? I chuckle. It's practically a competitive sport in Sumac Falls.

"It's not funny, young lady. She said if you go through with it, she's not coming to the wedding."

"Did you tell her she wasn't invited?"

"Of course not. That would be rude. She's threatening to disown you."

"*Oh no.* I'm really going to miss that ten dollars in every birthday card." I say it with a sarcastic edge, but at this point in my life, every dollar counts. Ten dollars pays for almost a half a tank of gas, if nothing else.

I'll buy a bicycle, though, before I'll walk away from this opportunity to get Gin and I out from under this house just because my elderly aunt is chirping about *the Gamble legacy* and how I'm disgracing it.

"We might need her generosity someday," Gin says quietly, which is as close as I've ever heard her come to admitting we're not okay in this house. There's also the fact we *will* be okay thanks to Hayden's generosity, but she's always been a people pleaser when it comes to anybody born a Gamble—except for me, of course.

"Mom, she's never given us a dime for this house and she never will. Except for those ten dollar bills in my birthday cards and that twenty dollars when I graduated from high school, she's never given us *anything.*"

"She's under no obligation to—"

"She didn't help us bury Dad or offer to help with the medical bills," I say, and then I pause before dealing the death blow to this conversation. "And she didn't come to his funeral."

All the fight goes out of Gin in a long, defeated breath. My mother can embrace varying degrees of denial when it comes to issues of money, but her husband's aunt not showing up to pay her respects was not only an emotional blow, but an affront to that Gamble legacy everybody claims to care so much about.

I wrack my brain to come up with something to talk about as

the silence drags on. Usually I'd ask about Sherry and the shop, but they're probably working on the flowers for my wedding.

"I had the cutest border collie pup in the shop today. It was his first time going to the groomer," I say, because Gin doesn't like dogs, but at least they're a safe topic. She'll probably ask who owns the dog and since it's not a Reilly, she'll tell me everything she knows about the people.

"Is that man going to let you keep your business after you're married?" she asks sharply, stabbing a chunk of pork chop with an enthusiasm that makes me wince.

"One, he's not going to *let* me do anything because, you know, partner in life and not my boss and all that. And two, *that man* is going to be your son-in-law in two days, so maybe you can use his name." I take a deep breath, trying to smooth some of the edge out of my voice. "Hayden knows Pampered Pets is important to me, and we'll work it out."

She doesn't ask any more about it, and I can't think of any topic that might not circle back to Hayden, so we finish the meal in silence. Then she leaves me to clean up without another word, which is fine with me. Her bitterness is like a smog cloud tonight —as it often is after a call from Aunt Tess—and I can breathe easier when she's not in the room.

After drying the last of the dishes and putting them away, I'm not sure what to do with the rest of my evening. I don't really want to go watch TV because it might draw Gin back downstairs. And I just ate, so it's too soon to hide in the garage with my secret stash of snacks.

I pull out my phone, intending to text Mel, but I type out a message to Hayden instead.

CARA

I hope your life is as ridiculous as mine so I'm not suffering alone.

HAYDEN

Ice cream in our spot?

Is he serious? We're adults now. And also, we've already forced our families to accept that we're getting married. There's no reason for us to sneak out and go hide in the woods with quickly melting ice cream.

CARA

I'm on my way.

Chapter Thirty-Seven

HAYDEN

I bring Penny with me. She doesn't love being out in the woods very much, but she hasn't loved the general vibe of my mother's house lately, either.

I can't blame her, and I decide she'd rather be out in the woods with me than alone in her bed again.

Thanks to past me hoping a trip to the river might happen—or maybe I'd simply surrendered to a moment of nostalgia-induced weakness—I already have ice cream in the freezer. I toss two of the small tubs in one of Colleen's insulated shopping bags, along with one of the frozen doggy treats I picked up for Penny.

I pass on the idea of dragging my old bike out of the garage, though. For one thing, it doesn't have a basket for Penny, which I'm sure she would hate anyway. And also, the last time I rode that bike was the last time I'd ridden any bike at all. I don't even like the stationary kind at the gym in my building, choosing instead to spend my workout time on a treadmill.

I drive instead, parking behind the closed post office because the lot is closest to the path I need to take. I don't see Cara's car anywhere, so she either walked or she hasn't arrived yet. After clipping Penny's leash to her harness, I grab the bag from the backseat and head down the path into the woods.

I'm not sure where Cara parked, but as I get close to our spot, I catch a glimpse of her through the trees. She's sitting on our rock and my pulse quickens with each step I take.

I'm tempted to stop and lean against a tree for a moment to get myself under control, but Penny's already spotted her. Rather than giving me a look that conveys her annoyance at dealing with woods *and* other people, she starts straining against the harness, eager to get to Cara.

Not in a million years did I imagine Penelope Louise being so excited to see a human who isn't me.

"Penny!" Cara's just as excited as my dog, and she doesn't even look at me as Penny climbs into her lap, licks her hand a few times, and then curls into a ball.

"I brought the ice cream," I say, trying not to sound like I'm sulking because Cara likes my dog more than me. I'm not sure I succeed because she laughs when she finally looks up at me.

"Sorry, and hello. But you must be used to being sidelined while people love on this sweet face."

"Not really," I tell her as I climb onto the flat-topped boulder. "I wasn't kidding when I said she doesn't like anybody but me."

"And me," Cara says as she scratches the sweet spot under Penny's chin. The dog stretches her neck, asking for more, while giving me a smug look I try to ignore.

Sitting on this rock with the river gurgling past, it's harder to ignore the memories of that summer flooding my mind. I rub the tattoo on my chest through my shirt for a few seconds, as if I can make the ache go away.

Cara and I shared our first kiss on this rock—the first of many.

How naive I'd been in high school, daring to believe that the intense feelings Cara and I had for each other would be strong enough to withstand our parents' objections. I thought we'd wear them down until they gave us their blessings, and then we'd get married and raise our kids in Sumac Falls. I'd daydreamed about our future so much, my grades had actually dipped.

But I'd underestimated just how dirty Marcus Gamble was willing to play when it came to keeping his daughter away from a Reilly boy.

"You look like you're having a worse day than I did," Cara says, jerking my attention back to the present.

"Just a lot on my mind, I guess. Are things getting worse with Gin or did you just need a break?"

She shrugs one shoulder. "Mostly I just wanted a break, I guess. But my great-aunt Tess told her she was going to disown us and even though that means exactly nothing except me not getting ten dollars in a birthday card every year, it upset my mother."

"Tess. That's short for Tennessee, right?" he asks, remembering our conversation about the women in her family being named after states. She nods. "So just lie and tell your Aunt Tennessee that Penny's full name is Pennsylvania. She'll think it was fate."

I'm rewarded with her laughter, which never fails to send warmth flooding through my body. It also makes me aware of a fundamental truth—if I could hear Cara laugh every day for the rest of my life, I'd consider myself rich beyond my wildest dreams.

I don't want her to see that emotion on my face, though, so I busy myself opening the insulated bag. I set Penny's frozen treat on the rock between us, open so she can lick at it. Then I hand Cara a small carton and a spoon before opening my own.

"I needed this," she says after savoring the first spoonful. Almost as much as I savored the way she closed her eyes and made a delicious little moaning sound.

"I know it's been hard, but we're almost there."

She pauses with her spoon in her mouth to give me a look. "We're almost to the wedding part. We still have to go through the selling the house part and the getting divorced without Gin suing you to get her house back part."

The urge to remind Cara that her mother doesn't have the resources to defeat me in a legal battle is strong, but it's smarter to deescalate. "It'll be worth it. Think about down the road, when you can do something you love."

"I *am* doing what I love, actually. I like Sumac Falls and I would never give up Pampered Pets. It's the only thing that's really mine."

"It's just the house, then? That you would change, I mean."

"It's not even so much the house." She stares into her tub of ice cream for a few seconds, stabbing at a chocolate chip with the tip of her spoon. "I love that old house, actually. Generations of Gambles have lived there, so my family history is basically baked into the bones of it. But it costs a lot to maintain and by the time I was born, that battle was already being lost. I'm tired of living every single day knowing we're one household disaster away from not being able to fix the furnace or the roof or pay the tax bill."

I know from researching the property that the tax bill on the Gamble house isn't insubstantial. While the house might be in a state of disrepair, it covers a lot of square feet and it sits on a large plot of private land. The homeowner's insurance is probably no joke, either, because they base it on replacement cost and rebuilding a house like that with current construction costs is painful for even me to imagine.

But I don't want to talk about the property anymore.

It's one thing to take the house away from Gin. As far as I'm concerned, she deserves to lose it. But it'll be harder to sleep at night knowing Cara actually loves the house, and it's only the financial aspect she wants to get away from.

"What would you do if the house and money weren't an issue?" I ask, wanting to remind myself I'll actually be doing her a favor by taking the house off her hands.

She sighs, her face softening as her lips curve into a dreamy smile. "I'd want enough land to move Pampered Pets to a stand-alone business rather than it being in a Main Street storefront.

SHANNON STACEY

And I'd fence the outdoor spaces and also foster shelter animals to help get them ready for their forever homes."

When we were young, sitting in this same spot, she loved to talk about how—when she was an adult and moved out—she was going to adopt a bunch of cats and dogs. She'd always loved animals, but could never have a pet.

"I'm going to make sure you get to do that," I tell her, and even though she shakes her head, a wistful smile curves her mouth.

"Did Aaron tell you we ran into each other at the market today?"

"He called me on his way home. Said after years of pretending you and Gin were invisible, he didn't know what to do."

"Same," she says. "Your niece and nephew are adorable, by the way. Listening to AJ's excitement about kindergarten was worth the stress of that dinner."

My brother's kids give us something neutral to talk about while we eat our ice cream, and it's easy for me. I love talking about them, and Cara seems to get a kick out of my favorite stories.

But too soon, the ice cream is gone and I know she's going to tell me it's time to go any minute. As much as I hate to bring up the subject when we're both so relaxed, the clock is ticking.

"Have you written your vows yet?" When she freezes in the act of stowing the debris from our ice cream binge in the bag, except for a widening of her eyes, I sigh. "You didn't read the *entire* email, did you?"

"I thought I did. In my defense, you send a lot of emails, and you pack a lot of information into them. I think I'd remember that, though." She sends a fierce scowl in my direction. "What's wrong with the standard vows?"

"Don't you think it's more romantic to write our own?"

Cara's quiet for a long time, staring at the rushing water while absentmindedly stroking Penny's back. "I don't think I can do that, Hayden."

"I could write something for you. Stuff about my chiseled jaw and—"

"No." She turns to look me in the eye. "It's going to be hard enough to stand up in front of everybody and make vows we don't mean. But at least if they're the standard, generic ones it'll... I don't know. It'll feel like a movie or something. Less personal, and maybe less fraudulent feeling. It's hard to explain."

"I get it." And I do. I've been so focused on convincing our friends and family we're madly in love, I haven't considered how it was going to feel to have Cara look me in the eye and recite wedding vows. I think she's right that stock vows will be *slightly* less painful.

She stands, signaling an end to our interlude in the woods. Penny looks expectantly at me, and I can see that she's done here, too. Both of them are obviously waiting for me to stand up, so I push myself to my feet.

"Tomorrow morning, I'm heading to Boston. I have to grab a few things, and also get Penny settled with her sitter. We probably won't see each other again until the ceremony."

Cara blinks a few times, and then laughs. It isn't her usual laugh, but one that sounds panicky and disbelieving. "We're really doing this?"

"We're really doing this." I don't want her to start spiraling into second thoughts, so a subject change is in order. "Should we practice the 'you may kiss the bride' part before we go?"

If the way her gaze drops to my mouth and stays there is any indication, she's considering it and my body tightens with anticipation. I'm doomed to disappointment, though, because she slowly shakes her head.

"I'm not kissing you on this rock, Hayden, because the last time I did, it was real. At least for me, anyway. And even though it's painful, I want to keep those memories separate."

"It was real," I say in a low voice. But I don't want to wander down that particular Memory Lane any further, either, because it ends with me telling her what really happened that night. Or it ends with her angry with me all over again because I won't have a good reason. Either way, I don't want that.

"I walked, so I guess we're leaving in separate directions," she says, obviously not wanting to look any further into the past than I do.

I pick up my dog, intending to carry her until we're back on the path. "So I'll see you Saturday, then."

Cara manages a smile, maybe because I'm holding Penny, which puts her at the perfect height for more scratches under her chin. "I'll be the one everybody's staring at."

There's nothing I can say to lessen her anxiety about that, so I just smile as she gives Penny a final head rub before walking away. I watch her for a few seconds, and then force myself to head back toward my car. The next time I see Cara, we'll leave together as a married couple.

And the next time I kiss her, she'll be my wife.

Chapter Thirty-Eight

CARA

Today's my wedding day.

I blink at the ceiling fan, waiting for my mind to start spinning in time with the fan's blades. Today is the day I'm going to stand up in front of my family, friends, and neighbors, vowing to love and cherish Hayden Reilly until death do us part.

There should definitely be spinning. Instead, I'm strangely calm.

Maybe it's because the last two weeks have been an emotional whirlwind, whipping up more chaos than my personal life has seen in years. By late this afternoon, it'll be over. Even though there are more items to check off the master list, the outrageous fake marriage plan will have been executed.

Of course, I'll have a husband at that point, which should be triggering some kind of panic. A buzz of anxiety, at the very least. Knots in my stomach. Butterflies. Anything.

Numb. That's what this is—not a sense of calm, but numbness. I've been on a wild rollercoaster since Hayden came back to town, and the idea of becoming his wife today has finally short-circuited all of my emotions.

That's the only rational explanation for why I'm not freaking out.

I close my eyes, trying to picture a big, fenced-in yard behind a cute little building housing Pampered Pets Grooming. I've been practicing, learning to imagine a future I'll have a chance to make for myself.

A little house of my own, where I don't have to strip in the garage and the hot water heater works. My business, flourishing once I have the space to handle more than one dog at a time, with grooming stations and maybe even an assistant. Plus, I won't have to pay rent in the Gamble Block. There are several dogs running around my imaginary yard—fosters that I'm getting to know so I can help them find forever homes.

Then, in my daydream, I turn to look at my house and I see Hayden and Penny sitting in the shade of the deep front porch, watching me.

I open my eyes because the butterflies are definitely dancing now. Hayden and his dog can't be in my imaginary future because they won't be a part of my *actual* future.

I'm saved from the fluttering escalating into full-blown panic by the sound of two car doors slamming in my driveway.

Georgia's here.

Crap.

I throw myself out of bed and I'm halfway to the stairs when I remember the tank top I'm wearing with no bra is so old and many times washed, it barely exists.

After turning around to throw a baggy sweatshirt over my threadbare tank and boxer shorts, I sprint down the stairs. Seconds later, my arms are wrapped around my sister and she's squeezing me so hard, I can hardly breathe.

"You came."

"Of course I did," she says, easing the embrace enough so I can breathe, but not letting me go.

We look enough alike so a stranger could probably place us as sisters, though Georgia's taller and less curvy. It broke my heart when she left Sumac Falls for college, even while I was happy for *her* because she'd gotten away.

"Shouldn't you be getting ready?" she asks when she finally steps back, looking me up and down. "We hit some traffic because of an accident, which means we're running behind. And that means you're *really* running behind."

I look at my wrist, which makes no sense because I haven't worn a watch for years. And then I pat the sides of my sleep shorts for my phone, which is also ridiculous because they don't have pockets.

"It's almost noon," Tony says, and I jump because I'd been so focused on Georgia, I'd forgotten about my brother-in-law.

I give him a hug, but then his words sink in and I gasp. "Wait. Noon?"

That explains how I tossed and turned for what felt like the entire night, and yet still woke up feeling fairly rested.

"We're going to head to the town square," Georgia says. "You need to go do something with that hair."

"Did you see Mom already?"

"She came out and said hello, and then muttered about finding something and then about her shoes before turning around and going back inside. We're sitting with her, of course, so we'll have time to catch up while we wait for the bride to get ready and arrive."

I laugh, but it's high-pitched, and I see the look that passes between Georgia and Tony as they walk back to their car. They don't think I can do it, but when your forty-gallon hot water heater coughs up maybe a gallon and a half of hot water, you learn to shower fast.

My hair takes the longest. I blow dry it for longer than usual, mostly because my scalp is hypothermic after my cold shower. Then I pull up the sides and clip them in a floral barrette. It's simple, but more elegant than my usual ponytail. And I keep my makeup simple, hoping I won't sweat and make it run down my face. I'm putting the makeup back in the drawer when my phone chimes.

MEL

I'm almost there!

I'm smiling as I slide the dress off the hanger. It's so pretty—probably the prettiest thing I've ever owned—and just the feel of the fabric makes me happy. That it was a gift from Mel and Lucas just makes it even more special.

I should probably wait for my maid of honor to help me put it on, but it's a sundress, not a formal gown. And Georgia wasn't wrong about us running late. I don't want to leave Hayden standing in the gazebo in front of everybody, wondering if I pulled a runaway bride.

I take a breath and give myself a final look in the mirror.

How many times, in this very room, had I imagined myself preparing to become Mrs. Hayden Reilly? With fake flowers in my hair and my hairbrush clutched in front of me like a bouquet, I looked into this very mirror and pretended the boy of my dreams was about to tell me he would be my husband forever.

Now that dream is about to come true, but the boy is a man now and he's not marrying me for love. It's all fake, and I just need to keep reminding myself of that over and over.

In the mirror, I see the door opening and because I'm expecting it to be Mel, I'm smiling when I turn. But it's not my maid of honor. It's my mother, and she's not smiling when she steps into my room.

I'm not sure what to expect, mood-wise, so I keep smiling. "How do I look?"

Her lower lip trembles and unshed tears make her eyes shiny. "You look beautiful, honey."

"Thank you," I whisper.

She looks into my eyes for a long moment, and I wonder if she's trying to come up with the right words for a last-ditch attempt at talking me out of this. I'm not sure anything would make Gin happier than me jilting Hayden at the altar—another humiliation served in the long-standing feud.

"You're doing this?" she finally asks.

"I am."

"Are you happy?"

Not in the way she means, but I *am* grateful to have a way to free us both from the bleak existence we've barely been eking out. "Yes, I'm happy, Mom. I really am."

She nods once—briskly, as though she's come to a decision. Then she lifts her hand and I notice the box for the first time. It's long and slim, made of a tattered cardboard with a faded, ornate pattern printed on it.

When she opens it, I catch my breath. The classic pearl necklace and earrings are gorgeous—clearly very old—and elegant in their simplicity.

"Mom, they're beautiful." As I say the words, I realize I've seen these pearls before, in my parents' wedding portrait.

"I know that maybe the Gamble name doesn't mean what it used to, but it meant everything to your father. It means a lot to me. I wore these at my wedding, and your grandmother wore them when she married your grandfather." Her voice trembles and she blinks rapidly a few times. "I should probably sell them, but it would mean a lot to me if you wore them today."

"I'd be honored, Mom." I slide the earrings in myself, but then I bend my knees so Gin can clasp the strand of pearls around my neck.

"They're perfect," she says, emotion making her voice hoarse. And right now, I don't care how many hot water heaters the jewelry could have bought. This is one Gamble heirloom we'll never sell, no matter how hard things get.

The door opens again, and in the mirror, I see Mel bounce into the room. She freezes when she sees Gin, but my mother turns and gives her a warm smile.

"She's ready now," Gin announces.

"Good." Mel looks at me and presses her hand to her stomach as she takes a deep breath. "It's time."

Chapter Thirty-Nine

HAYDEN

I've kept my composure in a lot of high-stakes business meetings over the years, but nothing could have prepared me for being in the Sumac Falls town square, waiting to see if Cara would stand me up at the altar.

At no point, right up to when Aaron was helping me slide my arms in my suit coat, did it occur to me that leaving me alone and humiliated on the gazebo steps would be excellent revenge for me standing her up for the homecoming dance.

It's occurring to me now.

Maybe she and Gin were even in on it together. It would explain why Gin had given in so easily. Why she'd been willing to cross a Reilly threshold and share a meal with us. Because she knew they were going to humiliate me and my family in front of all the residents of Sumac Falls who'd gathered to see a wedding.

Now that the idea has popped into my head, I can't seem to shake it.

I'm trying not to hyperventilate, and Taylor grips my hands in hers. She keeps her voice low, but her tone is intense. "You're going to pass out, Hayden. Unlock your knees and take a deep breath."

I try to do as she says, while her husband glances over to see how I'm doing. Taylor had tasked him with distracting Aaron while she calmed me down.

"I never would have pegged you for the wedding jitters type," she says. "You must really be gone for this woman."

I am, actually. "I'm marrying her, aren't I?"

I hope. If she shows up.

"As soon as you see her walking toward you, all the nerves and your awareness of everybody watching will fade away."

I nod because I know she's right, even though it won't be for the reason Taylor thinks. Once I see Cara walking toward me, I'll know it wasn't all some elaborate revenge scheme.

Well, it is, but the revenge is supposed to be mine. Not hers.

Aaron escapes Bill's conversation and joins us. "Hope says they're on their way, and rumor has it the bridal party was spotted getting into their cars."

She's on her way.

"I'm going to go meet Hope. I'll help her get Mom and the kids to their seats." Aaron grins and slaps my shoulder. "And then I'll meet you in the gazebo."

"I'm going to make sure everything's ready to go," Taylor tells me. "Then Bill and I will sit. If anything at all seems to go awry, you give me the look and I'll take care of it."

I laugh and pull her in for a hug. "You're here as my guest today."

Once she goes to make sure the kid with the playlist and Debbie—our officiant, much to my dismay—are in place and ready to play their parts, I turn to head toward the gazebo.

And I almost run straight into Georgia Gamble.

Or whatever her married name is. I have no idea if she changed it or not, but I know if there's anybody on the planet who hates me more than Gin does, it's her older daughter.

"Hi, Georgia."

"Hello, Hayden."

"It means the world to Cara that you could be here today." I look at the man standing next to her. "We haven't met. Hayden Reilly, groom."

He shakes my hand. "Tony Holt. Bride's brother-in-law. Soon to be yours, I guess."

Georgia snorts, but since I'm not wearing the glass of punch in her hand—yet—I ignore it.

"Tony, can you go see if Mom's arrived yet? I don't want her to have to sit alone. I'll be there in a minute."

Once Georgia's husband walks away, I glance around to make sure we're actually alone. And that nobody's within earshot, since I probably don't want my other guests hearing whatever she's about to say.

Georgia doesn't make me wait. "Listen, I'm not stupid. You wanted the house. Gin said no. Now suddenly you and Cara are rushing down the aisle."

I'd rather not lie to the woman who's about to be my sister-in-law if I can help it—especially since it sounds like she and Mel are the only supportive people in Cara's life—so I just arch an eyebrow and wait.

She arches an eyebrow right back at me, and it's an impressive look. Perhaps dealing with uncooperative patients is good practice. "What I want to know is whether you're both scamming Gin together, or if *you're* scamming them both."

I don't know what, if anything, Cara's told her sister—hopefully not the truth, since I couldn't even tell Aaron—and I don't want to get in the middle of that relationship. But I'm also an older sibling, so I try to put her mind at ease without confessing to anything. "This sounds like a conversation you should have with Cara. But she and I talked about our future, and how we can't wait until Gin sells the house to us—once I'm officially family, of course—so Cara can see her mother settled in a small place where she'll be comfortable and not having to worry about maintenance. Having Gin out from under that house will be quite a load off Cara's shoulders."

She must get what I'm *not* saying, because the corners of Georgia's mouth quirk, though she manages not to give me an actual smile. "Yes, it will."

The crowd shifts, murmurs spreading through the guests. And they make their way toward the rows of white folding chairs while chatting, which means somebody has spotted the bridal party arriving. I glance at the gazebo and see Aaron gesturing for me to join him.

"I need to get up there," I tell Georgia, who's still looking at me as though staring hard enough will make me cough up every secret I've ever had.

I don't wait to see if she has anything else to say. I need to be standing in the gazebo when Cara appears at the end of the aisle made by the gap between the chairs.

My heart hammers in my chest while my brother does a final check, ensuring my suit still looks as good as it did the first three times he checked.

I look out at the guests, Cara's side first—there's definitely a bride's side and groom's side at this wedding—where I watch Georgia take her seat between Gin and Tony. Mel's parents and her husband fill out the first row. Various other friends are behind them, and it looks as if guests kept the rear rows well balanced between the two.

My mother sits in the front row on the other side, and the smile she gives me helps chase away some of my jitters. But I also feel a twist of guilt in my gut. I wish this was real.

Daisy and AJ sit between her and Hope. Daisy has her hands clasped as if she's about to witness a fairy tale come to life, and AJ's swinging his feet and watching the birds swirling around the trees.

Instrumental music I don't recognize begins playing, and Mel steps between the last row of chairs. I take in a deep breath, hold it, and then slowly exhale, straightening my shoulders and relaxing my knees.

It seems to take forever for her to make the short walk down the aisle, but I keep the smile on my face. She finally climbs the steps and stands opposite me on the gazebo, giving me a beautiful smile.

Then "Pachelbel's Canon in D" blasts through the town square, the music swelling around us, and Cara is there.

She's gorgeous. Her dress is perfect, and her hair's pinned back, showing off what looks like old family pearls gracing her ears and neck. Cara Gamble has always been the most beautiful girl in the world as far as I'm concerned, but today she takes my breath away.

I can see the nerves. Her smile is wobbly as she looks around at the surprisingly large gathering of guests.

Look at me. I think the words over and over, willing her to hear me.

Then she does. Our gazes lock, and when I smile, she smiles back. Her back straightens, and she takes the first step toward me.

Here comes the bride.

Chapter Forty

CARA

I don't know how many people have come to watch me get married. I have no idea if there are more guests on the bride's side or the groom's side of the aisle. I'm not even clocking Gin's current facial expression.

All I can see is Hayden smiling at me.

He looks absolutely delicious in his suit, of course, but it's his expression that draws me down the aisle to him. Confidence. Certainty. A warmth that keeps him from looking arrogant.

And a glimmer of humor that's just for me. That look relaxes some of the tension in my muscles.

We can do this.

When I near the bottom of the gazebo stairs, Hayden steps down and offers me his hand. It's warm and strong, and when he feels the trembling in mine, he gives it a squeeze before leading me up the stairs to stand before Debbie. The opening of the gazebo is wide, and with the elevation, everybody can see us.

I pass my bouquet to Mel, who thankfully bought us brand-new matching tubes of waterproof mascara for the occasion because she has tears running down her cheeks. But no streaks.

Since she's guessed the truth of what's happening, they're probably tears of joy for my impending freedom. Or she just might be a wedding cryer.

Hayden still hasn't released my hand, and together we turn to face my cousin. I wish we'd been able to get anybody but Debbie, but all I can do now is smile as she launches into the standard wedding opening.

Everything goes smoothly until she gets to the objection part of the program. "Should anyone present know of any reason that this couple should not be joined in matrimony, speak now or forever hold your peace."

I stand perfectly still, my eyes on Debbie. Behind me, I hear clothing rustling. Several throats are cleared. The whispers blend together, sounding like a white noise machine. There are even a few snickers and what sounds like an explosive laugh-turned-cough from the back of the room.

But nobody speaks.

"Last call," Debbie says, and I can tell by the direction of her gaze she looks first at my mother, and then at my future mother-in-law. "Anybody?"

I swear, if I hear a single person mutter "*Bueller?*" under their breath, I'm going to chase everybody out of the town square like an irate goose and make this a closed ceremony.

"I think we can move on," Hayden says in a low—but *very* firm—voice.

Debbie startles, her eyes widening as she realizes she got caught up in the potential for a scandal and forgot her role in the occasion. But she gathers herself and smiles before leading us through the recitation of the standard wedding vows. I feel strangely detached, as though it's not even real, until Debbie says my name.

"Do you Carolina Marie Gamble, take this man to be your lawfully wedded husband, to live together in matrimony, to love him, comfort him, honor and keep him, in sickness and in health, in sorrow and in joy, to have and to hold, from this day forward, as long as you both shall live?"

My mouth is dry, and I have a hard time swallowing the lump in my throat. It's not as long as we both shall live, I remind myself. It's only until Gin signs the house over. "I do."

Hayden's expression doesn't change, but his sharp intake of breath doesn't escape me. I don't think either of us were sure what would come out of my mouth until I actually said the words.

"Do you Hayden William Reilly, take this woman to be your lawfully wedded wife, to live together in matrimony, to love her, comfort her, honor and keep her, in sickness and in health, in sorrow and in joy, to have and to hold, from this day forward, as long as you both shall live?"

Now his expression changes. As his gaze holds mine, the lines of his face soften and his icy blue eyes darken with warmth. "I do."

There are more words. The rings. More words. It's all a blur and I wish Hayden and I were alone on our rock by the river as we race toward one final hurdle.

The one I've been dreading. And also *not* dreading.

"By the authority vested in me by the State of New Hampshire, I now pronounce you husband and wife." She pauses, and I brace myself. *Here it comes.* "Hayden, you may now kiss your bride."

His hand goes to my waist, and I clutch his upper arm as he hauls me close. The very wedding-appropriate smile his mouth has maintained for the entire ceremony flashes into a wicked grin in the second before his lips touch mine.

Our second first kiss.

Just a quick peck, I think—a formality in front of almost everybody I know to seal the deal. But somehow, despite the overwhelming number of emails we'd exchanged about the wedding, Hayden apparently didn't get the for-show-purposes-only kiss memo.

This isn't the polite kiss of a man who's checking a wedding ceremony item off a list. And it's not the tentative kiss of a teenage boy by the river.

It's the kiss of a man who knows what he's doing, and heat floods through me as I clutch the sleeve of his suit coat. His mouth is demanding—hungry—and I yield to him, parting my lips as his tongue sweeps over mine. His hand slides up my back.

Somehow, the sounds of clapping and more than a few wolf whistles pierce the need that's clouded my mind, and I pull away.

The heat in his eyes sears me, and he's as breathless as I am. We came very close to stepping over some invisible line. But our mothers are watching.

"Ladies and gentlemen," Debbie yells over the crowd, "Mr. and Mrs. Reilly! Um, Gamble-Reilly?" She puts her hand over her mouth, and then shrugs. "Ladies and gentlemen, the happy couple!"

I take the bouquet Mel is holding out in front of me, and then I try to concentrate on both smiling *and* not falling down the gazebo steps as we make our way past the applauding guests.

This is bad—so very bad. Terrible, even. My husband kissed me and I liked it. And I want him to do it again.

I'm in so much trouble.

Chapter Forty-One

HAYDEN

I almost wish I'd taken the advice of our mothers and put off the wedding until September. Not because of the fall foliage, but because there would have been time to plan and host a formal indoor reception.

We could have had the kind of reception during which guests clink their silverware against their glasses to signal they want the bride and groom to kiss.

The guests would have provided the chance to kiss Cara at least a dozen times, or probably more.

One kiss hadn't been nearly enough.

I watch her laughing with her sister and Mel by the refreshments table, the sound carrying to me over the noise of mingling guests.

Even five hundred thousand kisses wouldn't be enough.

"If you keep looking at her like that, I'll have to cover my kids' eyes," Aaron says, nudging me with his elbow. "And Mom's, too."

"Don't forget, I was *your* best man, and I caught you fishing for the garter—or so you said—under the table before the first toast."

I laugh when my brother's face reddens. "Just because the first toast hadn't happened doesn't mean I hadn't hit the champagne yet. Speaking of, I haven't seen *you* with a glass in your hand."

"I'm driving us to Boston," I remind him. "I could have had hired a car, but then my car would have been here, and limiting myself to the one champagne toast felt easier than figuring out travel logistics."

Aaron chuckles. "Be honest. You didn't want to let your guard down during the first joint Gamble-Reilly event since before anybody currently living in Sumac Falls was even born."

"That might have crossed my mind."

Luckily, everybody is on their best behavior. While I haven't seen our mothers cross paths at all, I spot Georgia and Hope talking. The conversation appears to be a happy one, with both women smiling, so I relax and leave them to it.

"Hayden," my mother says, and I turn to find her approaching me. She does *not* look relaxed. "The big city photographer you just *had* to have is insisting on a photo of that woman and I together. She just tried to corner me again, for like the fourth time."

Actually, I just *had* to have Taylor hire a photographer who wasn't local precisely because I didn't want somebody who knew our families or the history between them. The wedding pictures might be performative—though I'll keep a few hidden deep in my phone, I'm sure—I was afraid we'd end up with either a lot of Reilly photos or a lot of Gamble photos. Or, even worse, a bunch of candid shots snapped whenever Gin and Colleen were near each other, hoping to catch a flare-up of the feud.

"I think that's a pretty standard picture on any wedding photographer's checklist, Mom," Aaron tells her, his voice light and a little cajoling in a way that often worked with our mother. I never mastered it the way he did and decided long ago it's just part of the second son toolbox. "But you both disappeared while we were doing the bridal party."

"I'll go find Cara and Gin." I don't bother trying to lighten

SHANNON STACEY

my tone. Neither mother is going to be happy about this, but they're doing it. And the sooner we get it over with, the sooner they can return to their own sides of the reception.

I don't have any trouble finding the bride. It's as if my body has some kind of inner Cara-detection system. And, as though she can feel my attention on her, she turns and our gazes lock. I nod my head, and she starts making her way toward me.

Meeting her halfway, I inform her the photographer would like for us to meet at the gazebo with our mothers for a group shot.

"You're kidding."

I glance around to make sure nobody's watching us. Of course people are, because we're the stars of today's show, so I lower my voice. "The photographer's insisting."

"Do we really need to do this?" she hisses at me. "It's not exactly going to be a treasured keepsake, you know."

"It would be strange if we didn't."

"Maybe to the photographer, who doesn't know us. But not a single one of our guests would be surprised by Colleen Reilly and Gin Gamble not wanting to be in a photo together."

"Valid point," I admit. "But I said we'd do it, so now we're doing it."

She rolls her eyes, but walks to where Gin is visiting with a friend. Cara speaks to her for a moment, and I hope nobody else notices how Gin's smile is suddenly one hundred percent more forced.

But they come, and we all line up at the bottom of the gazebo steps, still framed by the floral arrangements. We'd learned when attempting the initial photos of the bride, groom and bridal party that standing in the archway put the photographer below us, and there was a lot of talk about angles. We get it right this time.

"Okay," the photographer said. "I'll probably take a few shots, but I'll be quick so you can get back to the party."

"Tell your husband to tell his mother that her necklace is hung up on the collar of her dress," I hear Gin mutter to Cara.

Cara turns to me, but I just nod to let her know I heard. When I turn to *my* mother, she's already fixing the necklace. She looks to me to make sure it's hanging correctly, and I smile and nod again.

"Thank your wife's mother, please," she says in a tight voice.

Wow, this is fun. I lean forward so I can look across Cara to look her mother in the eye. "Thank you, Gin."

She doesn't smile, but her expression softens slightly. *Very* slightly. At least she doesn't look as though she's considering making her daughter a widow on her wedding day as the photographer calls for us to smile.

When she's satisfied she's got a good shot, everybody scatters again. I try to catch Cara's arm, but she gives me an apologetic look and goes after Gin.

While I'm careful to keep a smile on my face, my annoyance increases with every passing moment. It may be understandable that a generations-long feud between two families leads to a more stringent bride side versus groom side than one usually sees at a wedding, but that division among the guests is also keeping me away from my bride.

I distract myself for as long as I can, talking with Taylor and Bill, and trying to talk my nephew out of peeing behind the gazebo instead of walking to the very nice portable toilets we'd rented and had placed at the edge of the town square. I want a few minutes with Cara, so I climb the gazebo steps.

"If I could get everybody's attention," I say, broadcasting across the crowd with my boardroom voice. It works and everybody quiets. "First, I want to thank everybody for coming. It means a lot to us. And we hope you're all having a good time, but I think it's about time I get to dance with my wife."

My wife.

The pleasure of saying those words out loud is still pulsing through me when I find Cara in the crowd. Her eyes widen slightly, but she's smiling as she makes her way to the gazebo at the urging of the guests closest to her.

When she reaches the top of the stairs, I reach out and something deep in my soul sighs with contentment as she slides her hand into mine. And thanks to the crowd watching us, I don't have to mask what I'm feeling when I slide my hand around her waist and pull her close.

The song begins and, thanks to the speakers being on the gazebo with us, it's loud. But Cara laughs and leans into me as I lead her in circles. I'm careful to keep us away from the steps, while also staying within the flower-framed opening for the photos everybody's taking.

"I think this is the last thing on our reception checklist," I say. My cheek's practically pressed against hers in order to be heard, but I don't mind. "Especially since we already ate the cake."

"Daisy talked me into doing the cake early."

"She's hard to resist."

"She made a compelling argument. For one, she's been taught some strong opinions about food sitting outside. But mostly, she argued that eating cake would give us all energy and put everybody in a good mood."

I laugh, able to picture those words coming out of my niece's mouth so clearly. "Like alcohol, but fun for all ages."

"Exactly." She rests her forehead against my shoulder. "Is it just me, or is this a very long song?"

It's just her. As far as I'm concerned, it can't go on long enough. She's in my arms and if the music is the only reason why, I don't want the song to end.

"How are you holding up?" I ask, because she *does* sound tired.

"I'm running out of gas," she admits. "I know weddings are a lot for any bride, but having to watch everything I say and do—right down to being constantly aware of my facial expressions—is exhausting."

"We'll start working our way through the guests to say our goodbyes, then."

She laughs. "It's a little early for that. There's going to be a lot of cleanup."

"That's being taken care of."

"Of course it is. Are we going to tell our friends and family we have to get home to your dog?"

"I do miss Penny, but I don't intend to tell our friends and family anything. I couldn't wait to get you to the altar, so they'll assume I can't wait to get home for our wedding night."

She blushes and buries her face in my shoulder to hide it. My pulse quickens, and it takes every bit of self-control I can muster to not tighten my hold on her.

I'm taking Cara home with me. She's going to be in *my* home —in *my* world—for the weekend. I know it's all for appearances, but we're getting out of this town.

Together.

Chapter Forty-Two

CARA

The journey from being Cara Gamble—struggling to tread water while keeping my mother, our home, and my business afloat—to being Mrs. Hayden Reilly, standing in a shiny penthouse apartment in Boston, doesn't feel real.

Because it's *not* real, I guess.

Even the apartment doesn't feel real. The private parking garage. The elevator. The very open floor plan and perfectly coordinated—if a little boring—neutral decor. Honestly, it feels like what I imagine a high-end hotel would feel like, but I can't be sure because I've never stayed in one. The only motels I've ever stayed in had two stars and questionable bathrooms.

I'd expected walking into Hayden's home to be awkward after all the forced intimacy of going through the wedding motions, but I underestimated how happy Penny would be to see me. Her joyful spinning and yapping makes me laugh, and Hayden's mock hurt at his dog cutting their greeting short so she can welcome me makes me laugh.

Once Penny has sufficiently welcomed me and gone to sniff the bags Hayden set by the door, I look around the space he calls home. At first glance, the apartment had seemed impersonal, but now I notice the small pieces of his life on display.

Most of the photos on the wall are candid shots of Daisy and AJ over the years. There are a few framed Christmas photo cards that include Aaron and Hope. The largest frame holds a wedding photo, and it takes me a few seconds to realize it's Colleen and John Reilly. I want to take a closer look, but I'm aware Hayden is watching me, so I mind my own business. For now.

Seeing artwork clearly done by his niece and nephew taped to the front of a sleek refrigerator makes me smile, and I notice the quilt over the back of the leather sofa looks old and hand-crafted. A family heirloom, perhaps?

What really makes the apartment feel like Hayden's home— even more than the family touches—is how much Penny's comfort matters. There's a fleece throw on one end of the couch, clearly bunched into a Penny-sized nest. And there's a set of doggy stairs in front of it to make it easier—and safer—for her to get up and down. There are several fluffy beds arranged around the living and dining area. Toys are scattered everywhere, and under her food and water dishes is a mat with *Penelope Louise* written in a fancy font.

"It's nice of Penny to let you stay here with her," I tease, but I'm dismayed to hear the tremor that's been building in my muscles is also apparent in my voice.

"Have a seat," he says, nodding toward the sofa. "I'll get you some water."

I do as he says, and Penny runs up her stairs to join me on the couch. After letting me scratch under her chin for a minute, she digs furiously at the pile of fleece until it's just the way she wants it and curls up in the center.

Hayden hands me a glass of ice-cold water before sitting in the leather recliner with his own glass. Penny lifts her head, clearly trying to decide if she wants to join him in his chair. The fleece wins.

"You okay?" he asks after I've had a few sips of the water.

I nod, not trusting my voice yet. Even if I did, I can't really explain what I'm feeling right now. One night, years ago, I came out of a corner in a forty-five mile-per-hour stretch of road and almost hit a moose. It had been close, and I'd had to find a place to pull safely off the road until the shaking stopped.

This feels a little like that.

After being caught up in what felt like a hurricane of scheming and planning, it's done. I'm married to Hayden Reilly, and without the constant voice in the back of my mind screaming *are we actually doing this*, the sudden quiet is very loud.

Of course, it's just the eye of the storm. We'll have to face convincing Gin to sell us the house and then talk her into leaving it. And after that, a breakup and divorce. But at this moment, everything's calm and I can relax.

Or I could if I wasn't alone with Hayden, almost a hundred miles from anybody who cares about the Gamble and Reilly families.

"You're sure you're okay?" he presses, setting his glass on the table that's in the corner between his recliner and the end of the sofa.

"I'm sure. Today was just a lot."

"Yes, it was. I think poor Debbie was disappointed nobody objected," he says, and we both laugh. Penny snuggles deeper into her fleece blanket.

Hayden stands and tugs the hem of his shirt out of his pants as he walks toward the kitchen. His back is to me, but I can tell he's working at the buttons.

I can't make myself look away.

By the time he unbuttons his cuffs, I'm wondering if his expensive apartment came with a cheap HVAC system because it's uncomfortably warm in here. Even draining my glass of ice water doesn't help when he slides the shirt off and drapes it over a chair, revealing a white T-shirt that hugs his body. My mouth goes dry, and I regret not rationing my water.

It gets worse when he yanks the tee free of his pants and pulls it over his head. I'd barely gotten my heart rate under control from the T-shirt and now I'm being treated to a broad expanse of naked shoulders and back. My hands itch to glide over that skin, and I ball them into fists instead.

Hayden starts to turn toward me, T-shirt in hand and his mouth opening as though to speak. Then he freezes for a second before turning away sharply.

But not before I spot what looks like a tattoo on his chest.

"Sorry," he mutters. "Force of habit."

I set my glass on the table next to his and stand, wanting to get a better look. "Wait, was that a tattoo?"

For a long moment, I think he's going to ignore the question, but then his shoulders drop. "Yes."

The word comes out unusually terse for him, and combined with the way he's holding his shirt, I can tell he doesn't want me to see whatever he had permanently inked into his skin. Which naturally means I absolutely *have* to see it.

"What is it?"

"Nothing. It's just an old tattoo."

I move closer to him and smile when he takes a step back. "An old tattoo that just *happens* to be on your chest? Does it say *Mom* in a heart?"

He snorts, the corner of his mouth quirking up. "No, it's not a *Mom* tattoo."

"Can I see it?" I ask, taking another step forward. He doesn't say no outright, but he also doesn't drop the shirt. It's obvious he doesn't want to show me, but he can't figure out a good excuse not to. "You know, it would be weird if somebody mentions your tattoo and your own wife doesn't know what it is."

"Nobody you know is aware I even have one, never mind what it is."

Nobody I know? So he basically means nobody in Sumac Falls, but there have been women in his life who've seen it. Jealousy claws at me, but I don't let my smile slip. It's been a long time since I've had the energy to date, but I haven't exactly been pining for him all these years. "Show me what it is or I'll tell your mother how much I love your tattoo."

His jaw flexes as the tips of his ears turn pink. "That's playing dirty."

I laugh. "Says the man who married me to get my mother's house. Let me see it."

Reluctantly, he lowers the shirt, and I step closer as he reveals what looks like a pen and ink sketch of woods, with a boulder jutting out into flowing water.

"It's our spot by the river," I whisper, unable to stop myself from tracing the outline of the rock with my fingertip. "When did you have this done?"

"My junior year of college." His voice is low and raspy. "I went with some friends to Florida for spring break and there were beaches and women and parties, and all I could think about was how much I missed sitting with you on that rock by the river. I sketched it out on a napkin and carried it around with me until it got tattered. Then I found a way to make it permanent."

I rest my palm over the tattoo for a moment, feeling his heart beating as hard and fast as mine. And when I try to pull my hand back, he captures my wrist.

"It was the only place I was ever truly happy," he murmurs softly.

I stare at his fingers encircling my wrist because I can't bear to look him in the eyes right now. Letting him see how much the memory of that spot hurts me feels too much like letting him win. "You ended it. Not me."

"It would never work between us. Our families weren't going to allow it and sneaking around once they knew would have been harder. You would have gotten in trouble. By ending it when I did, nobody knew. If we'd gone to the homecoming dance, everybody in town would have known."

"Ah." I jerk my hand out of his grasp and turn away. "Saving me from my own bad decisions. How noble of you. And ghosting me on homecoming night to make sure I got the point."

"Cara, I—"

"I told you I don't want to talk about the past, Hayden. I meant it. I'm exhausted and I don't have the energy." I walk to the windows and look out over the view for a moment. Then I glance over my shoulder and see he's pulled his shirt back on, covering the memories engraved in his skin. "Since this is Boston, do you have that app where we just tell it what we want to eat and it magically appears on your doorstep?"

Chapter Forty-Three

HAYDEN

It's killing me not to tell Cara everything about the night I ended our relationship. I pieced together a long time ago that she thinks I stood her up—that I just never showed to take her to the dance —which means Marcus and Gin decided to let her believe that.

They both knew I was there when I said I would be.

But I don't want to push Cara's boundaries after a long, emotional day. "What are you in the mood for? There aren't many foods not in the delivery area, and there are even fewer foods I don't like. Name whatever you want and it'll show up on the doorstep."

Cara goes back to the sofa and plops down beside Penny. "That might be *too* many options. How am I supposed to decide?"

"I'd go for something you can't get in Sumac Falls."

"Oh sure, that narrows it down a lot." She laughs and scrubs her hands over her face. "Okay. Maybe a deep dish pizza. Or Chinese food. Or..."

"Just do me a favor and don't say b-a-c-o-n out loud or her majesty will be deciding what we have."

She laughs softly and reaches over to stroke Penny's fur. My dog sighs her happy sigh. While she talks through the options, I continue cursing myself for taking my T-shirt off. I'd stripped it off out of habit, not even thinking about the tattoo.

It's going to be a long time before I can remember the feel of her fingertips skimming over my chest without finding it hard to breathe. Resisting the impulse to put my hand over hers and hold it there so she could feel what her touch did to my heartbeat had burned through my self-control. What I need to do is remain fully clothed, out of arm's reach, and focused on the litany of take-out options Cara's cycling through.

"I really want a *great* pizza," she's saying. "But it's also been years since I've had crab Rangoon, so I'm torn. You might have to choose, Hayden, or I'll still be deciding between them come breakfast."

"We'll get both. You can have pizza and crab Rangoon and we'll put the leftovers in the fridge." I watch her struggle between wanting both and needing to reject what she probably sees as wasteful spending. "Trust me, they'll get eaten."

It only takes me a few minutes to place the two orders, and then I text the front desk to let them know there will be two deliveries. I'll wait until they've both arrived before I go down and collect them.

"Can you turn the TV on?" Cara asks after a few minutes of the quiet that descends while I gather what I'll need to set the table. "Today's been overwhelming and I'd really love to have something to focus on besides the chaos in my head."

I know I'm responsible for a substantial amount of that chaos, and there's nothing I can do about it. Empty words aren't going to make it better. After turning on the television, I show her how to navigate the on-screen guide and the different streaming app options, and hand her the remote.

Then I leave her to it, giving her both physical and mental space as I keep myself busy setting the table. She settles on a humorous action movie, and I can almost see the tension easing out of her body as she loses herself in it. With my dog's chin on her thigh, of course, because Penny seems to have found a person she loves almost as much as she loves me.

I try not to take that as a sign. I can't let my imagination start rewriting my future or I'm going to get my heart broken again.

Once the food's been delivered and I've fetched it from the front desk, Cara moves to the table. I tell her to leave the movie on, though, because it's a lot more relaxing to watch a car chase while eating than trying to force a conversation about anything *but* the fact we're now married and alone in my apartment.

It's nice, actually. We put a good dent in the pizza and the crab Rangoon while laughing at the movie and pointing out plot holes and bad dialogue to each other. Before long, any residual awkwardness is gone. Conversation flows as easily as it did when we were young and sitting by the river.

It isn't until I'm loading the dishes into the dishwasher and catch her trying to hide a jaw-cracking yawn that I realize I've been a bad host. Even though it looks comfortable, she's still technically wearing her wedding dress, and I haven't even shown her the guest bedroom. She popped into the guest half-bath while I was unpacking the take-out, but she never said anything about wanting to change out of the dress. I should have asked.

After hitting the button to start the dishwasher, I walk over and grab her bag. "I'll put this in your room for you, and show you around."

She laughs. "I don't usually go to bed this early, but I'm exhausted."

When I turn on the light in the guest bedroom, I can't help but wish I'd paid more attention to the space. It's very bland, with a queen bed covered with a beige duvet that matches the light wooden furniture. The lampshade on the nightstand is beige. It's a very clean look, but even a hotel room has more character, and I wince as she looks around.

"It's lovely," she says, and even though she sounds sincere, I have to assume she's only being polite.

"I guess the key to matching any potential guest's personal taste is to make the room as boring and bland as possible," I say, making her laugh.

"Maybe if you spent your life in an old house stuffed with clutter and antiques, you'd appreciate the appeal of a minimalist look."

"Good point. There's extra bedding in the linen closet if you want more pillows or another blanket. If you forgot to bring any toiletries with you, anything you need should be in the cabinets in the bathroom. The shower runs nice and hot, and it doesn't run out of hot water." I pause, trying to think of anything else she might need to know, but the smile that curves her mouth distracts me. "What?"

"So the thing that pushed me over the edge and made me agree to your utterly ridiculous plan was our hot water heater. It's on its way out and I can't remember the last time I took a long, hot shower without worrying about having time to rinse all the shampoo out."

"You married me because your hot water heater is dying? That seems extreme."

"Not if you spend your days covered in pet hair and more than a little dog drool." She chuckles. "Actually, it wasn't just the hot water heater. It was when my mother suggested we could heat water and haul it upstairs to bathe in, like being a pioneer would be a fun, new adventure for us."

I try not to laugh, but Cara does, so I give up and laugh along with her. While her circumstances—and her relationship with her mother—are no laughing matter, the concept of having to marry a man to avoid boiling bathwater on the stove is so ridiculous, I *have* to laugh.

"So I shouldn't get worried and call 9-1-1 if you're in the shower for an unusually long time?" I ask once our amusement dies down.

That makes her laugh again. "If you could *not* have a rescue squad barge into the bathroom while I'm naked in the shower, that would be great."

My intent was a chuckle, but the sound comes out a little strangled and hoarse. Imagining Cara naked in that shower, with water and suds running over her soft skin, is going to keep me up tonight—in more ways than one.

"Do we have plans for tomorrow?" she asks. "So I know how to dress in the morning."

"I didn't plan anything because I wasn't sure what you'd like to do. Taylor can probably get us tickets if there are any games in town, or a play."

She catches her bottom lip between her teeth, which doesn't help push that naked-in-the-shower version of her out of my head —and then gives me a sheepish smile. "I've never been to the aquarium."

"That sounds like a perfect way to spend the day." She could have said she wanted to spend the day counting the cracks in the sidewalks and I would have been okay with it. I'm just looking forward to spending a day with Cara, away from our mothers and their nosy neighbors. "We can have coffee in the morning. There are some pastries and fruit kicking around. Then, after we take Penny for a walk, we can go exploring."

"That sounds good."

When Cara walks toward me, there's a heart-stopping, delicious moment when I think she's going to kiss me goodnight. The bubble of anticipation bursts, though, when she reaches down and strokes Penny's back, not even making eye contact with me.

"Goodnight, I guess."

I almost make it out of the bedroom, but I can't help myself. "Goodnight, wife."

She *almost* smiles. "Goodnight, *fake* husband."

Then she closes the door firmly in my face. A few minutes later, I hear the faint sound of the shower running.

"Time for bedtime potties," I tell Penny, who sighs dramatically.

After her walk, I'll probably end up taking a shower myself. But unlike Cara's, it'll be a cold one.

Chapter Forty-Four

CARA

I'm laughing so hard when Hayden opens his door, I almost fall into his apartment. I'm utterly exhausted, slightly sunburned, a lot windblown, and I don't remember the last time I enjoyed a day so much.

"You have to delete that," Hayden says, and he's trying his best to sound stern, but the effort he's putting into not laughing takes the bite out of the words.

"I'm never deleting it." I slide the phone into my pocket just in case he tries to grab for it.

Not that it would do him any good. I emailed the video of Hayden trying to mimic the way the penguins walked to myself before we even left the aquarium. It was safely backed up long before I played it for him in the elevator.

I'll never show it to anybody else, of course, but I'm keeping it for myself. It's an adorable video, showing a side of the man I think very few people ever get to see. Daisy and AJ, for sure, but few others.

Luckily, Penny's joy at her favorite human being home distracts him, and he seems to forget my phone as he gives her belly rubs. Once he's done greeting her, she comes straight to me and we plop on the couch for a cuddle.

He looks at us getting settled in for some comfy time, and cocks his eyebrow. "We have reservations in a little less than two hours."

I groan and press my hand to my stomach. "You can't be serious."

"I didn't know you have a thing for food trucks when I made the reservation."

"In my defense, *I* didn't know I have a thing for food trucks until today." I feel bad now, because the reservation is for a very fancy restaurant, according to my sneaky Google search. I'd packed a decent dress and sandals, just in case, but I can't imagine putting more food in my stomach only two hours from now.

"Shall I cancel?" he asks.

I search his face for any signs of disappointment or annoyance, but I see nothing but amusement. Maybe even a little affection. "I could probably manage a few bites of your dessert if you want to go, but I wouldn't be eating a whole dinner."

"I'll just cancel. It's not a big deal, and I'm pretty sure I walked more today than I have in the last week, so I'm not sad about staying in. Movie?"

I'm so relieved, I melt a little deeper into the couch, which I didn't think was possible. Penny stretches herself over my stomach and chest and goes to sleep.

There are worse ways to spend an evening. Hayden has all kinds of streaming services, so I choose an action movie I would have seen in the theaters last year if we had a movie theater in town. Or if I could afford the gas and ticket price to drive to the nearest one.

"You have very bad taste in movies," Hayden says at the halfway point.

I laugh, earning a perturbed look from Penny. After huffing out a sigh, she decides to switch humans and goes to wedge herself between the arm of the recliner and Hayden's thigh.

"Okay, it's bad," I admit. "But at least it's funny in its badness and not just boring bad."

Since neither of have to pretend we're watching a decent movie, we talk through the rest of it—mocking plot holes and making snarky remarks about the dialogue. It's more entertaining than the actual movie and when the credits roll, I find myself wishing it was longer.

Once it's over, I force myself up off the ridiculously comfortable couch and go to the fridge to pour a glass of water. Though I didn't hear him follow me, I jump when Hayden peeks over my shoulder.

"Are we rummaging for snacks since we didn't have supper?"

I laugh, shaking my head. "We didn't have supper because we ate *all day*. You can't be hungry, Hayden."

"Not really." He reaches around me and plucks a branch of grapes from the container in his fridge. "Grapes are always good, though."

"I don't remember the last time I had grapes," I confess, closing the fridge door.

He smiles and holds one out in front of my lips. I open— purely reflex—and he pops it into my mouth. As I bite down and sweet juice floods my mouth, he runs his thumb along my lower lip.

Our gazes lock, and the hunger in his eyes makes me shiver. "Hayden."

"I don't remember when I've enjoyed a day as much as this one."

"Same, but that doesn't mean—" Doesn't mean what? That I don't want him? That I don't ache for his touch? I definitely do. "This is a bad idea."

He pops another grape in my mouth. "More chewing. Less telling me wanting you is a bad idea."

I'm not silenced that easily. "It is," I mumble around the mushed grape.

"Ever since I kissed you yesterday, I've wanted to kiss you

again. I want to hold you like I did while we danced. I want to run my fingers over those freckles on your shoulders."

Even though it's only a faint shadow through his T-shirt, I trace the tattoo over his heart. "It will make everything so much more messy."

"Not if we don't let it," he says, and I'm aware of him setting the grapes on the counter before putting his hands on my waist and pulling me close. His lips leave a trail of hot kisses down my neck and instead of pushing him away, I tilt my head to expose more skin. "Let me make love to you, Cara."

"What happens in Boston stays in Boston," I whisper, already lost.

Chapter Forty-Five

HAYDEN

I miss my wife.

My wife.

No matter how many times I tell myself it's not real, I'm jolted by pleasure and pride every time those words go through my mind. For better or worse, Cara Gamble is my wife, and I do miss her—fake vows or not. It hasn't even been thirty hours since the car service picked her up to whisk her back to Sumac Falls.

But every one of those twenty-eight hours has felt emptier.

We shouldn't have crossed that line. To be fair, it probably would have taken some kind of natural disaster to stop us, but blurring boundaries isn't a good idea in any business deal. Blurring the boundaries in a business deal that has me married to the first girl I ever loved—and maybe never stopped loving—has the potential to be a disaster. Leaving my feelings out of it has been a struggle the entire time, and to say having her naked in my bed didn't help is an understatement.

And to continue my streak of making bad decisions where Cara is concerned, I pull out my phone and send her a text message. Maybe it'll be enough communication to take the edge off.

HAYDEN

I'll be back in town tomorrow afternoon. The office is closed Thursday and Friday for the Fourth, so we can do the Fourth of July on the town square together.

She must be busy with a client because it's almost forty minutes before my phone chimes with a reply.

CARA

Sounds good.

I was hoping for more than that, but there are no dots indicating she's sending another message through. Frowning, I type a response.

HAYDEN

Should I pick you up or will you drive your own car to my mother's house?

The dots appear and disappear several times before they go away completely, deepening my frown into a scowl. We had a plan for navigating looking married when I was in town. The entire charade is pointless if we sleep in separate houses.

The dots come back, lingering for what feels like forever.

CARA

I have ten minutes until my next appointment. If you're free, just call me because I don't have time to text everything out.

That doesn't sound good, so I immediately flip to my contacts and tap the button to call her.

She answers on the first ring. "Hey."

"Hey. What's going on?"

Her sigh is loud through my phone's speaker. "I don't think I'm comfortable staying at Colleen Reilly's house, you know?"

"You can just call her your mother-in-law now."

"Whatever I call her, I know she'll hate having me there. The idea of it is like a lead weight in my stomach."

It's my turn to sigh, and I rub the spot between my eyebrows with my thumb. I understand what she's saying, but I don't see any way around it.

"I'm closed Thursday and Friday, too," she says. "Maybe I should just come back to Boston."

"I already promised Daisy and AJ I'd be there for the holiday."

"I don't—" She cuts off whatever she's about to say and falls silent.

I wonder if it feels worse because I'm not there. Without me at her side, it might feel like nothing's really changed. Four generations of animosity can't be shaken off by a ring on her finger. But if I'm there, she might be more confident about it.

"It's okay," I tell her, even though it's not. "I'll be back tomorrow and we can talk about it. We'll figure it out together."

"That sounds good," she says, and I can hear the relief in her voice.

Her relief sticks with me long after the call ends. Cara *really* doesn't want to stay at Colleen's. I know my mom, and she'll be nice, but maybe nice isn't enough. There's still going to be a low-key negative vibe in the air.

The problem of the optics stays in the back of my mind as I finish out my workday, and then it keeps me from getting a good night's sleep.

Maybe the feud is enough? The people of Sumac Falls might believe neither Colleen nor Gin will welcome the other's child into their home, and they can make it clear they haven't had time to find a place of their own yet—unless Gin's told everybody about his intent to buy the house. Then people might believe they're waiting until it's official.

It feels weak, though. We're supposedly so madly in love we

had to get married immediately, but we sleep separately under our mothers' roofs like teenagers?

That doesn't work for me.

By the time I drive into Sumac Falls the next night, I feel *mostly* prepared for the drama I'm about to unleash on the Gamble household.

"I guess we're doing this," I tell Penny as I pull into their driveway and park behind Cara's car. "I know it's going to be rough, but we're in this together, right?"

She just rolls her eyes at me, sighs, and then rests her chin on her paws. Hopefully seeing Cara again will help ease the anxiety of being in a strange house. And I won't leave her here alone. She'll be with me or with Cara at all times.

That doesn't make it any easier for me to unclench my fingers from the steering wheel and get out of the car.

I swore I wouldn't step foot on this property until I owned it, but that was before Gin's stubbornness changed the rules of the game. I might not have taken Marcus Gamble's house—*yet*—but I married his daughter.

My wife is inside that house, and her family can't keep me away from her anymore.

Chapter Forty-Six

CARA

The last pan had just been dried and put away when we hear a car door close, and it's obviously in our driveway. We look at each other, but it's clear neither of us were expecting company.

"I'll get it. It's probably Mel," I tell Gin, even though I know Mel always texts me first when she's coming over—mostly so I can meet her out on the porch and decrease the chances of her having to make small talk with my mother.

I'm halfway to the front door when I hear the car door close again. Or maybe it's a second door closing, like if the driver had to go around to the passenger side and get his dog out of her booster seat, for example.

There's no way he would come here, I think as I force my feet to keep moving. I knew he was coming back to Sumac Falls tonight. I'd thought about nothing *but* that since getting into the hired car outside his apartment building Monday morning. But I assumed he would go to Colleen's and let me know he was back in town.

When I open the door and find Hayden on my porch with

Penny tucked under one arm and a duffel bag slung over the other, my stomach drops.

"Hi, honey. I'm home," he says as if this is all a big joke to him.

I glance over my shoulder to make sure my mother didn't follow me to the door, and then step closer to him. "What the hell are you doing?"

"I'm the kind of husband who expects to live with his wife."

"You can't be serious."

"Who is it, Cara?" Gin asks a second after I hear the creak in the floorboard warning me of her approach.

I glare at Hayden like I'm trying to set him on fire with my eyeballs, and then step out of the way to let him in. "It's Hayden, Mom."

That stops her in her tracks, but Hayden's smiling as if he's happy to see her. "Hello, Gin."

"Is that a dog? I'm allergic to dogs." Gin clutches her chest as if just the sight of the dog sends her into instant respiratory failure. Or maybe it's finding a Reilly standing in her living room. It's hard to tell with her. "I can't breathe."

"Penelope's a Shih Tzu," Hayden says, and I can hear amusement in his voice. He's enjoying this. "She's hypoallergenic."

"Oh." Gin drops her hands, but the distressed expression sticks. "Why are you here?"

"Because this is where Cara is."

Gin looks at me as though she's expecting me to explain what's happening, but I've got nothing. My heart is still pounding because Hayden is actually in my house, and just seeing him brought all those naughty memories I've been trying to suppress to the surface. And my mind is still spinning because this is *not* going to be good.

I'm about to tell her Hayden's just picking me up to take me to Colleen's—even though I *really* don't want to do that, but I will if it keeps the fragile peace—when Hayden sets Penny on the floor. She immediately comes to me, looking for chin scratches.

Of course I crouch and give her some because dogs are always the priority.

"You have a bag," Gin says.

"I have another in the car, actually," Hayden tells her. "I'd rather not wear the same clothes every day for a four-day weekend. I also have a bag for Penny and two beds for her."

Gin is shaking her head, but she can't seem to make words. Finally, she looks at me, and then at Penny. "Do you have a cage for her, too?"

I know the dog is probably reacting to a sudden tension in Hayden's body, but I still have to stifle a giggle at the alarmed look Penny gives Gin. Hayden, on the other hand, is total ice. "Penelope doesn't have a kennel. She'll tolerate a leash to comply with town or city ordinances when necessary, but otherwise, she does as she pleases."

"This is still *my* house."

"Yes, it is. And Cara is *my* wife. Either Penelope is welcome here, or I'll take my wife and my dog and go elsewhere. You'll have the entire house, including upkeep and expenses, all to yourself."

I should object here. He doesn't get to *take* me anywhere. But I know what he's doing—the more uncomfortable and unhappy Gin is, the sooner she'll finalize the sale so I can help her get settled somewhere else. Since I can't be free of this farce of a marriage until that happens, I keep my mouth shut.

Without another word, Gin spins on her heel and walks back to the kitchen. Sighing, I give Penny a final scratch under her chin, and then straighten.

"I'll show you where to put your stuff, I guess."

I know I should be putting more effort into sounding like a newlywed reunited with her husband after a short separation, but I can't muster the energy. Instead, I pick up Penny and lead Hayden up the stairs.

It had never occurred to me he would sleep under the same roof as Gin, so my room has a very lived-in look. It's not *too* messy, but I clearly wasn't expecting company.

As soon as he closes the door behind him, I put Penny down. Maybe because she can tell this is exclusively my space, she's comfortable roaming around, investigating.

"I think you'd be more comfortable staying with Colleen," I say as Hayden sets his bag on the foot of my bed.

"I definitely would be, but you wouldn't be, so we'll stay here."

"Did you forget the part where I told you our hot water heater doesn't actually make hot water?"

I can tell by his wince that he did, in fact, forget that part, but he rallies quickly. "The goal is for your mother to not want to live here anymore, and it's not good business to invest money in a property you don't own. On the other hand, denying my wife something as simple as hot water is extremely petty behavior for a newlywed."

My pride wants to tell him to keep his hot water heater. It stings that I couldn't buy a basic item that's apparently *simple* to other people.

But I also really like hot showers.

"There's a compromise here," he says, almost to himself. "I'll replace the current hot water heater with a similar unit, but she'll know if I *owned* the property, I would have installed a high-end on-demand system."

"Like yours?"

"Exactly."

That shower was one of my favorite parts of the Boston weekend, and my dreamy sigh remembering it makes him chuckle. If anything's going to make me jack up the pressure on Gin to sell, it's that shower.

Eventually, I'd have to leave it, of course. After enough time has passed between Gin selling the house to us and our divorce so it all looks legit, the plan calls for me being the one to move out. Hayden will get full custody of the shower.

"I'll go bring in the rest of my stuff," he says, as if it's a foregone conclusion he'll be sharing this room—and this bed—with me until he goes back to Boston Sunday night or Monday morning.

"Penny's used to your mom's house. We should go there," I say in a last ditch effort to change his mind.

"She has you, so she'll be fine." He steps closer to me, presumably so he can lower his voice. "You and I spending our time together at my mom's would make this situation a lot easier for Gin."

And we don't want it to be easy. We want her to be uncomfortable so she'll *want* to sell the house and go live by herself. But having Hayden in *my* room might be even harder on me than staying at Colleen's.

Four nights, I think. Four nights of Hayden in my bed, with my mother across the hall.

Maybe, if I can curl into a tight enough ball, Penny will share one of her beds with me.

Chapter Forty-Seven

HAYDEN

Because it's getting late and Gin has already retired to her bedroom with a very enthusiastic slamming of her door, Cara gives me a very brief tour of the house.

It's about what I expected. Small rooms, all in dire need of updating. Generations of clutter. Old windows that probably don't even meet the minimum standard of efficiency. A lot of old, dark wood. The effect is claustrophobic, but I keep that opinion to myself.

This is Cara's home, and I know this isn't easy for her. The last thing I want to do is make it harder by insulting her home.

We end up in the kitchen, and I take Penny out the back door for potties. She's not pleased about it, so she takes her time finding a worthy spot. Being behind the house makes it obvious, even in the fading light, that they've been putting what work and money they can into the front of the house, where it can be seen from the street.

When we go back inside, Cara's leaning against the counter with her arms folded across her chest. She doesn't look angry, but there's clearly something serious weighing on her mind.

"You can't sleep in my bed," she says without preamble, though in a very low voice.

"I'm too old to sleep on the floor."

"You can sleep on the couch downstairs and I'll tell Gin we had an argument."

I shake my head. "We're not doing that, especially while we'd still technically be on our honeymoon if we'd taken a trip. Until we sign the papers, you and I are happy newlyweds looking forward to spending the rest of our lives in this house."

Her nose wrinkles at the reminder that pretense is her only way *out* of spending the rest of her life in this house. "Okay, I think there's an air mattress somewhere in the garage. My dad got it cheap at a yard sale because it has a leak, but if there's one thing we have a lot of in this house, it's duct tape. We can slide it under my bed during the day."

"I'm also not sleeping on an air mattress." I'm usually open to negotiation, but not when it comes to blowup beds.

She puts her hands on her hips. "Well, *I'm* not going to sleep on it. That is *my* bed and since nothing's been signed yet, that is still *my* bedroom. And you're the one who just showed up on the doorstep with bags, your dog and no plan."

Oh, I have a plan. She even *knows* the plan—get Gin out of this house. But, to be fair, I hadn't given a lot of thought to the sleeping arrangements before showing up on the doorstep.

Actually I had, but I'd been hoping the whole *what happens in Boston, stays in Boston* thing would be forgotten. Not that sleeping together again is a good idea—it's definitely not.

"We can't—" She pauses, waving her hand like she can't come up with the right words. "You know."

"I know." I hate admitting it, but I know she's right. We dove into the deep end of the pool with this marriage. We can't keep wading into even deeper water or we'll find ourselves dangerously over our heads.

"Penny can sleep between us," I tell her. "She likes to wedge herself sideways and stretch, so over the course of the night, she'll shove us toward opposite sides of the bed. As big as my bed is, there are still times I wake up clinging to the edge of the mattress, trying not to fall off."

She smiles at the dog, who's sitting by my feet and looking up at me as though to inform me this has been fun, but she'd like to go home now.

"A wall of Penny?" Cara says, smiling but sounding skeptical.

"We'll make it work."

It's too late to go anywhere at this point, but too early to go to bed, so we end up in the living room, watching sitcom repeats. We're at opposite ends of the slightly lumpy couch, with Penny stretched out against my thigh.

I'm starting to get drowsy, wondering if Cara will sit here and watch TV all night rather than face going to bed, when she moves suddenly. One second, she's leaning on the far arm of the couch and the next, Penny's sandwiched between us and her head's on my shoulder.

That's when I hear the creaking above us, and then the sound of Gin coming down the stairs. She doesn't even look at us while walking through the living room into the kitchen, and Cara sighs.

Two minutes later, Gin retraces her path between us and the television. Once again, she doesn't look our way, but she has a water tumbler in her hand. Without a word, she goes back upstairs. We follow the creaking and the door slamming, and then Cara moves back to the other end of the couch.

This is fun, I think to myself with a heavy dose of sarcasm.

"She'll be sound asleep by the end of the next episode," Cara whispers, and I nod.

When she finally turns off the TV, I take Penny outside one final time. She seems resigned to spending the night here, but she's not pleased with me and takes her sweet time doing her business.

When we go inside, Cara's nowhere in sight, so I pick Penny up and find the light switches to turn off the lights as I go. I hit the top of the stairs just as Cara comes out of the bathroom. She's wearing leggings and a long tee, and her hair's loose around her shoulders.

This is going to be uncomfortable enough for Cara without me stripping in front of her, so I follow her into the bedroom to grab what I'll need. After setting Penny on the bed, I rummage through my bag for the sleep pants I'd packed.

By the time I'm done in the bathroom, Cara and Penny have claimed their side of the bed, and I smile as I close the bedroom door as quietly as possible. It's hard not to be aware of how *right* this all feels, despite the circumstances.

It takes me a minute to find an outlet behind the table on my side of the bed for the charging stand for my watch and phone. Then I turn off the light and use the glow of my phone's screen to make my way around the heavy wooden footboard without breaking a toe.

After pulling back the sheet and sliding into the bed, I stretch out and listen to Cara breathe. It doesn't sound as if she's crying, but I can practically feel her tension radiating across the bed. I want to hug her, but trying to touch her in this bed right now would *not* help her relax.

"It'll get easier," she whispers, and I'm not sure if she's talking to me or trying to reassure herself.

"It will," I reply anyway, in a low voice. "Try to get some sleep."

It's a long time before her breathing becomes regular, though. And an even longer time before mine does.

The next morning, I do *not* wake up perched on the edge of the bed, about to roll off onto the floor.

I inhale the scent of Cara's hair as my mind shakes off sleep and I realize all three of us are in the middle of the bed. I can't move my arm because it's under Cara's neck, supporting her head —which is tucked under my chin. Her ankle is draped over mine, and my free hand is resting on her hip.

Penny nestles between our chests, her tiny snores making me smile, as they always do.

I should figure out a way to free my arm and get back on my side of the bed before Cara wakes up, but I can't make myself move. Instead, I close my eyes and breathe deeply, savoring the moment.

What would I give to wake up like this every morning for the rest of my life?

Chapter Forty-Eight

CARA

There are better ways to wake up than being startled out of sleep by the clang and clatter of one's mother taking her anger out on kitchen pans.

But there are worse ways than waking up in Hayden's arms. If not for the cacophony of cookware coming from the floor below, I'd think we were back in Boston. Wrapped in the warmth of his body, with an extra little bit of heat near my chest where Penny is curled up, I can't help but think of what an incredible kisser this man is. And how thorough he is with his hands.

Then he chuckles.

Since he's obviously awake, I disentangle myself and slide back to my side of the bed, ignoring Penny's disgruntled sigh. Maybe instead of a wall of Penny, we need a giant wall of pillows. Or a brick wall.

"Your mom's in a mood this morning."

"Yeah, she's a slammer. Doors. Cabinets. Pots and pans."

Hayden's phone buzzes on the nightstand. Before he can even reach for it, it buzzes again. Then again. After picking it up and reading the screen, Hayden drops back to his pillow.

"Bad news?" I ask, because he doesn't look happy. Instead of answering, he hands me his phone so I can read the text messages.

COLLEEN

Why are you staying at that woman's house?

COLLEEN

Hayden William Reilly, you better answer me.

COLLEEN

Why would you stay with that woman when you have a lovely room here?

As I'm reading, another text arrives.

AARON

Mom just called and told me to drive by the Gamble house and see if your car's really in the driveway because she can't believe you would actually do this to her. I take it this means I'm the favorite son again.

Laughing, I hand the phone back to him. "I think your brother's enjoying this."

I take advantage of Hayden being distracted by his family to snatch up some clean clothes and head for the bathroom. I don't usually get dressed for the day in the bathroom, but we haven't had a man in the house since my dad died. Also, stripping out of my pajamas and getting dressed in my bedroom while Hayden's in there feels far too intimate. He may have seen me naked once, but we're not making it a habit.

Once I'm wearing my armor of jeans and a blue T-shirt, which is about as festive as I get for the Fourth of July, I go back down the hall to my room. It isn't until I've stepped through the door I realize Hayden could be getting dressed, but he's still in bed.

He's sitting up against the headboard now, though, with his phone in his hand and Penny on his lap. "I didn't have a logical excuse ready to give my mother as to why we wouldn't stay in the very nice guest suite I specifically made so I could stay there when I'm in town."

That woman.

That house.

There's a very logical excuse for me being nervous about staying at Colleen's house, though. She doesn't like us, and her son marrying me didn't magically change that. "What did you tell her?"

"I told her I was fixing a few things around the house for my *mother-in-law* so it was easier to stay here, and then I got a text from Aaron letting me know Mom told *him* to tell *me* she's no longer speaking to me."

"I'm sorry." If I'd just sucked it up and agreed to stay at Colleen's for the weekend, I'd have the only mother throwing a temper tantrum.

He waves away my apology. "It's not that serious. If she was upset enough to actually impact our relationship, she wouldn't have dragged Aaron into it. Is she mad? Yes. Will she get over it? Also yes."

"Considering our mothers are kind of known for holding grudges, I doubt that, but I'll take your word for it. So what's the plan for today?"

He grins, giving his face a boyish charm that weakens my knees. "Fourth of July in Sumac Falls! Ice cream. Family. Popcorn. Lots of booths to explore."

"I do like ice cream, popcorn and exploring booths," I say, and he chuckles to let me know the omission wasn't lost on him. "You didn't mention the fireworks."

"About them," he says. "Like most dogs, Penny isn't a fan. And being away from home... Even in Boston, we hang out and watch movies together. You're a dog person. You know how that is. So I'll be here with Penny, and if you want to go with Gin, you have a valid reason for having a little time away from me."

I don't confess I don't actually *want* time away from him. I just wish our time together didn't involve lies, anxiety and fraud. Or my mother. "We can play it by ear."

"We'll enjoy the daylight activities, though, won't we, Penny?" She lifts her head and licks the back of his hand once.

"Maybe you'll run into some old friends."

"I only had two really good friends in school and, like me, they got the hell out of Sumac Falls. Unlike me, they didn't come back. Their families moved away, too."

It's tempting to argue that Hayden didn't actually *come back*. Boston is definitely his home, and he has no intention of making a life here. But I don't bother because I have enough stress in my life without picking a semantics fight with Hayden.

Plus, it sounds like Gin just pulled everything out of the pan cabinet and let it clatter on the floor. "I should get down there. She's definitely trying to communicate with me because we don't even use that many pots and pans for Thanksgiving dinner."

"I'll be down in a few minutes."

"If you plan to shower, you should do it *before* she starts washing dishes. And don't get too good a lather up, or you'll be half-frozen by the time you rinse it all off."

I can tell by his expression he forgot again, and I'm laughing as I walk out the door. One look at Gin's expression when I walk into the kitchen kills any lingering amusement, though.

"I was going to make pancakes," she says in a clipped tone. "But I can't find the pan and I promised Sherry I'd help her set up her booth, so I'm going upstairs to find my sun hat and then I'm leaving."

And then she walks out, without me ever saying a word. I hold my breath, dreading her and Hayden running into each other in the hallway, until her bedroom door slams.

Hard.

Whether he planned it or was just lazily scrolling his phone in bed, Hayden doesn't come downstairs until my mother's gone—her departure announced with more doors slamming. He's dressed in well-worn jeans and a casual, short-sleeved button-down in a soft sage that's suddenly my favorite color. It looks really good on him.

"Apparently, the good pancake pan is missing," I tell him. "But we do have some eggs. And cereal."

"Let me take Penny out for her morning walk, and then we can grab something at the diner."

"They're not open today."

He frowns. "With everybody in Sumac Falls converging on downtown? They should at least be open for breakfast."

"Nope. And before you pull up that magic food-on-your-doorstep app, don't bother. I'll make some scrambled eggs and toast while you walk Penny."

By early afternoon, I'm running out of steam. There are very few people in the town square that one or both of us doesn't know, and the people Hayden knows are eager to catch up. I think it's even more exhausting to play out this charade now than it was for our wedding because everybody wants to talk to us. And we don't have other guests to use as an excuse to step away.

At least our mothers are behaving. I'm not sure if they've both snapped out of their bad moods or if neither wants to appear ungracious to their child's new spouse in public, and I don't care. When we stopped by Sherry's booth to thank her again for such gorgeous floral arrangements on short notice, Gin managed a smile. And when we ran into Colleen by the Little League's fundraising game, she was slightly cool, but not so anybody else would notice.

"How come you don't have a booth?" Hayden asks when we have a few blessed moments to ourselves, walking hand-in-hand through the crowd.

I try not to dwell on how right it feels for our hands to be clasped together.

"There's really no benefit for me," I explain. "The people with pets already know I'm here. They're either existing customers, already travel to another groomer, or they do it themselves. And the people who don't have pets don't need me. No matter how awesome my booth is, nobody's going to go out and buy a dog just so they can give me business."

He nods. "Good point."

I reach over with my free hand and scratch under Penny's chin. Because she's so little and easily stepped on, Hayden's been carrying her since we arrived, and she's a little smug about it. "Though some people might drag their dog up from a different state to get her nails done just so they can talk to me."

He chuckles. "And now you're my wife, so my plan clearly worked."

My wife. There's something about the way he says those words that still heats my skin.

"Cara!" I see Mel walking toward me, her hand in the air.

"Uncle Hayden!" we hear at almost the same time.

"We've been found again," he says, and then he winks at me before heading toward his niece and nephew, giving me time with Mel.

"I didn't think I'd ever find you," she says after giving me a quick hug. "I wasn't even sure you'd be here, actually. I meant to text you, but then I got distracted. A few minutes ago, I heard a woman talking about the little dog Hayden Reilly is carrying around, so I started hunting."

"I knew I'd run into you eventually. You're always here. But where's Lucas?"

"One of the old classic cars that's going to be in the parade won't start, and he was so excited to get his hands in an engine that's not all computerized, I didn't have the heart to remind him he promised to spend his entire day off with me."

I'm trying to pay attention to what she's saying—she's my best friend and I haven't gotten to spend much time with her lately—but over her shoulder I can see Hayden.

While I could probably summon the willpower not to watch him if he was alone, watching him with the kids is too hard to resist. I can't tear my attention away from the joy on their faces as he swings AJ up on to his shoulders, while Daisy forces a leashed

Penny to accept a kiss on top of her head. He's unguarded—love practically shining from him—and staring at him is like standing outside in a lightning storm. You know it's dangerous, but it's too mesmerizing to look away from.

He'll be a great dad someday, when he has kids.

With some other woman.

"Oh, hey. Why do you look like you're going to cry?" Mel moves closer to me, and sees where I'm looking. "Dammit, Cara. We talked about this."

"I'm not going to cry, Mel."

She leans close enough to hiss in my ear. "You said you wouldn't fall in love with your husband. It hasn't even been a week."

"I am *not* in love with my husband." I tell myself it's the truth, but I might be lying.

"Did you sleep with him on your honeymoon?"

"Mel." I'm not answering that question, best friend or not. "We are standing in the middle of the Sumac Falls Fourth of July celebration. Literally everybody we know is around us right now."

"You better call me later."

"Sure. I'll talk to you about it when I'm in the house that has zero sound insulation while my mother and my husband are in another room."

Her eyes narrow. "This level of snark from you tells me everything I need to know about what's going on."

I force myself to look her in the eye. "Nothing has changed regarding our situation."

"I'd call you a liar, but a lot of people are looking at us right now, probably afraid we're having an argument." She fakes a laugh. "How was that?"

I paste an obnoxiously fake grin on my face. "They'll never suspect a thing."

When I look for Hayden again, he's no longer playing with Daisy and AJ. He's talking to an older guy I've seen around town for years, but can't actually place. I say goodbye to Mel and head over, but by the time I reach him, he's already shaken the man's hand and started walking my way.

"Who was that?"

He smiles and shifts Penny to his other arm. "He's the man that's going to install a new hot water heater at nine o'clock tomorrow morning."

"You're kidding. A Friday in the middle of a holiday weekend, with no advanced notice? Hayden, that'll cost a fortune."

"I'm pretty sure you know how I feel about hot water, since you've been in my shower."

Heat floods my face and I lower my head to kiss Penny, hoping Hayden won't notice. His low chuckle tells me it didn't work.

"She's trembling," I tell him, scratching under her chin.

"She's a good sport, but she doesn't love strangers. Or crowds. Or people. Or, believe it or not, being outside. Unless there's snow. She likes snow."

"Should we take her home?"

Something I can't decipher flashes through his eyes—perhaps a reaction to my use of the word *home*—but he smiles. "She'd like that. You can stay here if you want, though. I've gotten a few snide comments about spoiling my dog, so if anybody asks where I am, they won't bat an eye if you tell them I took her home because she needed a nap."

I think the only thing worse than having to look happily married in front of all of Sumac Falls would be answering questions about my husband's whereabouts. So far Hayden has done most of the talking, reminding me yet again that he's a very smooth liar, and I'd rather not be here without him.

"No, I'm ready to go, too. Maybe if I put all the pans away before Gin gets home, she'll forget she was mad this morning."

Chapter Forty-Nine

CARA

I'm not going to survive this long weekend. Being caught between two people who *really* don't like each other isn't fun, and I have a new appreciation for people who struggle with in-laws when they actually intend to stay married for the rest of their lives.

For us it's temporary, I remind myself as I stand in the kitchen and listen to my mother rant while we wash the breakfast dishes. A breakfast Hayden didn't appear for because his mother called and I just left him to his conversation.

For the fourth morning in a row, I woke up wrapped in his arms. When I finally fell asleep, we were on opposite edges of the bed, with Penny *and* a pillow between us. But once again, when I opened my eyes this morning, he was holding me. Penny was happily wedged between us, and the extra pillow was on the floor.

It's been a rough day already and we just barely finished breakfast.

"The toilet seat is always up now, Cara."

"Always? He just got here Friday night. How many times could either of you possibly have needed to pee?"

"Every single time I go into the bathroom, the seat is up. I almost fell in."

Keeping a straight face while imagining the splash and Gin's outrage isn't easy. "I'll mention it to him. He's a guy who's been living alone for years, so he probably doesn't think about it."

"I don't think he's even using the toilet that often. He's just going in there and putting the seat up to annoy me."

"Do you hear yourself right now?" I have to force the laugh, though, because I honestly wouldn't put it past Hayden. "Why would he do that?"

"Because he's a Reilly."

Her tone tells me there's no thought behind the words coming out of her mouth. She's running on pure emotion. "I'll talk to him. In the meantime, remember we have hot water now thanks to him. Just kill him with kindness."

"It would be faster and easier just to kill him."

"Mom!" I'm pretty sure she's just venting, but with Gin, I never really know.

"I'm just saying."

I'm washing the scrambled egg pan before the eggs can fuse to the tattered nonstick coating—our dishwasher died eight years ago—when Hayden enters the kitchen. I don't need to turn and see him to know it. I can hear Penny's nails on the floor, and also my mother's body tenses, her shoulders rising toward her ears.

"You missed breakfast," she snaps. "I'm not cooking again."

"Good morning, Gin," he says, and his hand on my waist is the only warning I get before he nuzzles my hair out of the way and kisses my neck. "Good morning, wife."

I shiver, but I don't stop scrubbing the pan. I don't need to turn around to know Gin has stormed out of the room. Even in her house slippers, her stomping away is unmistakable.

"Gin planning to murder me wasn't part of the deal," he murmurs close to my ear.

Since she's not watching, he really could step out of my personal space. "You heard that?"

"She's not a quiet woman," he points out, making me laugh.

"I'm mostly sure she was just venting." I shrug. "And you know how she feels about your family. When you came into town trying to buy her house and ended up marrying her daughter, you had to know her taking you out was on the table."

"You two coming up with a secondary scheme to get me to the altar and then off me would void the agreement," he teases.

"Would it, though? I read all those documents you made me sign *very* thoroughly, and I didn't see that anywhere."

His laugh fills the house, and even though I love the sound of it, I know it will just annoy Gin even more. I rinse the pan and put it in the rack to dry while pulling the plug with my other hand. After rinsing away the last of the suds, I dry my hands and turn to face my husband.

"So, I guess Colleen's speaking to you again?"

"About that." He leans against the counter and shoves his hands in his pockets. *Uh-oh.* "Fair warning. This might make you mad."

"So, *all* the women in your life will be mad at you? Maybe you're the problem, Hayden."

He actually grins. "Oh, I'm definitely the problem. And I don't think Hope's mad at me…yet. She's mostly trying to ignore us all, which isn't easy because Mom works for her."

"Oh, that's fun. But why am I going to be mad?"

"Well, my mother decided if I'm going to be going back and forth between here and Boston, that every other time I'm here, we should stay with her."

I was afraid of that. But if Hayden can put up with Gin, I can put up with Colleen. He deals with conflict better than I do, but I can handle it. "That's fair, I guess."

"I appreciate that. *But*, I think me being in *this* house is… helping."

I can't deny he's annoying the hell out of Gin. Enough to sell the house to him? That remains to be seen. "Obviously you can't explain why to Colleen."

"No, so now we're too the part that might make you mad."

"Oh, none of that was it?"

"Funny." He snorts. "Hold on to that sense of humor for the next part. Which is me telling my mom that we're trying to mend old relationships. And because Colleen Reilly is a wonderful woman who will be warm and gracious to you no matter who your mother is, it's more important for me to be here and try to bring your irrational, unkind mother around."

I know I should be offended on my mother's behalf—and yes, mad—but I have to laugh. "And she bought that?"

"She did. And you don't seem mad."

I shrug. "I probably should be, except it's all so ridiculous. It's really hard not to laugh."

"Good." He's quiet for a moment, watching me. "I've been thinking."

"Please stop doing that. My mother wouldn't sell you this house, so you *thought* about it, and now we're married and sleeping in the same bed with the world's worst chaperone between us."

He tries to look chagrined and utterly fails. "That's what I've been thinking about. Well, not the bed part. Actually...no. Never mind that."

It's not often I see Hayden flustered. It's adorable.

"Anyway," he says firmly. "I was planning to leave for Boston early tomorrow morning. But it would have to be *really* early to make my first meeting of the day. You have appointments in the morning. And the stress level has been high for all of us. I was thinking of heading back today. I can get Penny settled back in. Maybe we can all get a decent night's sleep to kick off the week."

As much as a part of me doesn't want him to go, he's not wrong about any of it. "That actually sounds like a good idea."

"And I'll be back Thursday night."

I hadn't even gotten my entire sigh of relief out yet. "Of course you will."

"Any chance you can see me off with a tearful goodbye on the curb? Maybe wave a handkerchief as I drive away?"

"Nope. Any chance Penny can stay with me?"

"Nope."

I had to try.

Chapter Fifty

HAYDEN

Three weeks later...

"Did you move all the stuff around in the kitchen drawers?"

Hearing Cara's voice behind me makes me smile, even though she sounds thoroughly exasperated with me. I turn to face her, doing my best not to look smug. "I reorganized the drawers in a more logical way as a favor to my mother-in-law."

She laughs. "You are so full of shit right now."

"Tell me the way I have the utensils and cutlery doesn't make more sense."

"It's not about making sense and you know it. You would never do this to *your* mother's kitchen." She arches her eyebrow, waiting, but I keep my mouth shut because I don't want to admit I wouldn't dare move a single spoon in Colleen Reilly's kitchen. "This game you're playing needs to stop."

"What game is that?"

"The game where you're behaving like the worst roommate ever in an effort to get Gin to move out faster."

"Is it working?"

"You're not funny."

"Not always, but you should hear me after a few drinks. I'm hilarious. And I think it's starting to work. I'm pretty sure people across town could hear her yelling about that plastic bag of old twist ties she was saving."

It's not working fast enough, though. It's been three weeks since I showed up on their doorstep with my bag and my dog, unofficially moving in, and we've fallen into a routine. I leave for Boston on Sunday night, spend four days in the office, and then return Thursday night to work remotely and torment Gin Gamble. While she fought me at first, Cara finally agreed to scheduling appointments only for the days I'm in Boston and I pay her the difference as a retainer for Penny. It looks better for our marriage and, as a bonus, I get to spend a *lot* of time with Cara.

But it's exhausting and the sooner Gin surrenders, the better.

"I understand what you're trying to do, Hayden, but maybe you could take it down a notch. Or maybe you could give us all a break and claim you have a work crisis that can only be dealt with from Boston and requires you to work next weekend."

"And take the pressure off just as she's nearing her breaking point?"

"You're assuming that reaching her breaking point means moving out, and not clocking you with a cast iron skillet." She snorts. "Me joining her in tragic widowhood, the two of us pining away in this decaying house together, might hold some romantic appeal for her."

"I wish you two would stop talking about killing me."

"Maybe stop rearranging the kitchen drawers." She sighs. "I did notice she's engaging more when I show her potential properties, though."

"See? It's working."

"I know. It's just... It's a lot. And I'm hungry, so put on your best fake happy face and let's go eat. Dinner's on the table."

Penny follows us into the kitchen, and she starts to head for her bowls, which are near the back door. But Gin's in her path, so she turns back and goes all the way around the table to get to them.

Of course Gin notices. "Your dog isn't very friendly."

"Penny doesn't really like people, except for me." I pause, just for a beat. "And my wife."

"My daughter has a name," Gin snaps.

I'm about to say *yes, her name is Cara Reilly* when the woman in question catches my eye and gives me a pleading look behind her mother's back. My goal here is to nudge Gin out the door, not make Cara throw herself off the roof, so I let it go for now. I can play nice for her sake.

Then I sit down and get my first look at tonight's meal, which puts a serious hurt on my good intentions.

I stare down at the plate, the lump of elbow macaroni, mayonnaise, tuna and peas killing my appetite.

Tuna casserole was a constant staple in the Reilly household after my dad died. Money had always been tight, and it got tighter. Overwhelmed by grief and stress, Colleen had understandably done the bare minimum for a while. And just looking at the casserole on my plate brings me back to those dark days.

Was that Gin's intention? Had she somehow guessed the Reilly family had lived on food that was cheap, easy and could be stretched to cover multiple meals? It's exactly the kind of thing Gin would do in an attempt to subtly remind me of *my place* in her world.

Anger boils up, threatening to make me forget I'd just decided to give them a break and play nice. I look at her, a comment about bringing a personal chef with me next week forming.

Gin's back is rigid. Her jaw's clenched. She's clutching her fork and her eyes are on her plate as she pokes at the casserole.

I recognize that body language, maybe because my mother looked the same for a long time after my dad died. A woman who feels beaten and is clinging to her tattered pride with everything left in her. In my peripheral vision, I see Cara, looking much the same, and my heart breaks a little.

I scoop up a forkful of the tuna casserole and shove it in my mouth. The texture turns my stomach, but I know it's only the taste and feel triggering memories of the hardest time of my life. I shove back the emotions, swallow and then wipe my mouth with the napkin.

"This is very good, Gin," I say, and it's not *totally* a lie. As the dish goes, hers isn't horrible. "We used to eat it as a kid, but I haven't had it in a long time. It brings back memories."

Not good memories, but it's worth the half-lie when she relaxes slightly and even gives me a weak smile. The true reward is the warmth in Cara's eyes when she gives me a *genuine* one.

I eat the entire plateful of tuna casserole, an excruciating experience made worse by the awkward silence around the table. Every time I glance at Penny, who's curled up in the corner, she gives me a questioning look. *Can we go home now?*

When the meal is finally over, Gin leaves us to clean up, claiming she's going for a walk. I glance at Penny when she says the w-a-l-k word, but my dog immediately closes her eyes and pretends to be asleep.

"I've been thinking about what you said," I tell Cara when we're about halfway through doing the dishes—with me washing this time because I put everything away in the wrong place last time I dried. "Maybe you're right about a little break."

"What happened to not letting up when she's close to cracking?" Cara holds up her hand. "Not that I'm disagreeing. Just wondering what changed your mind?"

"I'm afraid *you're* close to cracking, and that's not what I want. Maybe it's time to shift strategies. I can spend a little time away. Things calm down a little. And maybe I can make her like me. That might be easier than driving her out."

Cara's laugh doesn't bode well for the plan. "I'm not sure what it would take to make my mother like you, but it'll be more than being a good sport about the tuna casserole."

"Hey, I made *you* like me," I tease.

Her smile slips away. "But I never hated you. I was hurt by you and angry with you, but I never hated you."

Again I feel the urge to tell her the truth about homecoming night, and again I tamp it down. Since I can't say that, I'm not sure what to say, so I bring it back to the conversation at hand. "Either way, I think a break from the stress would be good for everybody. Instead of coming back Thursday night, we'll say a situation came up and I have to work the weekend."

"You know, Penny could stay here with me."

I laugh, shaking my head. "Not a chance. I know she loves you, but I wouldn't be able to function that long without her."

"It actually *is* a good thing you addressed custody of her in the prenup. I'd probably fight for her."

I laugh because I prefer playful Cara to stressed out Cara, but the mention of the prenup is like a blow to the gut.

It's too easy sometimes to forget this isn't real—that Cara isn't my forever wife, and that the time we spend together is just a means to an end. And maybe giving Gin's nerves a break isn't the only reason some time apart is a good idea.

Even though I'll miss Cara, I clearly need some time in Boston, reminding myself of what my *actual* life looks like.

Chapter Fifty-One

CARA

When I get home from work a week later, I find Gin sitting on the floor in the middle of the garage, frantically trying to scrub her face with her sleeves as I walk through the door. It's obvious she's not only been crying, but crying *hard*, and fear clouds all of my senses. My mother is *not* the crying type and the last time I saw her like this was the day my dad passed away.

Georgia or Tony would have called me if it was either of them. Hayden's in Boston right now, so it couldn't be anything he did. Or that she *perceived* he did.

"Mom? What's going on?" She looks as if she's going to get up, but I'm sitting on the floor with her before she manages it. "Did you fall? Are you hurt?"

When she opens her mouth, a hiccupped sob comes out instead of words, but she shakes her head to let me know she's not injured. An emotional meltdown, then. It's very unlike her, so I simply wait, keeping her company while she gets herself under control. Sitting on cement isn't ideal for either of us, but I can't leave her here like this.

"I'm fine," she says about two minutes later.

"You're clearly not fine, Mom. What's going on?"

"Sherry told me that adorable house down the road from her is going on the market, and the real estate agent said I can have first dibs before it's even public."

Excitement bubbles up inside of me, but I tamp it down because I'm a lot happier about this news than she is and I'm not sure why. "This is what you wanted, Mom."

"I can't," she wails, waving her hands around the piles of junk filling the garage. "I tried to do just one box and there's so much and I can never do this."

Nope. The three of us are absolutely *not* living in this house— with me caught in a fake marriage limbo—for the rest of Gin's life because of decades of junk. "You don't have to go through all this, you know."

She sniffles, her lower lip trembling. "Why? Because your husband will just hire somebody to haul it all to the dump? Even the Gamble family heirlooms?"

It takes everything in me not to laugh at her. She definitely wouldn't appreciate that. "Mom, there's a difference between Gamble family heirlooms and generation after generation of Gambles living here, meaning nobody ever threw anything away. When people don't have to move, they don't have to get rid of accumulated junk."

Her lips tighten and I wince. "It's not junk."

"Nobody's throwing anything away without you. And we don't have to do it all at once, you know. Buy the house and we'll pack up just what you need—*your* belongings. We'll get your new home set up just the way you want it, and then we can start sorting through things, deciding what you want to keep, what should stay in the house, and what to sell or donate."

I can never be sure when it comes to my mother, but I think there's a good chance once this house is in her rearview mirror and she has a cute little home of her own, the last thing she's going to want to do is fill it with all this stuff.

"You won't throw anything away without asking me first?"

I rest my hand on her knee. "I promise. Once everything's settled, maybe we can have one or two nights a week where we do a set amount of time of going through stuff, and then we have dinner together."

She brightens. "That sounds doable."

"See? Now, how about I loop Hayden in, and he can get his real estate person to make the offer for you and set up the closings so the money for this house pays for that house, and the leftover will make a nice nest egg for you."

I'm not surprised when she nods instead of saying anything about some of the egg coming my way. That's just not how her mind works, plus she probably assumes I'm all set because I married a man with money. She doesn't know that's temporary, and I don't want to think too hard about whether that would make a difference or not.

"Let's get up off this cement floor," I say, pushing myself to my feet. When she groans, I put out my hands and pull her up.

She brushes off her pants. "I'll go text Sherry and get the contact info for the agent."

"That sounds good." Instead of heading into the house—my mother always leaves her cell phone on the kitchen counter, as if it's a landline—she's still for a long moment. "You okay, Mom?"

When she faces me, her lips curve into a smile. "I'm terrified, Cara. But I think I'm a little excited, too."

For a moment, all of the resentment and hopelessness of the last few years fades, and I think about how trapped my mother must have felt. Trapped by her promise to her husband, her sense of obligation—misguided as it was—to her daughter, and fear of learning a new way to live her life.

"I'm excited *for* you, Mom. You're going to have so much fun living in that neighborhood. And it's not only Sherry. You know more than half the people who live there. And you won't have to worry about anything."

Once she's gone into the house, I strip out of my work clothes and pull on clean shorts and a tank top. A full load has accumulated, so I start the washer before pulling out my phone to text Hayden.

CARA

The good news: Mom's ready to make an offer on a house near Sherry. The bad news: She'll be coming back one or two nights a week to go through all this junk, which might take four or five years.

HAYDEN

Even better news: She lets me hire somebody to haul it all away?

CARA

Worst news: She specifically made me promise I wouldn't let you do that. Circle back to the good news.

HAYDEN

The best news: You're almost free.

It's unclear to me if he means I'm almost free of the house or almost free of him. Or maybe he means both.

Of course I should be happy about both. Especially since it means I'll be free to do whatever I want, within reason. But, even though I'm genuinely excited for my mother, my happiness bubble loses some of its shine as I go into the house to figure out what we're making for supper.

While I would never admit it to anybody—not even Mel, or maybe *especially* not Mel—I like being Hayden's wife. And even though our marriage isn't real, the divorce will be.

I knew this plan was a bad idea.

Chapter Fifty-Two

HAYDEN

It takes another two weeks to line everything up. My team had done as much of the prep work as possible, and they kept on top of the people handling Gin's purchase. It's fast, but that's what I expect from my people. I want it done.

Not just because I want to own the Gamble house, but because Cara had told me it might be easier on Gin—and therefore her—if I made myself scarce while they tried to gather what her mother would need for the initial move. Coming up with reasons to be in Boston hasn't been hard.

But being away from Cara has. Not waking up with her in my arms *definitely* has.

"Hayden."

The sharpness in Taylor's voice tells me it's not the first time my assistant has tried to get my attention, and I tear my thoughts away from Cara.

"They're about five minutes out," she says.

I nod and then inhale deeply, trying to settle my nerves. I don't usually have anxiety walking into any business situation, but this is different. I've wanted this on a personal level for a very long time, and Gin could still change her mind.

And I'm going to see Cara.

Using a car service had been my suggestion, and Cara readily accepted on their behalf. It was almost an hour from Sumac Falls to the office handling the closings, and neither of them drove in cities often. And I didn't want them getting lost or having a car break down throwing off the timing of the back-to-back closings.

The schedule is set. The first closing, during which Gin sells the Gamble house to Cara and me. After that, I'll leave since I'll no longer be necessary, and so my presence won't tarnish Gin's excitement for her new house. Taylor will take them out for a celebratory lunch while the first deal is finalized, and then they'll do the second closing on Gin's property.

I'll be heading back to Boston tonight because Penny's there, and to give the two women some alone time to process the events of the day.

When the black SUV pulls in, I practically jog across the parking lot to meet it. Somehow I got lucky and Cara's on my side, so I get to help her out while the driver opens Gin's door.

I grin and pull her in for a tight hug, kissing her neck. "I've missed you. That was way too long for us to be apart."

And not a word of it is a lie.

"Mom's a little shaky today," she whispers. "Please be kind, but also give her space."

"I will."

Taylor had already been inside, making sure the meeting room was in order. Because I'd spent some time remembering how my mother dug in her heels when I suggested she sell the home she'd shared with her husband and buy something nicer, I do have empathy for Gin. Usually I sit at the head of any table I'm at, but not this time. Gin will be at the head, with the man from the title company and Taylor on her right and Cara on her left. I'll sit on the other side of Cara and, whenever possible, let her lead.

No matter how much the thought of this moment has driven

me over the years, I won't be rubbing my Reilly roots in her face today. I even hang back when we enter the building because Gin takes Cara's hand and their interlaced fingers are locked so tightly, their knuckles are pale.

For a moment, I'm tempted to stop it. I could give Cara a divorce settlement that would keep the house going for the rest of Gin's life, and then Cara could do what she wanted with it.

But Cara needs this. She wanted it enough to marry a man who'd already broken her heart once, and to put up with me causing chaos in their lives. If it was just for me, I don't know what I would do as we take our seats and Gin sniffles into a tissue.

But for Cara's sake, I'll be the bad guy.

The process goes smoothly. I know Taylor has vetted every single document herself, as well as having my team go over them, and there are no surprises. When it comes time for the very last signature, I hold my breath while Gin stares at the paper. Then she looks at Cara and holds her gaze for a long time, until Cara squeezes her hand.

"It's okay to let go, Mom."

The breath Gin lets out is almost as shaky as her hand, but she signs her name and it's done. The Gamble house belongs to me.

"Congratulations," Taylor says as we all stand. "If you want to go out in the reception area or outside and relax, I'll join you in a few minutes."

Gin holds it together until we step out into the sunshine, and then the tears start. Cara holds her tight while I hang back, out of the way and out of Gin's sightline. Tears stream down Cara's cheeks, as well, but I tell myself they're both going to be a lot happier in the future than they were before I set this all in motion.

"Take good care of that house," Gin says as they disentangle themselves.

"I will, Mom," Cara says in a hoarse voice before giving me a stricken look.

I can't hang back anymore. I step forward so I can rest my hand at the small of her back, trying to offer silent support. But before I can think of anything to say that might help the situation, Taylor joins us.

"We'll have a nice break now," she says softly, having taken the emotional temperature of the group at a glance. "I found a nice, comfortable spot for lunch. We can relax and then we'll come back and that pretty little house down the street from your friend will be all yours, Gin. I saw the photos, and I'm so excited for you."

Gin brightens and moves with Taylor toward the black SUV. Cara follows for a few steps, and then seems to remember I'm not joining them. She turns and hesitates.

I force a smile and lift my hand. "Enjoy your lunch, sweetheart. I'll talk to you soon."

I wait until the SUV pulls out of the parking lot before getting into my car. The plan was for me to head straight back to Boston, but I don't fight the urge to point the car in the direction of Sumac Falls. I can spare the time to savor my victory.

As I walk up the steps, across the porch, and through the front door of the house I now own, I wait for the sweet flood of triumph, or at least a sense of satisfaction. I've waited for years to take Marcus and Gin Gamble's precious house away, and today I accomplished that goal. The papers are signed.

It's mine.

But the taste of victory is soured by an aching awareness that, as of this moment, the clock has started ticking down on my marriage to Cara.

Chapter Fifty-Three

CARA

I'm surprised to see Hayden's car in the driveway when the driver he hired drops us off in front of the house. I know Hayden legitimately has some pressing things on his plate, work-wise, and the plan was for him to drive up for the closing and then go back to the city.

I'm even more surprised when we haven't even gotten up the porch steps before Sherry's car pulls up and stops out front. She honks the horn and waves, her grin visible even from the porch.

"Sherry and I are going to go see my house," Gin says, waving back at her friend. "We need to measure for curtains and figure out where things will go."

It feels abrupt—she hadn't mentioned this plan to me—but Hayden had clearly been right. With the painful part behind her, Gin is excited to move on. "That sounds fun. Do you have the keys?"

She pats her handbag and then kisses my cheek. "And you and your husband can celebrate in peace."

She's gone before I register she'd called him my husband and not *that man* this time. It's progress.

Of course, progress doesn't matter at this point. Before long, Hayden will be my *ex*-husband and his former mother-in-law's opinion of him won't matter.

And on that depressing note, I go inside, only to find Hayden in the living room, obviously waiting for me. "I thought you were going back to Boston."

He shrugs. "I am, but I wanted to see you before I go. Where did Gin run off to?"

"Sherry picked her up and they're going to roam around the new house. She seems happy now that it's over."

"I hope you are, too. I know it's been hard, but it's done. Your mother—and therefore *you*—are free of this house."

"It's not over yet. Sure, my mother is excited about her new house, but that's because this house is mine now, as it was always meant to be. But when we decide to end this fake marriage and she finds out the house will be *yours* and yours alone, it might all blow up in our faces."

"There won't be a thing she can do about it, legally."

I shake my head, not sure why I expect him to understand. "Maybe that's all that matters in your world, Hayden. But she's my mother. And Sumac Falls is my home. You can go back to Boston, but I'll be stuck living with the fallout."

He closes the distance between us and takes my hands in his. "That's not a worry for today. Or tomorrow. Judging by the amount of stuff Gin owns, it's probably not even a worry for next year."

He gets the laugh out of me, and then wraps his arms around me. I relax into the hug, soaking in the strength of his warm body. His hands don't wander. He doesn't nuzzle my neck or try to kiss me. Hayden simply holds me until my breathing calms and the tension seeps out of my muscles.

"Let's get out of here. We'll go to the diner and have cheeseburgers and salty fries."

"I had a cheeseburger and salty fries for lunch," I mumble

into his shoulder. "It was a big lunch, actually, but I wouldn't mind dessert for supper."

"I'm always up for dessert." He pulls back and drops a gentle kiss on my forehead. "I'm ready whenever you are."

"No, you need to head back to Boston. What about Penny?"

"Penny is being taken care of until I get there. Even if we take our time over dessert, I won't be too late getting back to the city."

I feel like I should argue more. He's had a long day, too, and he still has that drive ahead of him. But I'm reluctant to let him go, and not only because I really don't want to be alone in the house right now.

Signing the papers has triggered a hurricane of mixed emotions swirling around in my head. Relief that I'm not going to lose any more sleep worrying about the house falling down around us or calculating just how low a thermostat setting we can tolerate in the winter. There's also loss, not only of the only home my family has known for generations, but with a resurgence of grief for my dad. Sorrow for my mother. Elation I'm almost free.

And seriously conflicted feelings about the impending end of my fake marriage.

Even though I've known from the jump ours is a marriage in name only, it's hard to imagine my life without him. Once the divorce is behind us, will I ever see him again? Based on the last almost-two decades, probably not.

And the fact my heart is aching in advance is proof I'm already screwed. But I can't resist just a little more time with him today.

The diner's busy, but since we're not having a full meal, we sit on the stools at the counter. I order the strawberry shortcake with vanilla ice cream and extra whipped cream. Hayden chooses the cherry pie with chocolate ice cream.

"Really?" I ask when Lorene goes to hand off the order to whoever's making desserts. "Cherry pie with chocolate ice cream?"

"Trust me, you have to try a bite." I must look skeptical

because he chuckles. "Do you think chocolate-covered cherries are weird?"

He has a point. "Okay, I'll try one bite."

We end up sharing both desserts—the bowls between us—and he wasn't wrong about the pie and ice cream combo. And I appreciate that he doesn't talk about the house. There's no discussion of a timeline for Gin or about which part of the renovations he'll tackle first.

We just talk about desserts and Penny and random things. It's a perfect way to end a rough day, and when he drops me off at home, it's hard not to ask him to stay one more day. Or two. If he'd brought Penny with him, I might have caved.

Instead, I smile and wave as he drives away.

Fifteen minutes later, Gin walks through the door. She's practically glowing, and she talks more in the next hour than she has in the last week. With measurements in hand, she talks about what furniture she'll need and other things she'll have to bring with her.

Days later, when it comes time to actually move my mom's things to her new home, I'm not surprised she's suddenly a lot more mercenary about what she considers hers and what's just junk collected by the family over the decades.

I don't even care that she's leaving the bulk of the mess for me to deal with. That's pretty in character for her, honestly, and it'll be easier for me to sort donations from trash if she's not taking everything back from the trash pile for her emotional support pile.

Your father and I bought this lamp at a yard sale on the way home from playing mini golf for your sixth birthday. All it needs is a new electrical cord and it'll be good as new.

There's no doubt everything in the house and garage has a similar origin story. And if she can't remember it, she'll probably make something up. The woman does *not* like to let go of anything from the past.

She seems content to make a fresh start in her new house,

though, and the faster we can make it feel like home, the faster she'll forget about the junk in the garage.

Meanwhile, I'm alone in the house, waiting for Hayden's return. And dreading the next phase of the plan.

Chapter Fifty-Four

HAYDEN

Returning to Sumac Falls to find that my mother-in-law had already moved into her new house was a pleasant surprise. Discovering my wife had moved all of *my* belongings into Gin's old room was much less pleasant.

"I don't like it," I say, standing in the open doorway of the bedroom that *was* ours, but is apparently just hers now.

"So you've said. Twice." Cara's standing in the hall, arms crossed. "But we don't need to pretend to be a real married couple if there's nobody in the house to know."

It's a valid point. And I can't argue with it because I don't want to tell her that, even in my condo in Boston, I have trouble sleeping without her warmth next to me. I don't want her to know how many hours I spend lying awake, wishing I was in her bed.

But I still don't like it.

"Penny will be confused," I tell her, knowing my dog would be okay with me throwing her under the bus in this instance. "She's gotten used to sleeping with both of us."

"She'll be fine. She still sleeps alone with you in Boston." She shakes her head and heads down the hall, but she stops at the top of the stairs to look back. "We need to leave in ten minutes."

"Right," I mutter, and I hear her laughter as she goes downstairs.

To make the evening even more fun, we're having dinner with my family tonight. Honestly, without Gin and her pickles present, it shouldn't be too bad. Aaron and Hope both like Cara, actually, and Colleen's seemingly warming to the idea of our marriage.

It's seeing Cara with Daisy and AJ that'll get me. Every time I think about my brother's kids now, I build this vision of the future in my head. Family cookouts. Cousins playing together in the yard. Cara and Hope laughing while Aaron and I argue over who's better at grilling burgers.

And then I have to remind myself none of it's real.

I move Penny's booster seat to the backseat before we leave. She's mad about it, but doesn't refuse to get in the car because it's for Cara, who is her second favorite human.

At least I hope she's her second favorite. Sometimes I wonder.

We're halfway to Colleen's when Cara turns to say something to Penny and sees the box sitting on the seat beside the dog. "What's in the box?"

"Wedding photos."

"Oh." She snaps back around in her seat, staring out the windshield. "That's fun."

"I got them by email, too, but I'd prefer to show them to the family without getting fingerprints all over my laptop. I did forward the link to the online album to your email, though, so you'll have them."

"Why are we showing them to the family at all?"

"Because it would be strange not to. Going through the wedding proofs and everybody picking the ones we want high-res copies of for framing is part of the fun."

"I don't see anything fun about encouraging our mothers to choose their favorite wedding photo of us to hang on their wall."

She sounds like she's going to cry and we're almost to

Colleen's, so I reach over and cover her hand with mine. "I know, Cara. I don't love it, either. But my mother and Hope have both asked me about them, multiple times. Maybe I can drag my feet on actually getting the prints. Hell, maybe I can make up a story about data corruption and how all the photos were lost. I'll figure it out, but right now, we'll just get through this."

"You could have come up with the data corruption story instead of bringing the photo book," she mutters.

"Contrary to what you seem to think, I'm not that great at lying."

She barks a humorless laugh. "I've seen no evidence that you're *not* great at it."

So we walk into my mother's house annoyed with each other —me carrying an anxious dog and Cara carrying a box she wants nothing to do with.

Of course Colleen zeroes in on the photographer's name on the side of the box immediately. "They're here!"

We manage to talk her into eating first, since the meat's already on the grill. The tension doesn't ease between Cara and I, and she spends most of her time talking with Daisy and AJ or cuddling Penny. Nobody seems to notice, though Hope sends me a few questioning looks. I just smile.

When it can't be put off any longer without Colleen spontaneously combusting, we all gather in the living room to look at the proofs of the wedding photos. My mother plops herself right in the middle of the couch with the book, with Daisy under her arm. Hope sits on one side, and Aaron looks between me and Cara.

"I have the digital album," I tell him. "I'll follow along on my phone."

"Me too, since I've already seen them," Cara lies, earning an arched eyebrow from me. She gives me one of her own while pulling out her phone. "You can all look at them together."

There's a lot of oohing and aahing from the couch, but I can't resist watching Cara's face as she slides from photo to photo. I know it's hard because I've already done it three times. Each trip through the album broke my heart a little more, but I saved a few of them to my phone, even though they're not the final product.

"A Sharpie could fix this one right up," I hear my mother say, and I know she's come to the one of us with both of our mothers.

"Mom," I snap, and her head jerks up, as though she'd forgotten Cara and I are in the room.

"Sorry," she says, sounding sincere, but thankfully, Cara's pretending she didn't hear any of it.

I know when they reach the photo that's my favorite because Colleen and Hope both gasp, and my mother touches her fingers to her lips. It was the first one I saved to my phone, and I've lost count of how many times I've looked at it. I'd probably make it my lockscreen wallpaper if I was younger and didn't have my phone out in professional settings so often.

A moment later, Cara catches up on her phone because I hear her sharp intake of breath. She looks at me, and even though the shimmer of tears in her eyes breaks my heart, I give her a warm smile before turning to my family.

"Our favorite, obviously."

The photographer caught us dancing, framed by the flowers adorning the gazebo's arch. Cara's head is back, as if she's laughing, and I barely recognize the soft, warm expression on my face as I smile at her. We're in each other's arms, the rest of the world forgotten, and we look like two people *genuinely* in love.

"That's the one," Colleen says. "That's the one I want for framing. An 11x13."

"Hey," Aaron says. "You framed an 8x10 of me and Hope's wedding portrait."

"I'm the oldest," I say just to annoy him. "Mine should be bigger."

"I framed the size you gave me," Colleen tells my brother. Then she turns to me. "Fine. I'll take an 8x10, then, so they match. My two happily married sons and their beautiful brides."

It hurts so much I can't look at Cara, and I'm not surprised when she gets up and offers to take Penny out for potties. Penny looks confused because she didn't ask for that, but she loves Cara enough to follow her out to the backyard. I want to go with them, but instead I give Cara her space and keep my eyes on my phone while my family flips through the rest of the book.

"I'm going to go through it again later," Colleen says. "I need a notebook so I can mark down which other ones I want prints of."

"No problem," I tell her. "You can keep it for the week and then we'll give it to Gin so she can choose her favorites."

Colleen's lips purse, but she keeps her opinion on that to herself. Unable to stand it anymore, I get up and go to the kitchen so I can check on Cara. I can see her out the window, playing fetch with Penny in the shade of an old elm.

It's Penny's version of fetch, of course. She loves sticks, like any dog, but she doesn't like the sticks thrown very far. And she's really only in it for the belly rubs and chin scratches she gets when she brings the stick back.

But the important thing is that Cara is laughing. If my mother's reaction to that picture had made her cry, there's no evidence from this distance.

I didn't hear Colleen follow me, but suddenly she's at my side, watching my wife play with my dog. "I'm so glad you two came over tonight. I enjoy having you so close by."

"Don't get used to it."

Her frown and the way she tilts her head cues me in to the fact I spoke too quickly, without thinking. For a second, I try to come up with a way to walk the statement back.

But then it hits me—like it or not, it's time to start showing some cracks in my hasty marriage. After an intense few weeks of convincing our family and friends we were so madly in love we wouldn't delay the wedding, and then the fake domestic bliss, it's time to start convincing those same people we might have made a mistake.

"You know I have no desire to live in Sumac Falls, Mom. I

don't think you're alone in hoping I'll change my mind, but I've been clear about it. My *home* is in Boston."

"I wish you'd just try it. You've always looked for the worst in this town."

"The worst isn't hard to find."

"Not if it's all you're looking for," she shoots back. "You focus so much on the people that didn't like you—or didn't like our family, actually—that you don't leave room for the good memories. Especially the way this community rallied around us when your dad died. I couldn't have gotten through it without help."

"You were strong," I tell her, because *that's* what I remember. "You got me and Aaron through it, too."

"I was strong because I had so many friends propping me up. And it wasn't just the casseroles, Hayden. They say it takes a village, and the village of Sumac Falls made sure I knew I wasn't alone."

"I bet the Gamble family didn't show up."

"That's one family. Plus, rumor had it at the time that Gin Gamble was spotted dropping some dollar bills into the collection jar the market put out to fund a gift certificate for us." I must not do a good job of hiding my surprise, because Colleen laughs. "That's my point. Even people who enjoy watching you fall down will give you a hand up if you actually hit rock bottom."

I nod, but I don't add to the conversation. It feels cruel to let her believe there's a chance I'll settle down with Cara in Sumac Falls and raise a family here. But the alternative is telling her the truth, which I can't do.

The emotional fallout from my driving need to own the Gamble house is starting to weigh on me. I'm hurting people I care about—including Cara—and for the first time since I walked into her shop for a nail appointment Penny didn't need, I can't wait to get back to Boston.

Chapter Fifty-Five

CARA

"Okay, you. Neither of us are leaving here until we get this done, so how about you just surrender to the inevitable?"

Jazz blinks at me, her head tilted. The blue merle border collie is stunningly gorgeous, and one of the most intelligent and obedient dogs I've ever worked with.

As long as I don't try to touch her feet.

She won't nip at me. She doesn't growl or show any signs of aggression. But she's smart and squirrely, and doing her nails is a test of my patience and resilience. And her owner's scheduled to return for her in five minutes. Just this once, I wanted to have her nails already done, but it's not going to happen.

Jazz gives me a smug look that reminds me so much of Penny, I have to laugh. I miss that saucy little Shih Tzu so much when she's in Boston.

I also miss her owner. I haven't really heard from Hayden, and I assume it's because I'm in the house alone. There's nobody to track how often he communicates with his wife. Nobody's watching our relationship. It makes sense on a logical level, but I still miss him. Living alone in the house for half the week, I miss having Hayden around even more than I miss my mother.

The bell rings and Jazz's owner walks in. She gives me a hopeful look and I shake my head, making her sigh. A few minutes later, we've wrangled the dog into the hiking backpack they use for longer hikes with rough terrain. It leaves Jazz fairly immobile, but with her feet accessible. It's still a battle, but I have the advantage. And luckily, her human doesn't hold it against me and still tips generously.

After they've departed, I clean up and head for the market. It's hard to muster the energy to shop and cook for one, but I also can't live on cereal alone. I roam the aisles, searching for things that look good. It's a bit of a novelty to be able to impulse buy fresh fruit and produce, thanks to all of the house-related expenses being transferred to Hayden's name the day of the closing.

Taylor also sent me a credit card with my name on it, with a note that it was a *joint account* to be used freely, but I haven't touched it. I don't know how much Taylor knows about the status of our marriage—I assume a lot because somebody did that legal paperwork—but she knows *joint* actually just means Hayden's money.

Once I've gathered a decent amount of food that doesn't come in a cereal box, I get in line and wait for my turn to load everything onto the squeaky conveyor belt.

"Well hello, Mrs. Reilly," Shawna says as she scans my first item. "How's married life?"

Lonely. "It's wonderful. How are you doing?"

"Isn't it hard with Hayden gone all the time?" I'm not surprised she totally ignored my attempt to turn the conversation to her. "Living in two different states can't be easy."

Curiosity wrapped in concern. There's a reason Shawna always has the best gossip. I shrug. "By working in the city four days, he gets to spend a full three-day weekend here with me. If he commuted every day, we'd actually have less quality time together because he'd spend so much time in his car."

"Will he keep doing that when you start a family?"

My breath catches, not only because the question isn't even remotely subtle, but because a scene of what could be flashes through my mind. Hayden. Me. Babies. Dogs. The house restored to its glorious former self.

But none of that is going to happen. At some point in the future, I'm going to come in to buy more cereal and Shawna will be bemoaning my divorce and fishing for details on what went wrong.

"We just got married," I remind her, and I can feel the tightness in my smile. "We'll cross that bridge when we come to it."

"Of course," she says, rallying as I shove my debit card into the reader. "I hope you enjoy your weekend."

My weekend of separate bedrooms and Hayden making lists of what needs to be done around the house—which is pretty much everything. He hasn't given me a timeline for when strangers will be showing up to start tearing the house apart. I'm not sure if it's out of respect for the fact it's currently my home, or because we haven't put much of a dent in emptying it out yet. Probably a little bit of both.

I'm putting the groceries in my trunk when a familiar voice calls my name. "Cara!"

Emily, Mel's mom, is heading my way and I brace myself for another round of pretending I'm doing great and sure, this is totally the way I saw my life playing out. My mom in a shiny new house. My fake husband and his dog in his shiny Boston apartment. And me, alone in the shabby house at the center of it all.

"I have no time," Emily says, clearly in a hurry. "But I'm so glad I ran into you. It's good to see you, honey."

"It's good to see you, too. I've been busy with the house and all. Trying to...sort stuff."

"I heard you successfully pried Gin out of that house, and I want to hear *all* about it. You should come for dinner Saturday night. Mel and Lucas will be there, and we've barely seen you and Hayden since the wedding."

I wince, guilt warming my cheeks. "I'm sorry. I've been—"

"Oh, honey!" Emily rests her hand on my forearm. "Of course you've been busy. You're a newlywed and you're supposed to disappear into your own bubble of bliss."

I wouldn't exactly call it a bliss bubble. I spend most of the time I'm not at Pampered Pets alone, sorting through stuff in the house and garage to give Gin a head start by pulling whatever is obviously junk. So far I've made two trips to the dump without her finding out.

"So Saturday, about four o'clock? We'll visit a while and then throw some burgers and dogs on the grill. Nothing fancy."

I should probably ask Hayden, but I've missed the Pearsons, and I nod. "Can I bring anything?"

"Just your handsome hubby! And his cute little dog, of course." She kisses my cheek. "I have to run now because I still have to get to Shelly's and get another damned cactus."

"Is this Harry 8.0? Or 9.0?"

She rolls her eyes. "I've lost track. I swear, I never should have started this. But we'll see you Saturday, okay?"

It isn't until later, when I'm eating a grilled chicken salad for one alone at the kitchen table, that I admit to myself the real reason I'm looking forward to eating with Mel and her parents.

Come Saturday, we'll have another situation during which we'll masquerade as newlyweds. Hayden will smile at me, and hold my hand. He'll rest his hand at the small of my back in that way he does. He might even kiss me.

I don't care if he's pretending. It won't be long before we begin the process of looking as though our hasty marriage is crumbling, and I'll take every minute in the bliss bubble I can get.

Chapter Fifty-Six

HAYDEN

I'm late getting back to Sumac Falls Thursday night. A meeting ran long. Taylor insisted I sign off on some reports before I could leave for the weekend, which meant reading them all. And an accident tied up traffic on the highway in a place there was no jumping off to take back roads.

When I finally pull into the driveway, Penny perks up. She's accepted the new routine—four days with me in Boston, and then three days with Cara and me in Sumac Falls. As soon as I get her out of her seat, she finds a patch of grass within the glow of the porch light because it's dark and if she pees now, she won't have to come back outside.

The house is quiet when we go inside, but the lights are on. I don't call out for Cara in case she's already gone to bed, and instead let Penny go hunting for her.

When I reach the kitchen, Cara's sitting cross-legged on the floor in front of an open cabinet, surrounded by a mountain of plastic bowls and lids, with my dog on her lap. Penny's licking her hand with enthusiasm, while Cara uses her free hand to stroke her head.

"I missed you, too," she was murmuring. "The house is lonely without you here."

I wish she was talking to me instead of to Penny, but she hasn't even looked in my direction. "Planning on having a lot of leftovers?"

Cara chuckles and finally looks up at me, her eyes crinkling at the corners. "I got bored and decided to tackle the Tupperware cabinet. Strangely enough, there's no actual Tupperware in here, but there are approximately six hundred empty butter containers. Some of them even have lids."

"Yeah, while I was finding creative ways to rearrange the kitchen, I opened that cabinet. Then, after shoving in the lids that fell out, I closed it very quickly and swore to never open it again."

"I'm taking it all to recycling. We've been using the same two or three glass storage bowls for the last I don't know how many years because they're microwave safe. But how was *your* week?"

"Good." After sniffing around the bowls long enough to determine there was no food in them, Penny has gone to make sure nobody disturbed her bed, so I put out a hand to help Cara up. "Busy, actually, which is part of why I'm late. Did you already eat?"

"Yes. Did you?"

"I grabbed something on the road."

I hate this stilted, awkward conversation. I want to walk through that door and have Cara throw herself in my arms so I can give her a proper kiss hello. But that's how a real wife greets her real husband who's been away.

And this isn't real. Now, when we're behind closed doors, we're just roommates with a common objective. And not once has she given me the impression she'd like me back in her bed.

Bad idea or not, I'd be there in a heartbeat.

"I ran into Emily at the market," she's saying as she nests bowls so they'll fit in the box for recycling. "We're invited over for a cookout Saturday afternoon. I should have asked you first, but there was no good way to get out of it in the moment."

"I like cookouts," I tell her. "I don't get invited to a lot of those in Boston."

"They have barbecue grills in Boston."

"I didn't say they don't have cookouts. I said I don't get invited to them." She pauses in her task long enough to roll her eyes at me, making me laugh. "We'll have fun Saturday."

I'm already looking forward to it, actually, because it means, for several hours, Cara and I will be a loving couple again. I don't even care that she's pretending. I just want to feel like it's real for a little while longer.

After we've finished filling the box of plastic for recycling, Cara gives Penny a good belly rub and announces she's going to bed and she'll see me in the morning. It hurts to watch her go up the stairs alone, leaving me to watch TV or lock up or whatever I care to do, but it's the deal I made.

Friday and Saturday morning aren't fun at all. Cara seems hell-bent on getting rid of a lot of the obvious junk, cutting down on the amount of belongings Gin will have to make decisions about, and I mostly fetch and carry boxes and bags.

"Has Gin been coming by during the week to go through stuff?" I ask when we're taking a break after dealing with a box of Halloween decorations that might have been older than me.

Cara's lips tighten for a moment. "Not yet, really. She's settling into her new house. But she's happy and she loves it, which is the important thing."

In other words, Gin made a new life for herself and, in typical fashion, hasn't even looked back to see how her daughter's faring. If the house didn't have historical value, I'd do us all a favor and burn it all to the ground while Cara's at work.

By the time we leave for the Pearson house, I'm more than ready to step out of the Gamble mess for a while. When I offered to pay a professional and Cara refused because it all belongs to her mother, I was relieved. The longer this takes, the longer she and I stay married. But I'm starting to have regrets because it's too much of a workload for Cara.

When we arrive and I take Penny out of her booster, she's low-key annoyed with me because I moved her to the backseat again and she runs straight to Cara. It doesn't seem to matter to my dog that Cara's the reason she lost riding shotgun. She just knows I'm the one who actually moved the seat.

She's also not thrilled about being in yet another new place, so she sits down and refuses to move. I have to scoop her up and then, with one arm cradling my stubborn dog and the other around Cara's waist, we head around the house to the backyard.

"It's the Reillys!" Bob hollers when he sees us.

"Or the Reilly-Gambles," Emily says, making her way across the grass to greet us. "Or the Gamble-Reillys. Or the Gamble and the Reilly. I'm not sure where you landed on that. Oh, who is this?"

"This is Penelope Louise, but we call her Penny." Because she's tucked safely in my arm, Penny begrudgingly accepts Emily rubbing between her ears and babbling baby talk at her.

"Where have you been hiding?" Mel asks, hauling Cara in for a big hug.

"You're, uh, not supposed to ask newlyweds that," her husband says, and they all laugh as I shake his hand.

Lucas was a couple of years ahead of me in school. We knew each other, of course, but we were neither friends nor foes. We just happened to be two guys who went to the same school. I know he's been good to Cara, though, helping keep her and Gin's cars on the road.

There's a lot of mingling and small talk while Bob puts the burgers and dogs on the grill. He refuses help, claiming the grill and the basement are the only parts of the house that are his domain, so mostly I listen to the others chatter and keep an eye on Penny, who's staked out her place in the shade under Cara's chair.

"I'm convinced Mel's been waiting for you to get married so you can have babies at the same time and raise them to be best friends like you are," I hear Emily say, and that certainly gets my attention.

"Mom is starting to get anxious for grandchildren," Mel explains, rolling her eyes. "And I'm going to get cheese for those burgers so Dad doesn't forget again."

I watch Cara's best friend walk away, finding it oddly telling that she didn't show any excitement at all about the prospect of her and Cara maybe getting pregnant at the same time.

It reinforces my suspicion that Mel knows the truth of our marriage. She hasn't said anything or given me dirty looks—not since the night I found them drunk and she accused *me* of stealing poop bags before *she* stole Penny's snacks—but that in itself is suspicious. She knew us in high school, so me sweeping into town and marrying Cara before buying the Gamble house should have at least earned me sideways glances at the wedding. Maybe even a few threats about what she'd do to me if I hurt her best friend again.

Getting nothing but smiles? Mel's not worried about Cara because she knows the truth.

It's a little annoying because my own brother doesn't know. I don't know if Cara told her outright or if she guessed, but it doesn't seem as if anybody else has found out, so there's no point in me confronting Cara about it.

Penny—who heard the c-h-e-e-s-e word and has abandoned her hiding spot—makes a break for the house. Me scrambling after her to keep her from charming their hosts out of giving my spoiled princess every single piece of cheese they own distracts everybody from talk of babies.

But it doesn't stop me from thinking about what it would be like to have children with Cara. It's a strain on my meager acting skills to sit with these lovely people who don't know a divorce is in our future, and pretend my heart's not breaking.

Chapter Fifty-Seven

CARA

Today's my four-month wedding anniversary—not that we're celebrating those milestones—and this limbo we're stuck in is quickly becoming more stressful than worrying about heating costs and a shabby roof had ever been.

We never really defined how long we'd continue the charade after the closing. We thought we'd both know when the time was right. But our lives have become routine and my nerves can't take much more.

It's almost impossible to spend long weekends with Hayden, sleeping across the hall from him, and not... I don't know. Throw myself at him? I lie awake at night, remembering the night I spent in his bed in Boston, aching to do it again. I think about what it would be like to have children with him, and raise them with Mel's as little besties. And, more than anything, I wish our marriage was real.

It gets harder to maintain the façade every time he walks through the door on Thursday nights. And it's hard for him, too, I think. We obviously have sexual chemistry, and attraction isn't the problem. But wanting to sleep with me doesn't mean he wants to spend the rest of his life married to me.

So I'm determined to start moving this process along so I can maybe get some peace back in my life. Sure, my heart will be broken, but he won't know that. And everybody else in my life will accept it because divorce is *usually* heartbreaking.

Even though I'm expecting Hayden home any time, I'm making one last run to my mother's house with a few boxes of things I know she wants to keep. The last time I brought things over, she grumbled about not wanting to fill up her new home with old stuff, but I told her I'd stack them neatly along the garage wall to keep them out of the way. And then, after the renovations are done, we can figure out where it goes. Just one more lie on top of the ones I've already told her.

"I can't believe you brought more stuff here, Carolina," Gin says, watching me add the boxes to the top of the stack with her hands on her hips.

"We can't renovate anything until we've cleaned out most of the house," I remind her.

"Where is he going to start?" she wants to know. "And when?"

"I'm not sure, but it can't be until I've made space for them to work."

She sighs. "He should be helping you with this."

She should be helping me, actually, but I keep my mouth shut about that. "He's not even back from Boston yet. My late afternoon client rescheduled because the dog may or may not have swallowed an AirPod and they're taking him to the vet, so I thought I'd get a little done. You should come over and see how it's looking."

"I might, when I get a chance."

"There are four days every week Hayden is not there, if you're avoiding him."

"I'm not avoiding him," she snaps, but then her shoulders

drop. "Maybe a little bit. I thought the day your father threw him off our porch would be the last time I ever saw that boy."

Wait...*what?* "What are you talking about, Mom? When was Hayden on our porch?"

She twitches, as if my question startled her. "Never mind."

Hayden left Sumac Falls right after he graduated, and my dad passed away five years ago. That means the most likely time for Hayden to have shown up on our porch was back when we were in high school. Even during fundraisers with cool prizes—like the year the person who sold the most wrapping paper won a scooter—the Reillys going door-to-door did not include *our* door, and vice versa. It doesn't make sense. There's only one reason I can come up with for Hayden to have knocked on our door.

So no, I am not going to *never mind.*

"When was it?" I ask again, because I still can't bring myself to ask the important question—the question with an answer that could mean everything I've thought about Hayden was a lie.

Was it the night of the homecoming dance?

"It was years ago. I don't remember and really, what does it matter?"

"It matters to me, Mom." I set the last box on the floor, not caring about the neat stacks anymore. "Did Hayden come to take me to the homecoming dance?"

"That's what he said he was there for," she says, and my stomach knots. For a few seconds, I'm afraid I might actually be sick. "But a Reilly? You knew better than that, so your father got rid of him. And we didn't want to fight with you about it, so it was easier to let you believe he never showed up."

My entire body is cold, and it takes an effort to make words form. "What did Dad tell him?"

"I don't know what Marcus said to him. All he told me was that we didn't need to worry about a filthy Reilly sniffing around our daughter ever again." She shrugs as if it's no big deal. "He'd said he'd taken care of it and that was the end of it."

302

"All this time you let me believe he stood me up?" The anger warms me, and I start walking toward my car. "I have to go."

"Carolina, it was for your own good," she calls after me.

I spin around, so angry I'm afraid to get close to her. "I don't want to talk to you right now. I'm leaving."

I tune out whatever it is she's saying in a futile effort to convince me she didn't do anything wrong. All the way home, I turn the information over and over in my head, trying to figure out *why* Hayden didn't tell me he showed up. I'm dismayed, but not surprised, by my parents' actions. But it makes no sense for Hayden to have let me believe he stood me up. Especially now.

I'm not sure if I'm pleased or even more angry that his car is in the driveway when I pull in. I could probably use a little time to process this new information, but I'm not going to get it.

Penny meets me at the door, and I pick her up to give her a cuddle. I miss her so much when she's gone, and the fact she's not going to be a part of my life much longer gets the tears flowing again.

Hayden comes down the stairs, stopping short when he sees my face. "What's wrong. What happened?"

I kiss the top of Penny's head and then carefully set her down. By the time I straighten, Hayden is halfway across the room, but I hold up my hand. "My mother accidentally told me you showed up at my house to take me to the homecoming dance."

The change is instantaneous. His body tenses, straightening his spine, and his jaw clenches. He's silent for so long I'm starting to think he's just not going to say anything, but then he nods once in a sharp gesture. "I did."

"Why didn't you tell me that?"

"It wouldn't have made a difference."

I hold up my hands, unable to believe the words coming out of his mouth. "You didn't think there would be a difference between my parents being awful and me thinking the boy I loved stood me up for what was going to be the most amazing night of my teenage life?"

"They were never going to let me see you, Cara."

"What did my dad say to you?"

More jaw clenching. Silence. "It doesn't matter anymore."

"It doesn't matter anymore," I repeat, sadness blending with my anger. "It doesn't matter anymore because you got payback. That's why you dragged me into this, right? He threw you off our porch, so now you *own* the porch?"

The way his chin lifts slightly gives me my answer. "You knew right from the start I wanted this house."

"Yes, the house. But I thought it was just because you loved the house and wanted to restore it. And me getting out from under it would be an added bonus."

"That part's true."

"But you really wanted to buy it because my father told you that you weren't good enough to even stand on the porch. So you bought it."

"Two things can be true at the same time."

"This is not okay," I yell, and then I take a deep breath because I don't like raising my voice, and I don't want to scare Penny.

"Why not? What does it matter what my motivation was? Look at this house. You can't deny it needs the attention I can afford to give it."

"I would never have gone along with this if I'd known."

"That makes no sense to me. What difference does it really make?"

"There's a big difference between you wanting to save an old house and you using me to send a giant *screw you* to my dead father."

"Is there really, though?"

The cold is back, seeping through my body. "I know we have to play out this pretense, but I don't even want to look at you right now. Obviously you can't drive all the way back to Boston when you just got here, but you can go sleep at your mother's tonight." There's a pang in my chest at the thought of him leaving, but I ignore it. "That helps sell the divorce, anyway."

"It's too soon, Cara. If your mother thinks—" His words break off and he takes a deep breath. "It's too soon for us to separate."

If my mother thinks we purposely defrauded her out of the house, she could sue him, I think. Honestly, I don't care right now. "I'm not filing for divorce tomorrow. I just need some space and everybody seeing how much time you spend in Boston is a nice little bonus for when I do file. You need to go."

I give Penny some extra pets, trying not to let tears fall into her hair, and then I turn away and go upstairs. A few minutes later, I hear them leave and the crying really starts.

Chapter Fifty-Eight

HAYDEN

My mother's surprised to see me, obviously, but it only takes one look at my face to convince her not to pry too much.

"Is everybody alright?" she asks from the kitchen doorway. It looks as if she'd been cleaning up from her dinner when she heard me come in.

"Just a spat," I lie. It doesn't feel like a spat. It feels like the end of the world. "No accidents or emergencies. But she asked for some space."

Colleen's mouth tightens, and I brace myself for an anti-Gamble rant I *really* don't want to hear. Then she inhales slowly through her nose and blows out the breath. "Are you hungry? There's some leftover ham and fried potatoes."

"I'm not hungry, but thank you."

"You're not hungry? Or you already ate? Nothing feels better on an empty stomach. How about a grilled cheese sandwich and some tomato soup?"

I wasn't lying about not having an appetite, but I recognize that my mom needs to do something to help me feel better, and I appreciate that she didn't give me an *I told you so*. "Are you sure it's not too much trouble?"

"Never."

After checking that Penny's bed is still in its spot—it is, and she's already curled up in it—I sit at the table and watch my mom go through the familiar actions of making my favorite comfort food.

Maybe it's the nostalgia that loosens the knot of emotion in my throat. I hadn't wanted to start down this path so soon— honestly, I don't want to at all—but it looks like we've arrived. "We might have rushed getting married."

To her credit, she only nods slowly and stirs a can of milk into the tomato soup while processing that. I can see that she wants to be careful with her words—always a good idea because she doesn't want to have said something awful if Cara and I reconcile after sleeping on it.

"One spat doesn't mean it's over," she finally says. "Learning how to fight and then move past it together is one of the most important skills to develop in a marriage. Usually you learn how to do that during the dating and engagement process, but you kind of skipped that part."

I don't really have a great reason to have skipped it, other than repeating the story that we fell so hard and fast, we couldn't wait. But I can't bring myself to say it out loud right now. Not with the memory of Cara's tear-stained cheeks and accusing eyes so sharp and fresh in my mind.

I just couldn't tell her all of it—I couldn't bring myself to tell her the rest of the story.

"Have you told your brother you're here?"

"No." It was only for Penny's sake that I came here instead of making the drive back to Boston. I'd rather not have this conversation and I don't want to explain it all to Aaron, either. "I might tomorrow if...I might talk to him tomorrow."

She sets the grilled cheese in front of me, followed by a bowl of creamy tomato soup. "Everything might look different in the morning. And I know how you are, so I'm not going to make you talk about it. But you know I'm here if you *do* want to talk."

"Thanks, Mom."

She leaves the kitchen and a minute later, I hear the TV come on. Even though I'm still not hungry, I eat the grilled cheese because I can rarely resist it. And I manage about half the soup before I add the dishes to the dishwasher and hit the button to turn it on.

When I walk into the living room for my bag, Colleen pauses the TV and smiles at me. "Did you have enough?"

"I did. Thank you. If you don't mind, I think I'm going to go upstairs. I'm not very good company tonight."

"You never have to be good company for me, but I also won't be offended if you want to be alone."

"Thanks. Goodnight, Mom." I look at Penny, who's glaring at me from her bed. "Come on, Penny Lou."

She ignores me until I start up the stairs and she realizes she's going to be left alone with Colleen. I hear her nails as she scrambles to catch up, and I slow so she doesn't have to rush on the stairs.

Her annoyance isn't soothed any by being back in our own guest suite. Sometimes I wish she could talk to me and then other times—like now—I think it's probably a good thing she can't actually say what she's trying to communicate with her eyes and body language.

Even though it's a little early for bed, I rummage through the clothes I've always kept there until I find a worn, comfy pair of sleep pants to change into. That's Penny's signal to use her stairs to go to bed, and she does. But she's not happy about it.

I kill the light and slide into the bed. It has the same mattress I use in Boston, and there's absolutely no logical reason why I should be missing the old one in Gin's former bedroom right now. And yet I am. Even if I'm stuck across the hall, I'd rather be sleeping under the same roof as Cara tonight.

Usually, Penny would cuddle up against my side, but tonight

she's sitting on what would be Cara's side of the bed, staring at me. It's ridiculous because the three of us haven't shared a bed since Gin moved out of the Gamble house.

"I know," I tell her. "But she doesn't want to sleep with us anymore."

My dog tries to stare me down.

"Yes, it's my fault. But you and I were going to be on our own again eventually, anyway." I don't tell her I know how she feels—that I miss Cara, too. "Penelope Louise, it's time to sleep. Lay down."

Penny gives me a derisive snort. Then she turns in a few circles and, after heaving a very dramatic sigh, settles down—still on the other side of the bed—with her back to me.

I've known the whole time we would end up here. It was the plan all along. But I hadn't expected it to hurt so much.

"I don't know how to make it better," I whisper to her, and then I close my eyes and hope sleep will come soon and dull the pain.

It doesn't.

Chapter Fifty-Nine

CARA

Sleep-deprived and heartbroken, I get through the next day on caffeine, belly rubs, and sloppy kisses.

While I haven't been taking clients on Fridays, I had one appointment on the books I hadn't rescheduled—they were heading on a long road trip—and I was happy to have a reason to get out of bed.

Thankfully, I'd been too numb to cry, so I was able to smile convincingly enough at the human who walked through the door. But my furry client sensed my sadness and gave me extra love.

And I've only looked at the wedding photo I'd downloaded to my phone six times. Maybe seven. I can't bring myself to delete it, but I had to stop myself from locking my door and crying all over my phone all day.

Now it's time to close up and go home to the empty house that somehow *I* ended up the only person living in. Beyond the fact that was the opposite of the plan, it's depressing as hell.

I drove today because I couldn't summon the energy to walk, even knowing it would have helped me feel better, so I sit in my car and debate my options.

I can go to the diner and drown my sorrows with ice cream. But Lorene will ask me where Hayden is and I might burst into tears.

I can go home and make a dinner for one.

And that's how I end up pulling into my mother's driveway. I'd been angry with her when we parted ways, but it wasn't the first time I'd gotten upset with her and it won't be the last. She's still all I have.

Her little house looks so cheerful, with hanging baskets of flowers and colorful quilts draped over the two wooden rockers on the porch. If nothing else, this disaster got my mother out of that house before it fell down around her.

Gin opens the door while I'm debating if I can just walk in or if I should knock first. "Cara!"

She pulls me into a hug that's over so fast, I don't even get a sense of whether she's just happy to see me after our disagreement, or if she'd somehow heard Hayden spent the night at Colleen's.

That would explain the smile on her face. I guess we're going with the traditional Gamble way of dealing with problems— pretending they're not happening.

Walking into Gin's new home is still a strange experience for me, even though I've been over several times since helping her move in. Freed from the accumulated "treasures" of multiple generations, my mother has found her own style. It's simple and bright, without a lot of clutter, and I'm actually a little jealous.

Okay, a *lot* jealous. She has a shiny new life, while I'm still stuck in the old one.

"So what's going on with you?" she asks as we walk toward her small kitchen table. I don't know why, but we never sit on the living room furniture when I visit. We hang out in the kitchen.

"Nothing, Mom. Everything's fine."

She turns to face me and her eyes narrow. "I can hear it in your voice, Cara. You're still upset. I'm sorry your father and I handled things so badly when you were a teenager. Did you have a fight with Hayden?"

I want to deny it. My emotions are too raw right now to share with anybody, especially Gin. But I guess showing cracks in the marriage helps lay the foundation for what's to come.

"We had an argument and he slept at his mom's house last night," I tell her. "It wasn't that big a deal."

"Sleeping on the couch isn't a big deal. Going home to his mother is a *very* big deal. What did you fight about? It can't be about that high school nonsense. That was years ago, and he wasn't at fault. Your father was."

I scramble to come up with something besides the truth. "I was already upset when I left here, and then he wanted me to cancel my appointments for the week and go to Boston with him, and I refused."

"Good for you. He might have money to throw around, but that's not only your business, but commitments you've made to your community."

Oh, *now* she respects my business choices. "We'll get past it, I'm sure."

Fortunately, she's setting two glasses of lemonade on the table and can't see my face. I know Hayden and I are *not* going to get past the bomb that had been dropped between us, and it takes me a second to shove down the urge to cry.

But after we sit down, her gaze goes right back to my face. "It's awfully early in the marriage for this big of an issue between you, honey."

"We had talked about it before, but I think there was something going on—a client dinner or something—that he wanted me in Boston for."

"You know, you rushed to the altar, and if you're realizing it was a mistake, then leave him." Gin's lips press tightly together for a few seconds, and then she waves her hand. "Let him keep the house, but make sure he buys you out of your half for a fair price so you can find a new place of your own."

I'm too stunned to speak. I'd sold my marital soul for this outcome, but I'm still shocked to hear those words come out of Gin's mouth. Except for the part where my heart gets broken, Hayden's plan actually worked.

"Our last name and that old house were all we had for so many years. And then it was all *I* had," Gin continued. "You know how, when you're driving in a winter storm and you hold the steering wheel so tight, you have a hard time letting go of it because your fingers are so stiff from clenching it?"

"I do."

"From the day I married Marcus, I had to hold onto that house. For decades I held on so tight, I just couldn't relax my grip and let it go."

"It's okay to move on, Mom. You're so much happier now."

"But you're not." She locks her gaze with mine, sorrow written all over her expression. "I'm sorry I couldn't let go even when it was dragging us both down, Carolina. And if this marriage isn't what you want, walk away. I don't care who owns that damn house anymore."

"Thank you." I reach out and take her hand. She squeezes my fingers in return. "I don't know what's going to happen going forward, but you and I are going to be okay."

"Of course we will. We always are."

I laugh, and then catch her looking at the clock on the stove for a third time. "Do you have plans tonight, Mom?"

"Just a casual get-together a few houses down. We all bring something to throw on the grill or a side dish, and then we play cornhole. Have you ever played that?"

I shake my head, smiling because it's hard to imagine my mom throwing beanbags at a hole in a board, but I can tell by the way her face lights up that she enjoys it. "I'll get out of the way. I just wanted to stop by and say hi."

Gin sighs. "I do miss living with you, honey."

"Me too," and it's the truth. It was my mom and I against the

313

world for a long time, and even though we were losing, we were together every day. "I told Mel I'd stop by, anyway."

That wasn't true, but I could tell she was about to invite me to join her at the cookout, and I might be able to fake it for a few minutes, but I'm not good company.

Despite knowing that, and the fact I hadn't told her I was coming, I drive to Mel's house next. My emotional mask is slipping, and she's the only person who knows the truth, even if I haven't outright confirmed it for her.

Lucas answers the door, and he smiles before stepping back to wave me in. "We just finished eating, but there's some left over if you're hungry."

"No, thank you."

I don't know if it's my expression or my voice, but Lucas nods once, as if to himself. "It's my turn to wash tonight, so I'll tell Mel you're here. Have a seat."

I sit on the couch, pulling my feet up so I can hug my knees. A moment later, Mel comes out of the kitchen, and I can tell by her face she knows something's wrong. I also know they don't take turns cleaning the kitchen after supper. They always do it together.

"Hey," she says softly, sitting next to me. "I heard Hayden slept at Colleen's last night and I thought it was all part of some master plan but I guess I was wrong."

"The plan went great. Except for the part where I fell in love with him."

Mel sighs dramatically, looking up at the ceiling for a second. "I told you not to fall in love with your husband, Cara."

"I know."

"Tell me everything."

So I do. With two short breaks to find a box of tissues and then to get some water, I confess the entire plan to Mel. And then I tell her about the night Hayden *didn't* stand me up.

"I wouldn't have gone along with it if I'd known his primary motivation was revenge on my dad," I end with. "I know it doesn't make sense. I mean, I always questioned his excuse that he just wanted to restore it because he likes old houses. But this is so much more personal than an old feud and the Gambles not liking the Reillys. He wanted to *hurt* us."

"I'm sorry," she says, holding out the supermarket bag she'd snagged for the used tissues and handing me a fresh one from the box. "What happens now?"

"I don't know. But I got over him once. I can do it again."

"Now that he's got his revenge house, he won't need to keep up the fake marriage bit, so he'll probably go back to Boston. It'll be a lot easier to get over him once he's gone."

My shoulders twitch in a really pathetic shrug. "What really hurts is that I don't think it's fake for him, either. Not anymore. He loves me too, Mel. I believe that."

"Then he should have respected you enough to tell you the truth about homecoming night. Even if he wasn't man enough to tell you then, he's grown now. There's no excuse for that."

"I know. But I love him," I manage to say before a fresh wave of sobbing hits me.

Mel wraps her arms around me, holding me close, which is how I can hear her mutter into my hair. "After all this, how the hell did *you* end up being the one stuck living in that house?"

Chapter Sixty

HAYDEN

"I'm going to talk to Cara," I announce the following evening because I can't stand the idea of a second night without her. And scrolling through the wedding photos on my phone is only making it worse.

I can't make myself stop, though.

Colleen pauses the TV and gives me one of those mom looks —like she's trying to see into my very soul. Usually when I get that look, she's trying to figure out if I've been up to no good, but this time her face softens.

"I never thought I'd say this, Hayden, but I won't wait up for you because I hope you two will work it out and you'll be staying at the Gamble house tonight."

The tenderness in her voice tightens my throat and I have to clear it before I can speak. "The Gamble-*Reilly* house."

"*Your* house."

I nod, feeling no satisfaction at all in hearing that. After all this time, I've had to admit I never cared about being worthy of stepping onto the Gamble's porch. I wanted to be worthy of Cara's love.

And I blew it.

I was going to leave Penny home, but she'd perked up when she heard Cara's name. And by the time I'm done talking to my mom, she's retrieved her harness, dropping it at my feet. She turns her face up to me, her expression breaking my heart.

After putting the harness on her and grabbing her leash, I pick her up. I don't know how this night will go, but Penny will never forgive me if I don't take her, so I carry her toward the door.

"Hayden?" When I stop and turn back to Colleen, she gives me a shaky smile. "Don't just say what you have to in order to smooth things over. Say what you *need* to say, because the Reilly and Gamble families both know that on any random day, you may run out of *somedays* to tell a person what you needed to say."

I'm such a wreck, it takes me two tries to clip Penny into her car seat. She gives me an impatient look, sighing like only she can, but she forgives me when I scratch under her chin and tell her we're going to find Cara.

That's easier said than done, though, because her car isn't in the driveway. And even though it's still light out, the interior of the house is so dim, I'd expect lights to be on.

She's not home.

I want to drive around Sumac Falls until I find her. Gin's house. Mel's house. The diner. Mel's parents. Anywhere I can think of she might be.

But I'm not going to ambush her in front of other people. And I don't want to go home in defeat. Colleen will have questions, and Penny will be disappointed. Since I have her leash, I decide I'll walk Penny down to the rock by the river and back, and then try again.

We find Cara sitting on the rock, her knees drawn up and her arms wrapped around them, as she stares at the slow-moving water. Everything about her body language screams sadness, and my heart breaks all over again.

Penny is beside herself with joy, though, and I unclip the

leash. I fumble with it, and she gives a sharp bark of annoyance, catching Cara's attention.

She doesn't look at me, but her face lights up as Penny sprints to her. I think it's the fastest I've ever seen my dog move, and fear jolts through me as I imagine her not being able to stop and going right off the edge of the rock, forcing me to dive into the river—cell phone, key fob, shoes and all. I hold my breath until she's safe in Cara's arms.

I hang back for a few minutes, letting them enjoy their reunion, before taking a seat next to her on the rock. Penny makes herself comfortable on Cara's lap, her back turned to me.

"I'm sorry." I should probably specify what I'm sorry about, but there's so much. And I'm sorry for all of it.

"You don't have to be sorry. We both knew what we were getting into. I just wish you'd been totally honest about your motivation from the start and we could avoided all of this." Her mouth twists. "But I guess that was the point. You didn't *want* to avoid this, and you got what you wanted."

"I did *not* want to hurt you. I always wanted you to know I showed up." She stills, and I want to take her hand, but I can't risk her pulling it away from me. "The night of the homecoming dance. I was there when I said I would be, but your dad wasn't really all that happy to see me."

"But we knew he wouldn't be, even though I told my parents you were coming. That wasn't going to stop me from going."

"You weren't ready when I got there."

"No, because my mom said my hair wasn't right in the back. I couldn't see it but she said she had to fix it. I knew I'd be a few minutes late, but I...I wanted to look perfect for you."

Cara has always looked perfect to me. I want to tell her that, but her expression is getting darker by the second, and I'm not sure now is the time.

"I can't believe you," she says, the words an angry blast. "Even if my dad was being a jerk, I wasn't worth waiting for?"

Now *that* I can't let stand. "Don't you ever say that again, Cara Gamble. Not to me. You were definitely worth waiting for."

Her face is flushed with anger already, but the pink of her cheeks deepens. "And yet you didn't."

I have to tell her what happened on homecoming night, even though I never wanted her to know. One, because I didn't want to say anything against her dad. But there was also my pride. What Marcus Gamble said to me that night hurt, and I'm not one to expose my wounds.

The idea of her believing I didn't think she was worth waiting for hurts even more, though.

"I would have waited hours for you, Cara. But Marcus wasn't having it. I would have stuck it out, even if I had to stand on the sidewalk on the other side of your gate. But he didn't just want me to not take you to homecoming—he didn't want me to ever speak to you again." I pause, taking a deep breath to keep so many years of anger from choking off my words. "When calling me names and telling me all the ways I was too filthy to even look in your direction didn't work, he told me if I ever spoke to you again, he and his buddy Frank would plant a distribution amount of drugs in Aaron's car and then bust him during a traffic stop."

Marcus's buddy Frank was the chief of police at the time, and they both hated my family. And Frank had the power to destroy my brother's life.

I watch her face as some of the anger seeps out of her expression, leaving behind confusion. Fighting the urge to keep explaining, I stay silent and let her process what I told her.

"No," Cara says, and I expected this. Nobody wants to believe a loved one would sink that low. "My dad wouldn't threaten your little brother's future just to keep you away from me."

"He started by threatening *me*, but I told him I wasn't leaving until I talked to you."

"But he knew you would protect Aaron."

"He's my little brother," I say simply.

"I'm sorry he did that to you," she says, and I didn't realize how much I needed her to believe me until so much tension leaves my muscles, they actually tremble.

"Us," I correct in a rough voice. "He did that to *us*. You and me, and what could have been."

"But why didn't you just *tell* me? All this time I thought you stood me up. I thought it was just some...elaborate Reilly prank on the Gamble family. You could have at least slipped a note into my locker."

"I'm so sorry." Even though they can't hurt Aaron anymore— Frank retired the year before Marcus passed away and died three years later—the old fear makes my chest hurt and I struggle to take a full breath. "If I told you, and then you told Mel or anybody else, Aaron might find out and I never wanted him to know. I was scared, Cara."

Her brows draw together. "If a corrupt police chief threatened to frame me for a felony, I'd want to know."

"Aaron was a kid. And he knew how I felt about you, so he would have felt bad or—even worse—tried to fix it. He probably would have gone to our mother, and she would have dragged the entire town into it. I knew that no matter what, I was never going to be allowed to talk to you, and I was afraid Marcus and Frank would get even more dangerous if they were cornered. The stakes were too high, so I had to let you go. As far as I know, your father and I are the only ones who ever knew."

"And my mother." I start to speak, but she holds up her hand. "She deliberately delayed me with the hair thing. She was in on it."

"Oh, she was definitely involved in running me off. But that doesn't mean she knew he threatened to ruin my little brother's life with a fake drug dealing charge."

Her sudden laugh echoes across the water and eases some of the pressure in my chest. "Hayden Reilly, are you actually defending Gin Gamble?"

"She *is* my mother-in-law, you know." And I want to keep it that way, so even though I may have said what I had to say to smooth things over, there's more I *need* to say. "And to circle back to us knowing what we were getting into, I guess I didn't because falling in love with you all over again was never part of the plan."

"Hayden—"

"Do you know what I felt the day we closed on that house?" I cut in, because even if she's about to tell me she doesn't feel the same and it's over between us, I want her to know. "I thought the taste of triumph would be *so* sweet that day, but when we walked out of that office and the house was mine, all I could think about was how from that moment on, the clock was ticking toward you and I going our separate ways. The satisfaction of finally owning that porch was nothing compared to how badly I wished our marriage was going to last forever."

"Why didn't you tell me?" Her voice is barely more than a whisper.

"I broke your heart once, Cara. And I made a deal with you. I blew my chance, and dumping my emotions on a situation that was already emotional for you wouldn't be fair."

She inhales deeply, her hand stroking Penny's back, before she looks at me. "That was so long ago, Hayden. I mean, I guess it was unfinished business between us, but we were kids. We're adults now, and the teenage version of you might have broken my heart, but the grown version of you won it back."

As her words sink in, my pulse races and it's hard to breathe. "Cara?"

"I love you too, Hayden. Not still, but again. And I didn't tell you before because, like you said, it wasn't part of the deal we made."

"I think it's time we amend the deal," I say after clearing my throat. "Cara, you're my wife. I love you, and I'm asking you to *stay* my wife, not just in name, but in my heart."

She presses her lips together for a few seconds before they curve into a quivering smile. "Yes. Yes, Hayden, I will stay your wife because I love you, too."

"Then let's do this right." I take her hand in mine, my thumb pressed to the rings she hadn't taken off. "Carolina Marie Gamble, I promise to love you until the last breath leaves my body. I promise that we're going to dream big and then work together to make those dreams come true. And I promise to show up for you, every day, for the rest of our lives."

Her breath catches in her chest, and she blinks away tears. "Hayden William Reilly, I promise to see you—to see the man you are and not who anybody else believes you to be—and I promise to love you for the rest of my life."

Cupping the back of her neck, I lean in and kiss my wife.

My wife.

For the first time in my life, I know what peace truly feels like. Cara in my arms, her lips against mine. Penny happily cuddled up between us. The water lazily swirling around this rock where I kissed Cara for the first time, so many years ago.

And when the kiss ends and I look into her eyes, shimmering with happy tears, there's only one thing left to say.

"Let's go home."

Chapter Sixty-One

CARA

Two years later...

Dogs barking and car doors closing are pretty common sounds around the Gamble-Reilly house these days, but the pitch of Penny's bark tells me what I need to know.

"Daddy's home!"

Ari hops in excitement, which is awkward since my daughter is currently tucked into a baby backpack, with her hands fisted in my hair. It's been a good way for me to work around the property while keeping my hands free, but Arizona Gamble-Reilly is six months old now, and she's getting heavy.

I turn off the hose I'd been using to spray down the windows of the long, low building that now houses Pampered Pets Grooming and drop it in the grass. Then, as I walk by the smaller, fenced-in building that's our kennel, I tell the three large-breed dogs to quiet down. The teenager who volunteers to spend time with them before and after school will be here any time, and they'll get a lot of love and attention. And walks, since their social-ization is going great. It won't be long before they're ready to find forever homes.

Ari squeals, digging her toes into my back so she can bounce harder, and the sound of Hayden's laughter drifts across the yard. Nothing makes me happier than the sounds of joy from my husband and daughter mingling together.

He's holding Penny in his arms while she licks his jaw in greet-ing. While she remains unsure about the tiny human and fostering dogs, Penny's accepted Hayden spending three days per week away in Boston in exchange for four days at home. She always manages to be the first to welcome him home, though.

Ari lets go of my hair so she can clap her hands when she spots her daddy in the shade of the house. It's been painstakingly restored to its original glory on the outside, and totally renovated and modernized on the inside. The interior was meant to be an ongoing process, but when we found out Ari was on the way, we temporarily moved in with Colleen and paid a ridiculous amount to fast track the work.

When we reach the porch, Hayden sets Penny down and walks down the steps to meet me.

"Welcome home, husband."

"I missed you, wife," he says—as he does every time he returns home, even if he only went to the market—and kisses me until Ari reaches around my head and starts grabbing at his cheek to get his attention.

Laughing, I turn so Hayden can unbuckle our daughter from the backpack and lift her out. Ari laughs when Hayden kisses her face because she loves the way his beard tickles.

I sit on the steps, scratching under Penny's chin when she joins me.

A perfect evening, I think as I watch Ari wrap her arms around Hayden's neck. My husband is home, everybody I love is happy, and together, we've built a beautiful life.

As for the feud, there is finally peace in Sumac Falls. When the reality of a shared grandchild sank in, Gin and Colleen got together and swapped apologies. According to the two women, they buried their old beef—buried it deep and then buried the shovel. Somehow, during that meeting, they'd also talked about what the grandchild would call each of them. Rather than one being Grandma and the other being Nana, they've taken the first two letters of each of their names and come up with GiGi and CoCo. Maybe it's silly, but it works for our family, and our mothers laughing together when they told us was one of the best feelings ever.

"I'm not sure what it means," Hayden says, sitting on the step next to me with Ari on his lap, "but I asked her how daycare went while I was away, and she laughed. It was a little bit of a cheeky laugh, though."

"Yesterday, our daughter tried to instigate a nap rebellion and her room ended up having a very cranky afternoon."

"So she didn't *try* to instigate a rebellion. She succeeded."

"You probably shouldn't sound so proud of that."

He laughs, and Ari laughs with him. "It's the Reilly in her, you know. There's a reputation to live up to."

I bump my shoulder against his. "Just wait until she's a teenager. People will be talking about that Gamble-Reilly girl."

Hayden puts his hand over his heart, wincing. "Will you still love me when our daughter has turned all my hair gray?"

"Of course I will. You'll look very distinguished, as men do. The question is, will you still love *me* when *my* hair is all gray?"

"Nothing could ever make me stop loving you." He puts his arm around me and kisses my forehead. "It's so good to be home."

* * *

Thank you so much for reading Hayden and Cara's story! (Okay, it was really Penny's story, but Hayden and Cara were in it, too.) If you enjoyed *That Reilly Boy*, please consider leaving a review on the retailer's site to spread the word to other readers.

And please subscribe to my newsletter to get all the last news on sales and new releases, and turn the page for a complete list of my available books! (If you're reading the paperback edition, you can subscribe to my newsletter via my website, www.shannon stacey.com).

Also by Shannon Stacey

To see the most current list of titles by Shannon Stacey, visit the Books tab on her website, shannonstacey.com.

* * *

Standalone Contemporary Romances

The Kowalski Family Series

This reader-favorite contemporary romance series is full of family, fun and falling in love.

The Sutton's Place Series

Three sisters come together to open the family brewery so their mother doesn't lose everything, but they don't expect to find love along the way. Friends, family, love and laughter!

Her Hometown Man — Book 1

An Unexpected Cowboy — Book 2

Expecting Her Ex's Baby — Book 3

Falling For His Fake Girlfriend — Book 4

Her Younger Man — Book 5

Married By Mistake — Book 6

The Blackberry Bay Series

Feel good romances about love and laughter in a small town.

More Than Neighbors — Book 1

Their Christmas Baby Contract — Book 2

The Home They Built — Book 3

Cedar Street Novellas

Fun, tropey hijinks in a small town!

One Summer Weekend — Book 1

One Christmas Eve — Book 2

Hockey Romances

Here We Go — Book 1

A Second Shot — Book 1.5

The Devlin Group Series

This action-adventure romance series follows the men and women of the Devlin Group, a privately owned rogue agency unhindered by red tape and jurisdiction.

72 Hours — Book 1

On The Edge — Book 2

No Surrender — Book 3

No Place To Hide — Book 4

No Way Out — Book 5

The Boston Fire Series

A contemporary romance series about tough, dedicated (and sexy) firefighters!

Heat Exchange — Book 1

Controlled Burn — Book 2

Fully Ignited — Book 3

Hot Response — Book 4

Under Control — Book 5

Flare Up — Book 6

The Boys of Fall Series

A contemporary romance series about football and going home again.

Under The Lights — Book 1

Defending Hearts — Book 2

Homecoming — Book 3

Holiday HEA Series

If you're in the mood for a festive read full of love, laughter and happily ever after, the HOLIDAY HEA series is here for you!

Stranded in a Small Town Christmas — Book 1

There's Only One Sleigh — Book 2

Standalone Christmas Novellas

Holiday Sparks

Mistletoe & Margaritas

Snowbound With the CEO

Her Holiday Man

In the Spirit

A Fighting Chance

Holiday With A Twist

Hold Her Again

Feels Like Christmas

Standalone Novellas

Through the Rain

Heart of the Storm

Slow Summer Kisses

Kiss Me Deadly

Historical Western Rom Coms

Taming Eliza Jane — Book 1

Becoming Miss Becky — Book 2

Subscribe to Shannon's newsletter

About the Author

New York Times and *USA Today* bestselling author Shannon Stacey lives in New Hampshire with her family. Her favorite activities are writing romance and really random social media posts with her dog curled up beside her, especially during the long winter months. She loves books, coffee, Boston sports, watching way too much TV, and she's never turned down an offering of baked macaroni & cheese.

facebook.com/shannonstacey.authorpage

instagram.com/shannonstacey

bsky.app/profile/shannonstacey.bsky.social

threads.com/@shannonstacey

Copyright © 2025 by Shannon Stacey

All rights reserved.

No part of this book may be reproduced in any form or by any electronic or mechanical means, including information storage and retrieval systems, without written permission from the author, except for the use of brief quotations in a book review.

This book was not created with AI, and no part of this book may be used to create, feed, or refine artificial intelligence models for any purpose without written permission from the author.